FREE BOOK OFFER

Get a FREE novella!

Sign up for my no-spam newsletter
and get *BREACH*.

Details can be found at the end of
SECOND LAW OF ATTRITION

SECOND LAW OF ATTRITION

BRONWYN LEROUX

1

Why won't Deran answer? Where is he? Desperate, I jab the comm link just below the skin behind my right ear and order the call again. Still no answer.

The questions I asked only seconds ago pump through my head like heavy bass at full volume. Relentless, inescapable, and invincible. *My brother, his sister, and Sarissa, all connected! But how? And what am I supposed to eat? Have I just stumbled onto the questions I should've asked Deran instead of running away from him like I usually do?*

Breathing hard after my headlong flight, I come to an abrupt halt. I'm halfway across the massive park surrounding Cirrian Conglomerate's headquarters, but I'm oblivious to the lush, rolling lawns, tinkling water in nearby fountains, and heady fragrance of sweet frangipanis. All I can see is the gaping chasm yawning in front of me as another realization hits home. Have I truly gone and done it this time? Alienated my only potential ally?

Why, oh why, did I have to lash out? Deran is the one person who may have the answers I want. Certainly the only one who's ever been willing to give me the answers I need.

Deran warned me the information I was after was dangerous. But did I listen? Nooo, I thought I needed it. Told Deran I wanted it.

Emphatically. Then what's the first thing I do after learning they abducted my brother? I blamed him. Worse, I kneed him to get away, to hide from the disastrous consequences of my own curiosity. Regretting my rash actions now, I know there's nothing for it but to apologize—and the sooner, the better.

I call Deran again, my foot tapping the ground impatiently as the ringtone drones on. *Come on, come on! Answer!* After ten seconds, I cut the link and check the contact. No mistake. It's Deran. I hit redial, then wait.

Listening to the endless ringing, I'm sucker-punched by another thought. Frantic fear twists my gut into knots. Whirling, I sprint back the way I came, doing my best not to give in to the gnawing dread growing inside of me. What if Deran isn't answering because he can't?

Now that I've acknowledged the danger, the questions cascade, a rushing torrent. Did a mindhunter hear his damning words? I know he was whispering, but don't some of them have insane hearing? If they caught what he said, have they seized him, taken him away?

My heart falters. Has Deran fallen prey to the same fate as my brother?

No! I can't think like that. I push myself harder, feet flying over the ground as I try to convince myself he isn't answering because he's mad at me. A far more palatable reason than the alternative and the only one I can accept if I'm to think clearly. Or as clearly as I can, given the circumstances.

When I crash through the double doors into the foyer of CC HQ, the serenity sentries on duty at the front desk startle, their eyes widening. Apprehension sweeps across their faces, contemplating what sort of crazy woman invaded their space.

Even as the SerSents draw their stun sticks, I dart toward the turnstile, waving my arm over the access panel. A muted beep. Then I'm through as the computer accepts my credentials and grants entry.

The SerSents seem baffled. Shouldn't they know I work here? As often as I've walked through these doors, I would've expected some recognition. After all, I'm not just anybody. Cygnus, CC's director, made me head of the R&D labs, didn't he?

Cygnus! The mere thought of the man reignites my fury. Gritting my teeth, I make a concerted effort not to think about him—the man at the center of all this trouble.

Instead, I focus on finding Deran. The best place to start is where I last left him. Despite my desire to race up the stairs, burn off the excess energy, the elevator will get me there faster. I pace the polished marble, trying to keep a clamp on the panic threatening to overwhelm me.

By the time the elevator arrives, I'm almost hyperventilating. I barge in, bashing into the exiting passengers. Ignoring their muttered complaints, I slap the button for the lab floor. Finally, the doors close, and I bounce from foot to foot, the trip seeming interminable, but in reality lasting mere seconds.

Then I'm there and barreling onto the lab floor, past my team's blurred faces all wearing the same shocked expressions. *Yes, yes, I know! I've never acted this way in front of you before. Then again, there's never been so much at stake.*

I skid into my office, narrowly missing the desk. No sign of Deran. Racing back out, I tear down the corridors to the workshop, where Deran and his team of mechanical engineers are assembling the cold fusion energy device I've been tasked with inventing. I didn't even believe I'd succeed in creating a machine capable of generating more power than it consumes, using only clean, abundant fuels to trigger the process.

More gaping from Deran's team, but I'm immune. "Where's Deran?"

Silvan, the most senior, answers. "I don't know. We last saw him when he left to find you."

My screech is feral. Deran's team take several cautious steps backward, and I want to cackle maniacally. But this is no time to lose control. I *must* find Deran. Stabbing my comm link, I order the call again. Same disturbing, infuriating result.

I make it all the way back to my office, still unable to reach him, but hoping I might find him waiting. When I discover my office empty, I slam the door behind me, then pace the confined area.

My initial desire to set up a meeting so I could ask those burning questions has morphed into spiraling worry. A pit only aggravating the desperation caused by my brother's abduction. I'm wearing grooves into my carpet, but I can't stop, can't stand still. I have to know, have to get answers.

But with Deran missing too, there's only one other option. Turning to the one person I can't abide. Exasperated beyond measure, I hurl the drinking glass on my desk against the wall, relishing the thunk as it hits. It shatters, showering glittering shards onto the floor.

I give the mug on my desk the same treatment, then follow up with a decorative glass orb, hollow except for the glitter in a thin casing around the outside. Sparkles follow the broken glass to the floor, an even more pleasing demise.

As I survey the carnage, panting, a deranged grin creases my face. That's how I'd like to see Cygnus. Broken and in pieces. His stellar career crashing to obscurity, sinking into the dust on the floor, lost forever.

The desire galvanizes me into action. Time for answers. I no longer care that I have to ask the one man who wants me to beg.

As I charge out of my office, I catch sight of my team again. "Stop gawking!" The command is sharp, but their constant surveillance is driving me nuts. "Get on with your work." A flurry of activity follows, and I hurry away, my grin turning grim.

Now if I can just behave the same way with Cygnus: the director of CC and the person I once believed was on my side. Fortunately, I've seen the light. Unfortunately, he's still my boss.

As the elevator whisks me to the top floor, I remind myself my failure to repeat my success with the cold fusion energy device was not the catalyst for Xanin's disappearance. Thanks to my mother's inadvertent slip, I'm certain of it.

Her error is also the reason Cygnus's goons barged into the meeting he'd "granted" with the rest of my family and removed them —because he didn't want them revealing more specifics.

The memory niggles. Why did my mom call them "security

people?" Surely she's familiar with SerSents? My gut clenches as I reach another conclusion. Perhaps it wasn't SerSents who took Xanin.

The elevator doors open, spitting me out onto the very top floor of CC HQ. Into the scrawny arms of Hag Lady. Startled, she glances up, but not even her stony stare can stop me. "You can't go in! Chiara! You're not allowed. Stop!"

Barely registering Cygnus's goons aren't flanking his door as usual, I ignore Hag Lady's shrieks. *You just try to stop me, Mrs. Jacobs!* My smile is devilish, thinking of the trouble she'll be in for this. Serves her right for always being such a hag.

Then I'm through the door, into the lion's den. However, Cygnus is clearly expecting me. Leaning back in his disgustingly expensive genuine leather chair, he smiles.

Except I see the smile for what it truly is. Not kindly or pitying. The smirk of someone about to snap the head off a doll.

"What have you done with Xanin?" I demand.

"Why, Chiara, so nice to see you again! Did you forget something?"

Aargh! I want to claw the hideous smile off that face others find so irresistible. Want to rip that dark hair out, scrape my fingers down his tanned face, break that perfect Roman nose so it's forever crooked. But I must submit, must do what's expected. If I end up in prison, or dead, I'll never free my family. If I ever learn where they live. Another detail that's been kept from me.

Clenching my jaw, I go through the motions expected of us peons when greeting Cygnus. The gestures stiff, the words ground out between clamped teeth, I pull my arms apart, then link my fingers in the squashed delta symbol. "All for one and work for all."

Throughout the entire belittling process, Cygnus gloats, enjoying every second of my misery. Then, as if remembering himself, the smile disappears, an earnest expression taking its place. "Chiara, you've been with me long enough to know how things work: just as you get rewards when you make progress, there's punishment when you don't."

Another hysterical laugh tickles the back of my throat. How could I ever have thought the Board were the ones giving the orders? How many years did I delude myself into thinking Cygnus only had my best interests at heart?

"Director, you took my brother before I even showed you the machine. Therefore, it follows it wasn't punishment. You had another reason, and I demand to know what."

"Chiara, Chiara, Chiara." He shakes his head. "You know you weren't making progress. Until this morning, I would classify your achievements as less than stellar. At the very least, not up to your usual standard."

Really? He had to say my name three times? Curbing the urge to scream, I bite the words out, my temper still in no way leashed. "A nice, convenient excuse, Director! Didn't you forego the deadline in favor of allowing the mech team to get the job right the first time?"

Cygnus reels back like I've slapped him. *Yes, you've never seen this side of me, have you?*

Spurred on by his reaction, I can't resist adding fuel to the fire. "Also, when I haven't met your expectations in the past, you've given me the opportunity to correct the problem. Why not allow me the same courtesy this time?"

Bronze glints in those hazel eyes warn of his anger. But I won't back down. Not this time.

"Director McQueen, you still haven't answered my question! What is the real reason you took my brother?"

While I'd love to mention the E-AMPS gene, I can't tip my hand or allow the director to know I have forbidden information. But the question's bored a hole into my head ever since I saw the accusation in my mother's eyes. She thought they took Xanin for the same reason they took me—and the only thing connecting my brother and I (beyond the obvious) is the mysterious gene.

Cygnus still hasn't answered. "Well?"

Voice cutting as sharpened steel, Cygnus stares me down. "Have you forgotten who you're talking to?"

No, I know you're the Director. You've just pushed me enough that I don't care if you're the most powerful man on the planet. While I think the words, I dare not voice them. Reason beats me over the head, screaming her warning: I'll never save my family if I'm dead. Besides, two can play this game.

With a deep, calming breath, I paste a suitably contrite expression on my face. "I apologize, Director. I'm sure you can understand I'm more than a little emotional. Although I concede that doesn't excuse my behavior."

For the first time, I see something on Cygnus's face I've never seen before. Uncertainty. In an instant, I understand why. He's not sure if my apology is real—but he desperately wants it to be.

Was I actually right those times I sensed his feelings toward me were more than superficial? I shiver, the thought of him viewing me in *that* way repulsive in the extreme. Yet an opportunity not to be squandered.

I offer a pleading smile. "Director Cygnus, I'm sorry for my outburst. Please, will you tell me where Xanin is?"

The name I've called the director since he "rescued" me from my previous life does the trick. While bile still taints my mouth, the bitter taste is worth the result. Cygnus relaxes, obviously feeling in control again. I suppress the fierce grin, careful to keep my features patterned like those of a hopeful child.

"Chiara, you know I can't tell you where they took your brother. But I promise when you produce a working machine, you'll see him again."

Interesting. He still hasn't given a straight answer. More interesting, would I have picked up on this subtlety a few weeks ago? Desperate as I am to believe the director took Xanin as punishment, his guile leads me to confirm my earlier suspicions.

His answer also further cements a recent realization. If I truly want to keep my family safe, I must free them from Cygnus's clutches. And Cygnus will never give them back without a fight. They've been far too useful to him over the years.

That's about to change.

Abruptly, I realize now would be a good time to leave. I don't want to overplay my hand. I need the director thinking he's in the driver's seat. He can't know my eyes have been opened. He mustn't even suspect it.

"Thank you, Director Cygnus. I will endeavor to complete the machine as quickly as I can."

"I'm pleased to hear that. You may go."

Careful to follow the expected motions and spit the hateful line, I leave. Outside, Hag Lady's frosty stare confronts me. I give a cheery finger wave. "Toodles!" I'm still grinning at her purple-faced outrage when the elevator arrives to ferry me to safer places.

2

By the time I step back onto the lab floor, my black mood has returned. All good and well to say I need to free my family from Cygnus, but how? Worse, my meeting produced no answers.

Feet slapping the floor, I stomp back to my office. Why does Cygnus threaten me every time he sees me? Insecure raccoon! He's a nasty creature, just like them. Considering the black rings around his eyes and those vicious little teeth, all he needs are the horrid little claws.

The mental image returns a smile to my face, but only until I notice the way my team regard me. No time like the present. "Okay, you can all stop staring at me like I'm a volcano about to erupt. I'll be fine. If you must know, I've had some upsetting news. I'll get over it."

No surprise when Tandize (their unofficial spokeswoman) speaks, but her question is unexpected. "Is there anything we can do?"

Honestly, I didn't think she cared. "It's kind of you to ask, but I just need time to process. If you could all give me a little space, I'd appreciate it."

Again, Tandize speaks for the rest. "We can do that."

"Thank you." I continue the long march down the corridor

between the lab benches, eager to escape their curious stares, but resisting the urge to run. When I eventually reach my office at the far end of the lab, I'm impressed with my self-control.

Shutting the door, I lean back against it with a heavy sigh. I don't know whether to scream or cry. I still have no idea where they took Xanin, and I doubt the truth of the why.

As for Deran...

For the umpteenth time, I call him. Still no answer. Driven to distraction by the gruesome possibilities my mind conjures, I close my eyes and try to remain perfectly still against the door, concealing my distress from those ever-present cameras. I'm all too aware I can't give Cygnus another person to use against me. With luck, any torment I've let slip will be attributed to my brother's abduction.

If only Sarissa were here! I'd have someone to talk to.

Shocked by the unexpected thought, my eyes fly open. Where in the world did that come from? I haven't thought about her since her suicide. And since when was it acceptable to miss someone who betrayed you?

Out of sorts, I flop onto my chair, then drag my cube toward me, tapping it, before flicking the data collected from our two most recent trials onto the wall behind me, more for something to do than because I really intend studying it.

While science is typically my sanctuary, today, I can't get with the program. I stare at the information on the holoscreen, split to show the results of both tests, but my mind can't make sense of it. *That's a first.*

Listless, I rise, then pace the restricted confines of my office again. For the sake of those prying eyes, I should pretend to analyze the data, attack the project as I told Cygnus I would, but I can't face the prospect.

I pick up my massage ball, then amble to the closest empty wall. Tucking the ball between my aching shoulders and the wall, I slide around on it, enjoying the release of tension. Another incidental advantage? Facing my screens, it might appear I'm contemplating the data.

The buzz of my comm link startles me so much, I roll too far. The ball pops out as my shoulder crashes into the wall. *Ow!* But the pain fades at the message blinking on my mental screen.

"Can't talk now. Meet you in our spot in an hour?"

Deran! He's alive! He's okay! I'm so elated I almost forget to answer. After sending the solitary, "Yes," I know there's only one way to release the boundless energy coursing through me.

In the gym, I pump up the pace on the treadmill, reveling in the sheer exhilaration as I drive my heart rate up. You'd never guess I'd already run a few miles today, but thoughts I haven't permitted myself to contemplate swirl.

Uppermost is the rebellious glint in Deran's eyes when the SerSents dragged me away. At least I know if he acted on any rash impulses after our argument, he wasn't caught, or he couldn't have sent that message. So, what has he been up to? Dare I hope he may have answers about where they took Xanin?

Twenty sweaty minutes later, I'm still asking questions. I slow the pace and start my cool down. Then I'm off the machine and into the locker room for a quick shower.

By the time I exit the gym, my mood is restored, hope and optimism filling me once more. Deran. The man with the answers. Also, to my relief, one who will still meet me, despite the way I behaved.

As I exit CC HQ, I'm abruptly aware of the people around me. Finally, Deran's almost cryptic message hits home, and I understand. I nearly forgot! How could I be so careless? No wonder he wasn't specific, considering CC's ability to monitor comm messages!

I rotate slowly, pretending I'm taking in the scenery, savoring its beauty by lifting my hands high and waving them through the air. I smile like I have no cares in the world, but I'm carefully studying those around me. With their faces etched into my infallible mind, I finish the rotation and then skip along to increase my pace.

By the time I reach the trundle, I've put significant distance between myself and the rest of the herd. Enough to notice three people who've kept pace, who all leap onto the departing trundle with me. One in a business suit, one in overalls, and one...

Maxwell's theory of electromagnetism is a gauge theory, where the gauge symmetry group is the abelian group U(1). If A represents...

Despite flooding my thoughts with math, the realization is a strident gong in the back of my mind. A min—minus man! No, get back to your calculations. All the while, I scan for an opportunity, a chance to escape.

The trundle zips up to a stop I recognize. Excellent! I couldn't have chosen better if I'd thought about it. I wait until the doors are closing before jumping up and darting through the narrowing space. With a grunt, I catch an elbow on one door, but I don't stop Then I'm outside sprinting down the platform, away from the departing trundle.

My eyes meet the gaze of the man still stuck on the train. Was he really following me?

But I can't permit any distractions. There could be other minus men. A term I use so they don't know I know their real name—*mindhunters*. It's knowledge I shouldn't have, and if they figured out I knew, Cygnus would hear about it. I can't even begin to comprehend the consequences.

Determined, I keep my mind on math problems, hoping I'm successfully thwarting any nearby mindhunter's ability to read minds.

As my mind picks away at the math, my feet carry me to the mall I've visited once before. There, I dart through the bustling food court, grateful it's late enough in the day crowds are taking advantage of the easy meal for an early dinner.

I remember a surveillance technique in a movie I watched once. Accordingly, I use any reflective surfaces to scan the people behind me. None of the three faces I flagged at the trundle stop follow me. So far, so good.

Doesn't mean I'm out of danger. Aware of time ticking by and knowing I still have a way to go before I reach "our spot," I pick up the pace. In the party store, I choose a wig, hat, and overcoat, trying to think about the items as little as possible.

I pay for my purchase with an untraceable cash card. Using the store's restroom, I change into my disguise, carefully avoiding looking at my reflection in the mirror, worried this may somehow convey a mental image to any nearby mindhunters.

Hidden in a group of boisterous teenagers, I exit the store. Who said being short didn't have its advantages?

I remain alert for fresh faces which may have replaced those I flagged earlier as I scurry out of the mall. Although I find no one suspicious, the nagging concern I missed something ramps up my anxiety. I must learn more about surveillance. I'm only guessing at what I think I should look for based on movies I've watched and fiction Sarissa shared with me, and who knows how accurate that was?

Sarissa! Not the first, or even second, time I've thought of her today. Perhaps because I'm wondering how she fits into what Deran said.

When I reach Northsummit Park, I'm sweating in my disguise. I'm two minutes, twenty-seven seconds past the agreed meeting time, and I've yet to reach the secluded spot Deran took me to for our picnic.

On the bright side, all the park's open space makes it so much easier to confirm no one's following me. At least, not in person. Eyes lifting, I scour the sky, searching for drones, but they're not always easy to spot. Their silver bodies reflect the sky and make them all but invisible.

Afraid of what I can't see, I seek the cover of nearby trees, working my way through the small wood in an inordinately long roundabout route until I finally reach the place I was aiming for. Still no visible sign of pursuit, but this only increases my anxiety. Sudden movement draws my eye, and I stifle a shriek. Then air whooshes out as I recognize the muscular frame, broad shoulders, long legs. *Deran!*

I raise a hand to my chest, calming a heart in overdrive. "Whew, you scared me!"

Wordlessly, Deran closes the distance between us and pulls me into his arms. I'm too startled to resist. Not that I would've wanted to.

Deran's voice is a murmur next to my ear. "I thought something had happened to you." Almost imperceptibly, his hold on me tightens.

Although I want to stay where I am and savor his warmth, the comfort of his arms, the sense of safety, I lean back far enough to smack him on the arm. "That makes two of us! Why didn't you answer my calls?"

A smile creases his handsome face. This time, I do take a moment to relish the sight. I didn't think I'd ever see him again, let alone that cheeky smile. And now, here he is, safe and sound and cradling me, whole and unharmed. Unlike my brother. "Deran, where's Xanin?"

His smile falls away, gray eyes turning slate as storm clouds roll across them. "I'm sorry, Chiara, I don't know where they took him." Discerning my disappointment, his arms tighten again, keeping me in place. "Don't run away again. Understand, I refuse to lie to you, to give you false hope. Believe me when I say I'll do everything I can to help you find him because I meant what I told you earlier."

This time, my voice turns soft. "You don't want him suffering the same fate as your sister and Sarissa?"

"Yes."

I hesitate—the one time he mentioned her proves how much speaking about his sister affects Deran—before succumbing to the need to know. "What happened to them?"

Deran releases me, running a hand through his rich auburn hair. The spikes on top of his head stand straighter than flagpoles, suggesting he's been doing this all afternoon. Sudden tension emanates from him in waves. Then his eyes scan our surroundings as he withdraws his specially modified music player.

My angst returns; I've been careless with my words. I should've waited until he'd set the machine up before asking him questions.

With a strained smile, Deran starts the music. Grasping my hand, he draws me into the area behind the machine where we can't be heard. Or, rather, where we hope his modified music player will prevent this.

Now that we're more protected, I remember there's something I must do before he begins. "I'm sorry I kneed you. I shouldn't have run away. Will you forgive me?"

Deran tugs me into his arms again, and I want to melt. How is it I found someone so wonderful at such a terrible time in my life?

"I understand. Although, next time, simply ask me to let you go?" At his teasing tone, I blush considering the damage I might've done.

I drop my head onto his shoulder, only to lift my chin so he can more easily hear me. "I'm also sorry for asking questions before you set your machine up."

Deran's hand brushes through my hair, soothing me. "Just don't make a habit of it."

I giggle. "Yes, sir."

Through my fingertips, I feel the reverberations in his chest as Deran chuckles softly. Then the sigh that follows. "I suppose I can't put this off any longer. Before we start, did you have any problems getting here?" He fingers the wig I still wear. "This would seem to indicate you did?"

Hurriedly, I tug the hat and wig off, eager to be rid of them. "I think they tried to follow me, hence the diversion to a costume store and this disguise."

"They followed you from CC HQ?"

"Yes. Three people kept up with me all the way to the trundle, but…" My voice trails off. I only focused on losing one of them—the perceived mindhunter. What happened to the other two?

"Chiara?"

I shake my head. "Sorry. I just realized I was so focused on the one I thought was a mindhunter, I didn't pay attention to the other two. Give me a second." Mentally, I replay the time between getting onto the trundle and hopping off to escape the mindhunter, thankful my mind works this way.

One got off before I did, and the other remained stuck on the train after my hasty exit. "Yes, I gave them all the slip. Although I remained vigilant, I didn't pick up another tail. Not that I'm exactly an expert in countersurveillance."

Deran's grim expression confirms what I already knew. Just because we can't see them doesn't mean they aren't there. But we've taken as many precautions as we can. It's time.

Sensing my change in mood, Deran tenses, before shocking me with a direct answer I didn't expect. One I'm totally unprepared for.

"The conglomerate murdered Sarissa. The same way they murdered my sister."

3

"What?" I'm still wrapping my mind around Deran's devastating revelation when the words hit home. The earth drops out from under me, and I sway. There isn't enough air. I'm barely able to get the words out. "They're going to kill Xanin?" Deran's arms turn suffocating, and I push against him, needing my freedom.

While Deran loosens his hold, he doesn't release me completely. His hands glide up to grip my biceps, and he shakes me gently, forcing my gaze to his. "No, they won't kill him. At least, not yet, and not using their own hands."

My brain refuses to think, wading sluggishly through the quagmire abruptly encasing it. Eyes unseeing, I stare at Deran, still unable to make sense of his words. Then my rising panic makes me struggle. "Let me go!"

This time, Deran's shake is rough. "Chiara! Snap out of it! If you're going to freak out before you hear the whole story, I won't tell you more."

The threat registers, and I freeze. I know—it's so sad! I'm so hungry for answers I'll even betray myself. Voice hoarse, I grate out a retort. "Fine. But could you speed it up?"

Deran releases me, only so his hands can rake through his hair again as he paces. Abruptly, I realize he's trying to figure out what to tell me and how, so I don't lose it.

I must fix this. Closing my eyes, I inhale deeply, hold the breath for a second, and then release the air slowly, repeating the process a few times until a measure of calm returns. Once it does, I order myself to maintain my semi-Zen state, no matter what he says.

Yeah, right! Like that's going to work.

I take another deep breath. *It can work, and it must. For Xanin's sake.*

"Deran, I'll be fine. I'm sorry I overreacted, but I think it's fair to say you could've started with a less explosive sentence! That said, going forward, I'll endeavor to remain composed and hear you out before falling apart." Gaze piercing, Deran assesses the truth of my claim, but he doesn't comment. "Please, just speak to me. Tell me something. Anything! The waiting is worse than hearing something awful." Still no response. "Please?"

Deran remains dubious. "Are you sure you're ready?"

"I am. Now can I get some answers?"

Expression grim, Deran takes my hand, then pulls me to the ground. We sit cross-legged, opposite each other and knees touching, like we did on our picnic. After one last look around, checking we're still in the dampening field created by his modified music player and that no one else is nearby, he sighs. "Do you remember how Sarissa's behavior changed before she died?"

The question throws me, but I don't know what I expected. I can hardly forget how Sarissa went from being my only friend and closest confidante to the sullen woman who no longer cared how important my family was. Her increasingly reckless behavior, first arriving at work drunk, then drinking at work, to unexplained absences. When I challenged her on this last offense, she only subjected me to more bizarre behavior. I shake my head.

Deran frowns. "You don't remember, or you didn't notice?"

"No, it's not that."

"What then?"

"I still don't understand how Sarissa changed so radically. One day she was the carefree party girl who took me shopping for silly, insanely overpriced dresses and made me smile with her insistence on paper schedules with ridiculous checkboxes. The next, she was a stranger who fawned over me one minute, then screamed obscenities the next." I shake my head again, then nod. "So yes, I remember. How's that relevant?"

"The same thing happened to my sister before she killed herself."

I'm a ship at sea again, tossed about by the storm. I flounder, out of my depth, unsure how to respond. Emotional trauma is something I've never known how to deal with. Instinct must take over because my hand touches Deran's of its own accord, providing the limited comfort our seating arrangement allows. "I'm sorry. I didn't know."

Deran's face is drawn, anguish tightening his features, but there's also determination there. Almost as if he came here today set on sharing certain things, regardless of the personal cost. "I know you didn't. But you need to understand what happened. Let me show you."

Deran touches his comm link, pulling up the holographic screen, but keeping it small and low where it can't be seen except from directly overhead. Safe from most prying eyes.

The still image before the video plays shows a young woman. The family resemblance is unmistakable. Tall, like Deran, with an athletic frame instead of his muscular one, her hair is a darker shade of his rich auburn. While her eyes are equally striking, they're green instead of his gray. Then I see her mouth, curved in that all-too-familiar smile, an exact replica of her brother's. A smile that transforms her face. "Your sister?"

Deran nods, tears shimmering on his lashes. "Carys." He taps the play button, and the scene comes to life.

Carys and Deran are with friends—more hers than his judging by the ages. The group socializes around a table covered with the remnants of a meal. Less than ten seconds in, and it's obvious she's the life of the party. The one everyone turns to, everyone wants a piece of.

Someone in this position could so easily preen. Carys does nothing of the sort. She listens, offers thoughtful answers, makes sure her brother is included by asking his opinion. Nothing seems to bother her, not the tough questions nor the little brother the others tease her about. A little brother whose hair she tousles and who she touches frequently. Every touch shows her unconditional love. Her smile comes easily and often, each instance reminding me of Deran, so quiet and still beside me.

I squeeze Deran's hand, and offer a wistful smile, thinking of my own siblings and what I wouldn't give to love on them now. No answering smile, just a bleak nod of acknowledgement as he stops this video and plays another.

A birthday celebration. Carys's. The cake is decorated with flowers— purple irises—and covered with pale pink frosting. Deran puts an arm around her, and she turns, hugging him enthusiastically as he wishes her happy birthday. Then she's cutting the cake, laughing, telling those with her she didn't deserve such an expensive treat. Since Deran's the only one visible in the frame, I'm not sure who else is there.

"Not every day my baby turns eighteen," a voice off-camera says, likely her dad.

I swallow the lump in my throat. The love and tenderness in his voice is unmistakable. Would my father have bought me a special cake and used the same tone if he'd been around for my last birthday? Granted, not my eighteenth, but what are a few months?

I'm still hoping for a glimpse of Deran's parents when he abruptly flips to the next video.

Eyes rimmed too heavily with eyeliner that's too dark, I almost don't recognize Carys. Her hair, previously a glorious auburn curtain down her back, hangs limp. Her face no longer glows with radiant health. Instead, she's made an ineffective attempt at hiding the acne marring that once-perfect skin.

"Stop hanging around! Find your own friends! Must I always take care of you?" Then she lurches forward, snatching at the camera. "And get that bloody thing out of my face!"

The shrieking shrew is a violent slap, and I rear back, appalled. I'm so shocked, I lose my breath. Speech is beyond me. I can't even offer Deran any comfort.

Next to me, Deran swallows. Silent tears roll down his face.

Employing every scrap of willpower, I grip his hand, but the touch is too distant, too impersonal. I want to hold him, bring him closer, provide him with the comfort and reassurance he's given me so many times before. I shift, nestling in his lap, my arms sliding around his waist as I draw him closer.

"Thanks." Deran gives me a squeeze, then clears his throat. "That argument made me confide in my parents. Turns out it wasn't me. Carys had not only been treating them the same way, but her friends too. Overnight, she'd become the girl everyone was fighting with, instead of the girl everyone loved. My parents and I knew we had to do something, but no matter how we tried to engage her, Carys just slipped further and further from us. Then she got into a physical altercation with a girl at school. That day, her food trays went from green to blue."

My eyes widen, my mind spins. "Wait, you're telling me... what? You said I shouldn't eat the food the conglomerate provides. Is this related?"

Instead of answering, Deran selects another video. "This is Carys two days later."

Carys sits on a park bench, a notepad on her lap. No makeup, but a serene expression, even though she looks exhausted. She smiles at the camera. "What you up to, D?"

Before I can take in more, Deran flips the video again.

"You're deceived! The world isn't what you think it is!"

Deran's patient voice off-camera. "What do you mean?"

Face blotchy with rage, she screams at him. "Can't you see? It's... they... figure it out!"

Then she shoves Deran out of the way, judging from the way the image bounces down to the floor, then up against a wall.

I can't help it. I never wanted to think about Sarissa again, but it seems I can't get away from her today. Wasn't this exactly how she behaved at the end? I thought it was because I'd rejected her. Instead, she was suffering through something unimaginable. Hollowness carves a pit into my heart, leaving me devastated. How could I have neglected her when she needed me the most?

Oblivious to my inner turmoil, Deran flips to another video. "And this is four days later."

This time, he didn't capture the footage. *An irate shopkeeper accuses Carys of shoplifting. Carys is louder, belligerent, proclaiming her innocence, until the shopkeeper leans forward and rips the bag off Carys's arm. Store-sealed packages spill out.*

"What do you call this?" The shopkeeper's voice is triumphant.

My eyes find Deran's. He fills in the blanks. "The store chose not to press charges, but it was the worst thing they could've done. Instead of learning from her mistakes and getting better, she deteriorated, to the point she became destructive."

"Destructive?"

I wish I hadn't asked. Deran's face is grey now, the skin too tight, his eyes too dark. "Here."

Another clip. *The raging lunatic onscreen smashes a collection of incredibly detailed porcelain buildings. Pieces fly in all directions, and she attacks the remains. With nothing left to destroy, Carys throws her bat at the wall, slamming a hole in it.*

Deran sighs. "Those buildings represented designs Carys spent years accumulating, pieces no one was allowed to touch. Not only did she pulverize every piece of her cherished collection, but she took to throwing anything that came to hand and actively sought physical altercations. She was violent enough to end up with a citation from a SerSent. That was the day—"

I freeze in Deran's arms, images from the past few months flashing past with relentless speed. Trashing the vent pipe. My irritation with my team. The unusual emotional outbursts. Even my little episode less than two hours ago, how satisfying it was to shatter every single piece against the wall.

Still reeling, I recall the day my food trays changed from green to blue. Dread sets in. Is Deran showing me a pattern?

Regarding me, Deran finishes his sentence. "Her food trays went from blue to yellow."

My blood runs cold, my voice is a rasped whisper. "Just like Sarissa's." With blinding clarity, I finally grasp what Deran was warning me about earlier today. "Let me guess—she was back to normal for a while again?"

Deran studies me, eyes probing, face grave. "Do you understand now why I warned you?"

I fight for air. Panting, I struggle to come to terms with this discovery. My distress must show because Deran moves without warning.

In one fluid motion, he rises, lifting me with him, my legs dropping to the ground, limp as a ragdoll's. He's smart enough not to let me go. Supporting my weight with one muscular arm, he cradles me, using his other hand to rub soothing circles on my back. "Breathe, just breathe."

A fish out of water flashes to mind, and I perceive their desperation, understand their mouths gaping open and shut, their failure to find what their respiratory system needs. In seconds, my lungs ache, begging for relief.

Air jolts back into my body as Deran thumps my back. The shock of the unexpectedly firm contact after the soothing circles breaks the cycle, and welcome oxygen floods my lungs.

Two full minutes later, I feel more like myself. Or rather, as normal as I can be, given what I've just realized. I glance up at Deran, still holding me. Those gray eyes cloud over as they study me. "Really? There's something in the food?"

Deran nods.

"And the tray color changes mean they're increasing the concentration of whatever they add?"

Another solemn nod.

Although my legs are shaky, I push away from Deran, needing movement. This time, Deran yields, but I don't go far. There's no need to run away from the one person I feel safe with. Besides, where would I go? I'd only be running closer to danger, to that increasingly high cliff others have thrown themselves over.

I quit pacing the small area Deran himself paced only a short while ago, stopping in front of him. "You're saying whatever they add to the food is the reason Sarissa committed suicide?"

With a shake of his head, Deran takes my hand. "No, there's more to it. Can we please sit again?" When I resist his tug, he shrugs. "Okay, we can just stand here while I destroy your world."

Something in his tone has me searching for an answer on his face. Lips clamped tight, eyes lifeless gray slate, muscle ticking in his jaw. My finger goes to the tic, the place I've wanted to touch since I first saw it, and I ease my finger along his jawline, soothing the tension.

The slightest change in Deran's stance tells me I'm succeeding. I gaze into those incredible eyes, still focused on mine. "Deran, you're not destroying my world. You're opening my eyes. You're the only person who's ever cared enough to do so. Please, there's no need for remorse. I'm the one who asked to know, remember? Besides, if I don't have the courage to confront my fears, how will I ever learn the truth?"

Finally, Deran's features relax. He tugs me closer, crushing me against his chest. "If I could've shielded you from this, I would've. You don't know how much I've argued with myself about this decision."

I recall the weeks I watched him watching me, how he always seemed on the verge of saying something. How I decided I needed to gain his trust so he would share his secrets. And now that he is, do I regret it? Am I still unsure of him?

Do I still think he's a spy for Cygnus?

4

I want to deny the allegation vehemently, but after everything I've recently learned, I'd be a fool to ignore that tiny part believing even all this could be a ruse. Granted, an elaborate one, but the timing of Deran's revelations seems a little too convenient. "Deran, why are you telling me these things now? You've had so many opportunities before, when things weren't so dire."

With another quick squeeze before he releases me, Deran tugs me back to the ground. This time, I don't resist. We're barely back in our familiar front-facing, knee-touching position before he clutches my hands, gaze earnest.

"I couldn't take seeing you in so much pain. I know only too well how much it hurts to lose a sibling. When I saw you after your family meeting, it brought back all too vividly the anguish I once felt. The circumstances demanded I share what I did because I wish someone could've done the same for me after my sister disappeared."

"Disappeared?"

"Yes, exactly like Sarissa."

"Sarissa never—" I break off, suddenly remembering the ten days she was gone. The way she vanished from work one Friday, then her extended absence afterward, supposedly due to "some nasty bug."

My eyes widen as I remember a detail that should've raised all sorts of alarms. "That's why a SerSent came and collected her things?"

"Pardon?"

Deran's confusion makes me realize I have some explaining of my own to do. "Sorry! I didn't think about it back then, but that Friday, when I found Sarissa's office empty, Tandize followed me in and told me Sarissa never came back after lunch. Then she said, 'A SerSent came and collected her stuff.'"

"Why?"

"My question exactly!"

"What did Tandize say?"

I wave a dismissive hand. "She guessed something might've happened to a member of Sarissa's family, but if she knew Sarissa, she'd understand that never would've been the reason. But Deran, Tandize was clearly afraid."

For a few seconds, Deran says nothing. What if I can't trust him after all? I've just revealed Tandize as an ally I can turn to if he betrays me. As the silence stretches on, my anxiety deepens, more so when I realize something else.

After my insight, Tandize brushed off questions about her fear of the SerSents, then told me Sarissa probably wouldn't be back before making a hasty exit. Was Tandize trying to warn me about what might've happened to Sarissa? Is it possible she may know as much as Deran? Or could it be *she's* the plant to replace Sarissa, giving me information to get me to trust her, because Deran isn't the spy after all?

Nervous energy prompts me to move again, but when I make to get to my feet, Deran puts a hand on my arm. "How well do you know Tandize?" His face gives nothing away.

"Not well. I hired her less than a year ago."

"Chiara, I'm going to ask something that may seem strange."

I nod acceptance, although I already know where he's going.

"Don't trust her with anything I tell you."

There it is. But who *should* I trust? The answer is obvious. Right now, myself and only myself. Caution is essential. Whatever Deran shares, I'll take with a pinch of salt, verify for myself, until I can confirm what my heart desperately wants to believe—that he's safe.

"I don't plan to."

Deran searches my face but must decide I'm being honest. "Before, when I asked why the SerSents would take Sarissa's things, I didn't mean what you thought I did."

"Oh?"

"I meant why would they telegraph they'd taken Sarissa?"

"Oh!"

Deran grins. "Are you aware you said the same word twice, but gave it two entirely different meanings?"

I laugh, bright relief from the black tension. "I'll have to work on that."

"No, don't. It's refreshing to hear so much in so little."

His statement just makes me giggle more. "Really?"

Deran rolls his eyes. "Well, you know how Silvan can talk. He uses a thousand words when he could use a hundred. Then there's Koni…"

I punch his arm lightly. "You know Koni only talks *at* you because he wants to be like you."

He rewards me with another gorgeous grin. Before I can fully appreciate it though, it fades, replaced by the seriousness I'm beginning to loathe. "You know, if Sarissa hadn't killed herself like Carys did, under the same circumstances, I could've kept all those feelings buried. But your devastation about Sarissa's suicide made everything that happened to my sister resurface. That was the day I decided it was time I had an ally, someone who could fight back with me."

"Then why did it take you so long to share things with me?"

A pained expression. "Aw, Chiara, you're really going to make me say it?" I don't answer, and he sighs. "I had to be sure I could trust you. Verify your oblivion to the situation was real, not something conjured to entice me into revealing my true agenda."

"I understand only too well, believe me," I mutter. The more Deran divulges, the more I want to believe he's genuine. Despite this, that little needle pricks, warning me to be careful. "What changed?"

"The director gave you that side project."

My turn to be confused. "The one you were so adamant I *not* take? How did that affect things?"

"Suffice to say, it was more than a confirmation you really were clueless about the real world."

"So that's why you invited me on a picnic? To set things straight?"

Deran nods. "Not that I got very far."

I recall the abrupt end to our picnic, when we realized CC could be listening to our conversation through our comm links. What a relief when my desperate measures confirmed our fears were unfounded. "This is the reason you whispered more secrets this afternoon?"

"The conglomerate taking your brother forced my timetable. I don't have the luxury of waiting anymore. We must find your brother before it's too late. To do that, you need to know everything I do. Only by working together will we get answers, because although I know plenty, there's just as much that's still a mystery."

While that tiny irritating part of me screams Deran's increasing the conspiracy angle, another voice gets more strident, yelling Deran's telling the truth.

As if to prove the second voice right, my mind returns to our initial discussion: food trays. Sarissa told me they changed color because we were getting older, so the conglomerate added "nutrients" to stop us from getting fat.

Deran confirmed they were adding something, but what? And why? Unexpectedly, a memory springs to mind, another "picnic," one Cygnus once permitted our family to enjoy. My focus hones on my mother's food tray. Green. Not blue or yellow, or the final color Sarissa's turned to, orange.

If I'd taken time to think about Sarissa's claim back when she told me, I would've recognized the lie. This only adds to my resentment, considering the way she betrayed me. *Stop! You're not focusing on the right problem!*

"Deran, what do they add to the food, why, and when?"

To my surprise, a laugh rumbles out. My head tilts up, and I lose my breath for an instant, his face incredibly more handsome now with that glorious smile. "If I had forgotten you like asking questions, that last sentence only emphasizes it."

I grin. "Isn't there something somewhere about women being the nosy ones?"

"Oh, I'm so not going there! But to answer: as soon as someone exhibits what CC considers 'rebellious behavior,' questioning this world we live in, they add the coercion serum."

Stunned, I stare at him. "Coercion serum?"

"Yes, that's what they call it. It dulls the part of your brain that asks those questions."

I purse my lips, a few things coming together. "So, when someone's food tray is green, they're compliant, and they have no additives in their food?"

"No, the color then is gray. You probably don't remember because trays usually switch from gray to green at the first sign of those teenage tantrums."

Another memory returns. The one and only time I rebelled against Cygnus's demands and the terrible consequences for my family. I was so disturbed by the whole event, I *didn't* notice, but my infallible mind replays my food trays in the Academy cafeteria before and after. Definitely gray to green.

Throat suddenly dry, I struggle to get the next words out. "I've been subjected to this chemical, this drug, since I was a kid?"

Deran's gaze remains steady. "Yes."

"Oh." I'm glad I'm already sitting down. Deran watches me, and I offer a tepid smile. "Don't worry, I won't renege on our agreement. Give me a moment."

Deran waits, the intensity in those gray eyes once again silvering them. Sudden amusement dances across his face. "I can almost hear you thinking I'm making up wild conspiracy theories. Why not test me? I can bring you untainted food to prove what I'm saying."

I raise an eyebrow. "How will you provide food that hasn't been contaminated?"

"I'll cook it from scratch."

Whoa! Never saw that one coming! "You can cook?"

Deran grins. "Can't you?"

Reluctant to confess all I've ever eaten has been provided by CC via my magic refrigerator or bought from a restaurant, I cock my head. "And how do I know you won't add things of your own?" My tone is light, but it's a genuine concern.

Deran takes my question in the spirit in which it was intended and doesn't get all bent because I'm questioning him. "Oh, I'll be adding things alright! Garlic and rosemary, some paprika if there's cheese, perhaps a bit of oregano if there's tomato. Definitely salt and pepper, or—"

The giggle slips out as I raise a hand. "Okay, okay, you've made your point."

His grin fades again. "Seriously, if you need further proof, have you ever wondered why nanites can't heal your *hypoglycemia?*" He spits the last word, like it's a curse.

"No need to get upset. I've had it since I was a kid, and it's quite manageable."

"Really?" Flint has replaced the silver, and Deran's eyes are as hard as the stone, making me want to wriggle. I tear my eyes away, ready to move, when his hand catches mine. "No, don't squirm away. Do what you promised and face the problem. I want an answer."

Resentment burns, abruptly replaced by flaring realization.

As my eyes go wide, Deran nods. "Exactly."

I slap a hand to my forehead, sickened. "Ugh! I'm such an *idiot!*"

"No, you're a victim of the system, same as most other people."

Unable to sit a moment longer, I leap up. "Deran, I know you hate it when I run away, but I'm seriously agitated right now. I need to run! As in, do intense physical exercise."

Suspicious glints dance in his eyes before he rises next to me. "There are plenty of ways to get exercise." A blush flames my cheeks. "But running seems like a suitable option, given where we are."

Without waiting, I take off. Deran's long legs easily keep pace as my far shorter legs pump out my anger. I'm hardly surprised when I run out of steam nine minutes and twenty-two seconds later.

"Tired already?" Deran teases, running in place next to me.

"Don't start. This is my fourth run today—no, maybe my fifth."

Laughter spills out, the sound rich and warm, soothing my ragged edges. "Maybe it's time you stopped then."

"Don't I know it!" I snag his hand to stop his bouncing, then lead him back the way we came.

Keeping quiet, we amble back to the safety of his modified music player. I must credit Deran's silence as he allows me time to process.

5

All these years, I've believed I've had a blood sugar problem. One Cygnus constantly blamed for my moods and unacceptable behavior, and which he addressed by making me eat. No wonder Cygnus always had that smarmy smile on his face every time he ordered me food! He was giving me another dose of the coercion serum with every bite he forced down my throat.

Instead, this disease could've easily been eliminated by nanites. Why did I never wonder before? *Because you were drugged.*

The answer is simple—and an endorsement of Deran's claims about the food.

When we reach the safety of our sanctuary again, the first thing I ask concerns the last thing Deran mentioned. "When you said I was a victim of the system, same as most other people, did you mean most other people are drugged too?"

"What do you think?"

"Don't answer a question with a question. It's annoying. I wouldn't ask if I didn't need corroboration." Realizing I was more than a little snippy, I grimace. "Sorry. Maybe I should eat some food now."

I'm rewarded with a grin for my pitiful attempt at a joke. "You're forgiven. I'd be cranky too if I found out even a fraction of the things you've learned today."

Squeezing his hand, I copy his earlier actions and pull him down to sit in our usual position. It's ridiculous, but I love this seating arrangement. Not only can I see every facial nuance, but the physical contact is reassuring. Heat rises on my neck again as I think about physical contact.

"Thinking things you'd rather not share again?" Deran's prompt reminds me how observant he is.

"Absolutely."

"I don't even get a hint?"

"No, not even a little one."

A chuckle as Deran shakes his head. "One of these days, I'll get you to tell me what goes on in that head of yours."

"A man can dream."

More laughter follows until I remember a question Deran still hasn't answered. "Deran, if this coercion serum didn't make Sarissa kill herself, what did?"

Deran considers the question. "First, you need to understand a little background."

"You mean how the coercion serum works?"

"Yes. You now know how the serum's concentration increases as the food trays change color, and that they use this serum to make people more compliant, so they do and think what CC wants. Some people never need more than the concentration in a green tray. But for the rare few, even the highest dose in the orange trays becomes ineffective."

"I got all that, and our food trays change color as soon as our behavior—" I halt mid-sentence.

"What?" Deran prompts.

"The day I met you, Cygnus called me to account in his office that afternoon."

Deran grins. "For what you did to that poor, defenseless vent pipe?"

I'm too focused on my revelation to offer my own smile. "Yes. But it was more. When I arrived outside his office, I didn't even have the chance to knock before he was there, holding the door open for me, inviting me in. I was so addled I forgot his greeting."

Shocked eyes stare back at me. "You didn't!"

"I most certainly did. After that, he made more random turns in the conversation than usual, keeping me so off-balance, I couldn't keep my reactions contained." Deran's silence makes me uneasy enough to ramble on. "I soon realized he was looking for an answer, but I didn't know what the question was. Then I reacted to something else, and I saw I'd given him his answer to that question I didn't know to be wary of. Now I understand."

Face set in grim lines, Deran nods. "He was checking where you were on the rebellion meter?"

"Exactly. My food trays went from green to blue within twenty-four hours of that meeting."

With a sigh, Deran rubs his chin. "Unfortunately, for most people, that's how it goes. They don't even know they're under a microscope until their food trays change color. Then they think it's normal because it happens to everyone else."

"You know the worst part?" Deran shakes his head. "CCs own lie works against them."

"How so?"

"Sarissa's a prime example. When her tray changed color that first time, she started eating less because she was afraid of the weight gain that tray color change supposedly meant."

Deran groans. "So because she ate less, the serum was less effective, and her tray changed color again?"

"Yes. Poor Sarissa! If only she'd known she could eat as much as she wanted, her trays wouldn't have changed so fast."

Sudden intensity marks tiny grooves between his eyes. "When you say they changed fast, how fast?"

I consider his question. "Less than six months for her trays to go from green to orange."

"Carys's changed even faster. Maybe this is a problem I hadn't factored in."

"What do you mean?"

"Until now, when you told me about Sarissa's reaction, I thought the late teens marked some sort of cut-off point, the time where the serum either took hold permanently or you shook it off. But now I see —all the pressure accompanying being a teenage girl, the desire to be thin and thus supposedly attractive, explains it. The less Carys ate, the faster her trays changed color. Maybe this is why there are so many teen suicides."

Aghast, I stare at him. "There are?"

"Unfortunately, yes. If this is true, then there's a flaw not only in CC's logic concerning the lie they sell, but the way their serum works. Based on our discussion, I'm guessing the brain can't keep up with all those rapid dose changes, so instead of conforming, the person rebels so violently, CC takes the next step."

"The next step?"

Deran gets a firm grip on both my hands. "This is the part that I'm unsure of, so don't freak out when I tell you my theory, okay?" I nod. "I think they subject them to some sort of brainwashing."

I remain as still as a statue, pretend I'm playing that silly childhood game with my siblings. If I don't allow myself to move, I won't lose. But that's all wrong. I've already lost. And more than I realized.

Tears sting my eyes. Xanin, my beloved brother, has already changed so much from the boy I grew up with. How much more will he transform if they succeed with their brainwashing?

I wheeze, the sound making me realize I'm holding my breath again. Air whooshes out before I gulp more in. Several deep breaths later, I'm prepared to hear the rest. I hold Deran's worried gaze. "See?" I squeak. "I didn't run away. Please, continue."

"Are you sure? We can take a break."

"No!" The single word is explosive, and Deran startles. "Sorry. I didn't mean to shout. It's just… I can't wait anymore. I'd rather hear everything now, get it all out in the open. I process better when I have all the information."

Although Deran nods, he still looks uncertain. I'm relieved when he decides to trust my judgement. "After Carys died, I wanted answers. I couldn't reconcile the person my sister was with the one she became. Even more troubling, how does a girl who loves living end up taking her own life?"

My grip tightens on his, and he gives a lopsided smile. "Thanks. I know it's been a while and there's nothing I can do now to change things for Carys, but your support means more than you know."

"I'm glad."

"Anyway, so there I was, mad at the world and desperate to find something to make sense of the lunacy. I remembered the rumors I'd heard before Carys's death. Whispers the increased suicide rate was a result of something the conglomerate was doing, but no one knew for sure."

"You confirmed it?"

"Eventually. Once I remembered the rumor, nothing could stop me from finding out if those rumors were true. However, they don't just let anybody into CC HQ."

A slew of pieces snap into place. "That's why you became a mechanical engineer, and not just any mechanical engineer, but one who excelled enough to be recognized and promoted to the position you now occupy?"

Deran grins. "Weren't you just saying you process more efficiently when you have all the information? I didn't even have to give you half of it!"

My grin matches his. "Maybe it's simply the way my quirky brain works. When things don't make sense, my brain files them away, until the day I get a snippet of data and *bam!* It comes together."

"What question did your brain file that this snippet answered?"

"How someone as young as you could be in your position. I once asked, and you said it only came through hard work and sheer determination. In your words, 'To make myself as invaluable as possible.' While those attributes would've gotten you far, they weren't the driving force propelling you beyond your peers. Your love for your sister was."

Deran swallows, then wipes at damp eyes, voice hoarse. "Thanks." He takes a minute to compose himself. "You're right, of course. If I hadn't wanted to know the reason for my sister's suicide so badly, I might've given up long before I was qualified. As it was, I made a long-term, strategic plan to get into CC HQ. After I was in, I stumbled on a way to get information without anyone being the wiser."

"Care to share? Or is this a secret?"

Deran grins. "I think we're a little past keeping secrets, don't you?"

I drop my head so he can't see my face, pretending my hair needs to be retied. I can't bear to admit his perception is still one-sided—and I don't want him to see my lack of faith. Although the more he shares, the more I believe. "I hope so."

If Deran notices my lack of enthusiasm, it doesn't show. Voice dropping to a conspiratorial whisper, he says, "On my second assignment, I accidentally discovered the ducts running through CC HQ make great sound conductors."

I frown, and Deran notices. "Don't worry—it's all one-way. While sound gets into the ducts easily enough, those on the outside can't hear what's happening in the duct unless I drop a tool. I think the builders were perhaps so paranoid about the director's insistence people not hear from one room to the next, they soundproofed the ducts better than the walls!"

"You've verified this?"

"Yes. Several times, I exited the ducts using the vents into the rooms I was working above, placed audio sensors in those rooms, then reentered the duct and tested how much sound registered in those rooms when I scrabbled up and down the duct making noise, spoke at various volumes, and then finally hit the duct with my spanner."

"And you hitting the duct was the only thing that registered on the recorders, regardless of the room?" Deran nods. "That was smart, not to take another person with you when you tested your hypothesis."

"I was still so new to the job, I didn't know who I could trust. Even now, with the exceptional team I have, Silvan's the only one I might confide in. But you know how that goes—trust the wrong person and it could be deadly."

My eyes meet his, wanting to confirm what he's thinking. When I do, that little voice trying so hard to shout its warning is finally smothered. "Indeed."

Deran takes my hand, running his fingers over my palm, tracing the lines there, the effect soothing. "I'm glad I found you."

I close my hand over his, drawing his gaze back to mine. "Me too."

Interlude over, Deran picks up his tale again. "After establishing I was all but invisible to those present in the rooms I listened in on, I accidentally found answers in the food distribution center at CC HQ."

"The food distribution center? You mean the cafeteria?"

"No, the food distribution center is where they pack all those meals you find in your refrigerator. Or, at least, I assume you have prepackaged meals in your refrigerator the same as I do?"

At his raised eyebrow, I nod. "Until today, I called it my magic refrigerator because it restocked itself. Now I'm reconsidering—perhaps monstrous refrigerator is more apt."

A grin flashes across Deran's face, and I lap up the sight. "Unquestionably, monstrous refrigerators considering what they do to the food they so conveniently place in our homes."

By now, I'm vibrating with anticipation. "So what did you see in the food distribution center?"

"Two men standing on either side of a conveyor belt, both holding these long, thin hoses with triggers at the end. There was orange goo inside the hose, and they would shoot a pre-measured amount of the goo into each tray as it slid past."

"The goo was coercion serum?"

"Yes, although I didn't know that then. In my ignorance, I thought it was just the 'additive' we've been told gets put into our food. But their discussion led me to discover not only its true nature, but a more sinister truth."

"What did they say?"

"They were talking about a man named Pegrow Green, the name stamped on lids of the trays they added after they'd injected their poison. They said they couldn't believe the serum still wasn't working, and that if he didn't conform after this dose, he would 'undergo treatment.'"

"I can't imagine what that must've been like, hearing two truths in one sentence."

"Pretty unbelievable! I thought I must've misheard. But when they continued discussing the apparent lack of efficacy of the *coercion* serum, I knew I hadn't."

"They actually called it that?"

"They did. Whether that's its official name, I don't know. But once I realized the coercion part was real, it explained my sister's behavior. Suddenly, I understood why she became so docile after her trays changed color."

"I'll bet you went home that day and tossed every tray you had."

Deran's bark of laughter is unexpected.

"No, that would've looked a little suspect, don't you think?"

Icicles form in my blood, my body stiffening again. "You think they have cameras in our homes too?"

Deran's quick to refute the notion. "No, they don't."

"How would they know then if you tossed your food?"

A raised eyebrow is answer enough.

"Oh! The people who restock your refrigerator would've noticed!"

"Yes, and consequently, the information probably would've made its way to places I didn't want it to."

I'm still worried all my recent "unacceptable" behavior in my apartment may have been recorded. "Are you positive they don't have cameras in our homes?"

"It was one of the first things I checked when I discovered them plastered everywhere at CC HQ. Absolutely no cameras in my home. To ensure it stays that way, I've set up my own monitoring system, so I'll know if they ever get into my apartment and install their own while I'm away."

"Smart."

Deran's grin is suddenly wicked. "I can set some up for you too, if you'd like."

Rolling my eyes, I chuckle. "Wouldn't you love that?"

Delighted I'm playing with him, Deran's laughter rumbles out, and comforting warmth and safety envelops me. Luxuriating in the rich sound and the wonderful feelings it evokes, I almost forget the seriousness of our discussion.

"I'm wounded by the accusation." Deran pretends to pull the knife from his chest.

I can't resist the giggle, and we grin at each other, simply enjoying the moment. We *must* savor every sweet thing while it lasts. I sense the rest of Deran's story will wrench this momentary bliss away all too soon.

6

———

Within seconds of thinking reality will set in, it does.

Deran sighs. "Actually, I only set up the cameras up in my apartment after watching Pegrow."

"Pegrow Green? The man the food distribution workers were discussing?"

"The same. I found out who he was, and where he lived. Then I staked out his apartment until I learned his routine. Easy, considering he went partying every night."

"Same as Sarissa." My voice is quiet as the realization hits home. "Did Carys do that too?"

Deran shakes his head. "She didn't have time to find the party circuit, or I'm sure she would've."

We're both silent for a moment. "For what it's worth, I think it was a blessing she didn't." I'm eager to turn Deran's attention away from his sister when I see his brooding expression. "What happened with Pegrow?"

"I broke into his apartment and set up the cameras when I was sure he'd left for the night."

"Deran! When you said 'watching' him, I didn't think you meant cameras! And B&E?"

A quirky grin. "Yes, a risk, but ridiculously simple when you know how. After all, what are tumblers to mechanical engineers?"

I raise an eyebrow, a smile on my face. "What indeed."

Deran squeezes my hand, and I know this is the part he's been leading up to. "Let's stretch our legs a little, shall we?"

Thrown by the unexpected question, it takes a moment to discern the subtext. "Sure."

Pulling me to my feet, Deran grabs his pack and music player, leaving no sign we were there. He leads me to a thick clump of trees, surprising me when he pulls me into their leafy embrace.

About to ask him what he's up to, he wastes no time setting up the music player again, then pulling something palm-sized from the pack.

"Sorry for all the cloak-and-dagger, but this is definitely something that would raise questions if anyone's watching."

I peer at the item in Deran's hand. "What is it?"

"An old video camera. Hardly surprising you haven't seen one before, but it was the only way I could think of to capture the recordings without leaving a signal that could be intercepted or traced."

Immediately, I understand. "It's independent of CCs system?"

"Yes."

I pull the device from Deran's hand, inspecting it. "And I'm guessing motion-activated so you can conserve battery and memory?"

A terse answer. "Correct on both counts but watch the recording—you can ask questions later. I don't want to be in the trees for too long."

The fear I've been able to forget for a while resurfaces, and I nod understanding.

Deran flips the screen open and starts the recording.

The image is nothing like the high-def resolution captured by our comm links. Despite this, I can still see the inside of the apartment clearly. Nothing unusual, just another apartment like mine or Deran's, except for the mess. The place is trashed!

Movement as someone enters the living area from the adjacent bedroom. From his disheveled appearance, bloodshot eyes, and unsteady gait, I assume this is Pegrow. Expression belligerent, he opens the door. Then it's chaos. Two men in dark clothes storm the room, Pegrow's arms flail. Light glints on the needle; then Pegrow sinks to the floor.

The door opens further, and a third man strolls in with a wheelchair. *A wheelchair! Like the one Deran procured when we were dealing with a drunk Sarissa at work.* I meet his eyes briefly, seeing the confirmation there before returning to the action.

Now that I have more time to absorb the scene, I realize these are not mere men. Mindhunters! Of course! Why would Cygnus trust anyone other than mindhunters, people he can control, to do things he shouldn't?

When Deran takes the camera, I want to snatch it back. But he fills in the blanks while he changes out the cartridge. Or is it tape?

"You can't see what happened next, but calm as you please, they wheeled the unconscious Pegrow down the corridor and outside to a waiting helivate."

"A helivate? I thought those were only for Board members."

"Think again. How do you suppose mindhunters always appear within seconds when there's trouble?"

"You forget I've rarely interacted with mindhunters. In fact, they've only featured in my life in the past few weeks."

"Ah, yes, I had. They really did shut you away from the rest of the world, didn't they? Here, watch the rest."

This time, the camera is further from its focus. Nevertheless, I gasp. It can't be! Ice slides through my veins, destroying life. Still shocked, I continue staring at the empty corridor. The one I found Sarissa in so often. The one holding the accursed door marked, "Janitorial."

The still-unconscious Pegrow is wheeled down the corridor and into the room. Is this what they did to Sarissa?

Sickened, I would fall if not for Deran catching me.

"Easy. You're okay."

Yes, I am. But what about those poor people who went through that door?

My voice is dull. "You knew I'd make the connection because you saw me at this door with Sarissa?"

"Yes."

My head spins, and I take a quick breath. "When? How?"

Deran's face is grim. "After placing cameras at Pegrow's apartment, I took the liberty of adding a few of my own cameras at CC HQ because I already suspected they did their brainwashing there."

I can't seem to get my breathing into a normal rhythm. Focusing on that single, life-threatening problem, I regain control, and as oxygen rushes back to my brain. I make the remaining connections.

"You hid your cameras in the ducts?" A nod. "So the conglomerate aren't the only ones who can watch people now?" Another nod. I sigh. "In that case, let's hope your cameras really can never be found."

"Indeed. Chiara, you don't know how much I wanted to explain things when I saw you there with Sarissa."

"But that was before you trusted me?"

"Yes." No beating about the bush, no apology, simply a statement of fact. "What did you see when you asked maintenance to open the door?"

"Nothing. A room full of cleaning supplies. I suppose I saw exactly what they wanted me to, what I expected to."

"But why ask them to open the door?"

"I thought Sarissa was using drugs. So when you saw me poking around in there, I was looking for evidence of a dealer, or her stash, not some hidden door into a sector that brainwashes citizens!"

"Believe me, I understand your anger. I felt the same when I learned they hide their despicable acts in plain sight."

I wish we had more time. "Anger aside, what's your theory about the room?"

"Same as yours—it's their path to restricted underground levels."

"You haven't confirmed that?"

"No!" Deran draws the word out, emphasizing it. "Not only do I not want them to see me showing any interest for obvious reasons, but once I knew to watch the room, I saw the mindhunters drag plenty of people inside. Anyone who enters never leaves—at least not the same way and, clearly, not without their personality irrevocably altered. I didn't want to be one of them."

Claws rake at my heart, shredding the vital tissue and sending an unbearable ache through my chest. "Did they take Xanin there?"

Deran's brawny arms tighten around me. In stark contrast, the thumb tilting my chin up is gentle. "No, they didn't. I couldn't answer your first hundred calls today because I was in the ducts, checking my surveillance recordings for exactly that. I don't get reception on my comm link when I'm inside. But I confirmed your brother never went through that door."

"How do you know? You don't even know what he looks like!"

"I don't need to. They haven't taken anyone into that room for the last three days."

Tears stream down my cheeks as I finally succumb to the sobs. Familiar hands rub my back, and I relax into their comfort. When the crying subsides, Deran pulls away to look at me. "Feeling better?"

"Yes, thanks. More so now because you confirmed something you didn't know to tell me. I never had a chance to mention it earlier, but they took Xanin last night, so it's reassuring to know that falls well within that three-day timeframe."

"Wait, they took him last night?" I nod. "But why? We only ran the test for Cygnus this morning."

"I know, meaning his abduction had nothing to do with the failed test today."

"Then what *was* it about?"

Deran searches my face. It's my turn to show a little faith in him. Time to tell him part, but not all, of the truth. "Remember how I told you I was in the academy?"

Dark storm clouds turn those amazing eyes turbulent again. "You mean how they imprisoned you there?"

I smile. "Agreed. What you don't know is they placed me there after bursting into our home and absconding with our whole family."

Shutters close over Deran's eyes, and wariness shows on his face, but I file the observations away.

Before I back out again, I must finish this. "I'm not sure what it was like where you grew up, but ours was a place of desperation, never enough food or water and air so foul your nasal passages were eternally on fire. When Cygnus came and 'rescued' us, he also separated me from my family. They put me into one APC and my family into another. We haven't lived together since."

Deran hugs me tight. "Oh, Chiara, I'm so sorry."

Swallowing the lump in my throat, I nod. "Thanks. From what you've shared today, it's obvious you and your family were close too, so I know you understand." I pause to swallow again. "But you know the worst part was?"

"What?"

"Not knowing why they separated us. I only recently learned something I invented to help my mother caught Cygnus's attention that day. A silly windy-drier was the reason he thought I might be smart. That's why he put me in the academy, kept my family as a 'reward' for when I 'pleased' him by completing the project he'd assigned."

The tic is back in Deran's jaw, and tension builds in his arms as he strains against himself in an effort not to crush me. His barely leashed anger warms me inside, these tiny signs further confirmations we're on the same team.

"Today, when I was in that meeting with my family, I saw accusation in my mother's eyes."

Deran stills. "Why?"

"I believe my mother thinks they took Xanin for the same reason they took me."

Incredulity filters through in Deran's voice. "Because Cygnus thinks your brother might be as smart as you are?"

I shrug. I haven't told Deran about the E-AMPS gene or my related suspicions because that would mean revealing a *lot* more than I'm comfortable with. Especially considering this fragment of information was only obtained employing behavior CC would definitely consider "rebellious."

"He's had time to watch Xanin all these years, and just recently, Xanin took his place at the top of his class. It's not so difficult to understand."

"I suppose, but it seems a little suspect Cygnus would wait all this time."

"I agree, which is why I confronted him just before you sent your message. Unfortunately, he gave no answer."

Shocked, Deran releases me, moving me enough so he can see my face, but still gripping my arms. I'm sure I'll have bruises there tomorrow. "You went to see Cygnus?"

"I did." Witnessing the rising panic on Deran's face, I frown. "You weren't answering your comm. What was I supposed to do? There was no one else who could tell me why they'd taken Xanin or where."

"So you went to see him and basically confirmed he'd found the correct way to motivate you?"

"Wait, are you angry with me, or Cygnus?"

"You, Chiara, you! Why on earth would you do that?"

My own temper flares. "If you'd answered your comm, I wouldn't have. I thought you'd been taken too!"

I almost laugh when Deran's tirade stops, his expression flipping from frowns and anger to surprise and pleasure. "You were worried about me?"

"Yes, you idiot!" I slap his arm for emphasis. "You were whispering secrets to me in CC HQ of all places—there was no way of knowing whether a mindhunter heard you. If they had, what do you think they would've done? What do you think I *imagined* they'd done?"

"I see your point." Deran crushes me back against his chest in one effortless movement.

Suddenly, I'm face to face with him, our lips mere inches apart. My breathing hitches, abruptly all too aware of every inch where our bodies touch. Before I can run, Deran dips his head and plants a soft, quick kiss on my lips. Nothing to scare me, just something to make me think twice about running. Because *astatine!* Our brief intimacy sends a heady rush of sensations through me, and the last thing I want to do is flee.

Grin wicked, Deran studies me for a second before dipping his head again. This time, the kiss is slow, deep, sensual. My toes curl inside my shoes, and my head swims. When I think I might pass out from the sheer pleasure of it, Deran breaks the kiss, his smile softer now.

"I've wanted to do that since the first day I met you."

My laugh is choked, the words sputtered. "You mean, after finding me with my best end facing you, then bashing my head when I saw you and just about breaking a bone on my massage ball after that?"

Deran's grin widens. "It was the cutest thing I ever saw."

I snort. "I'm glad you think so. Most people would've run a mile."

"I found it rather endearing." Deran uses a finger to push some wayward strands of hair off my face. "Nothing like the smartest girl in the city appearing completely helpless."

Laughter burbles out. "Really? That's how I came across?"

"Enough that I wondered if I'd perhaps been misinformed about the extent of your genius. But one look at that vent pipe, and I knew there was more to you than your brain."

Now I'm intrigued. "And what was that?"

Small lines of tension form around Deran's mouth again, and I regret asking, our moment of intimacy lost. "Only someone with more than a hint of mettle in them could do what you did. Not physical strength, but that inner strength of will."

His words give me pause. "Hmm, I wonder if Cygnus saw it the same way."

Deran sighs. "Possibly, considering his behavior when he called you into that meeting where you forgot his greeting. But we've digressed. And we need to get out of these trees, back out in the open."

7

When Deran releases me, I'm left feeling bereft. Stashing the camera back in his pack and retrieving his music player, Deran sets a punishing pace as he leads us through the trees to another secluded glade on the other side.

I think he's going to lead us out of the park, but he sets up his music player again. This time, he doesn't sit down, instead inviting me to stand opposite him. Eyes determined, he faces me. "Let me finish telling you about Pegrow."

I knew his not sitting down couldn't mean anything good.

Deran doesn't give me time to compose myself. "In less than a month, they took Pegrow back through that door three more times—"

"They took him through more than once?" The set to Deran's face tells me he's guessed what I'm about to ask. Barely able to get the words out, I do. "They took Sarissa there more than once, too?" Deran nods.

I flop forward and place my hands on my knees, gulping air. All those unexplained absences toward the end—were those additional times they abducted Sarissa to who knows where?

I flip up again, taking a moment to steady myself. "You said you thought they were brainwashing their victims?"

"Yes, it's the only way they can force compliance if the coercion serum's no longer effective."

"History would support your theory, so I won't argue. Why do you think Sarissa kept going back and standing in front of that door afterward?"

There go those hands again, raking through his rich auburn hair. "I couldn't say. Also, she wasn't the only one. Maybe they perhaps subconsciously knew this was the place where they lost a part of themselves, and they're returning to the 'scene of the crime' to reclaim it."

Wretched, I resist the sobs threatening to escape again. All those times I found Sarissa, and I never thought to wonder past her using drugs. Why didn't I question her never remembering walking there or the blank expression on her face? How could I not have seen her need?

Warm hands grip my own, bringing me back to reality. Deran's face is serious, his tone stern. "Chiara, you can't blame yourself. Not only could you never have guessed the truth, but you weren't the one responsible."

"Wasn't I?" My words are bitter, my regret already eating through the anger of her betrayal. Despite her actions, she didn't deserve what they did to her. "If I'd been a better friend, she might've confided in me. I could've helped her!"

"No, you couldn't have. She wasn't even aware what had happened, so how could she have confided in you?"

Despite Deran's words, I feel no reassurance. "I should've paid closer attention."

"Chiara, blaming yourself will get you nowhere, and it's ridiculous. Place the blame where it belongs: with those who ordered these heinous acts."

Not bothering to respond, I just stare at Deran. He seems beside himself, the spikes on top of his head more on end than ever. I don't expect his next question. "You know those mood swings of hers?"

I nod.

"I think the repeated visits cause them. From what I observed with

Sarissa and based on what happened to Carys, I think these also only happen right before the end. Total oblivion, then sheer frustration, has them bouncing from elation one moment to desperation the next because something's eluding them, and they have no clue what or when it happened."

"That sounds about right. It's the way I would react."

"Chiara, shake it off! The most you can do for Sarissa now—the most I can do for Carys—is make sure what happened to them is exposed. Although I'm not sure how we do that before CC kills us or subjects us to the same treatment. I'm hoping you can help me figure that part out."

Though I'm still not feeling any better, I at least hear the truth of Deran's words, spurring me to think beyond my regret. If we're going to find a solution, we need to know all the elements in play. "You were telling me about Pegrow. What happened after they took him through the door the third time?"

"He vanished."

"Vanished?"

"Simply didn't come home one day. I kept checking the cameras in his apartment, but nothing. Then, two days later, people transferred his things out. I was hoping he'd moved somewhere..."

"But that was a vain hope?"

Deran nods. "I waited three weeks before deciding I had to investigate. I finagled a way to 'bump into' one of his former neighbors in a store. Pretended Pegrow had introduced us once before, that I wasn't offended he didn't remember me. I didn't even have to ask. He was all too eager to tell me about Pegrow's suicide."

"People and their ghoulish fascination with death. Poor man!"

"My sentiments exactly. But it proved my theories. After subjecting him to whatever they did, he was never the same. His behavior became more irrational, not less, and the downward spiral continued. The same thing happened with Carys and Sarissa, until they took that ultimate step."

We're both silent, each stuck in our own heads with memories of those who were dear to us.

"Deran, if people disagree with the director, why don't they just leave?"

"Where do you think they could go that the conglomerate couldn't reach?"

"Uh, yes, I see your point." Until a few weeks ago, I would never have dreamed of going against Cygnus or the conglomerate. But now that I'm no longer so compliant… *Is this the reason they had such detailed records in my stolen file of what I ate and when? So they'd know when to up my dose of serum?*

Something about my epiphany must register on my face because Deran's suddenly alert. "What?"

Caught unawares, I fumble for an answer. I can't tell him I stole that file, let alone that I have it! For once, something plausible comes to mind. "Am I going to end up like Carys and Sarissa?"

"Oh, Chiara, no!" Deran sweeps me back into his arms, crushing me to him. "I'm sorry for scaring you. I won't let them do that to you."

Just the way he says that, the conviction in his voice, the implied threat of what he'll resort to should they try, makes me feel better than I have since he kissed me. I want that bliss again. Sliding my hand up and around the back of his head, I tip his face down to mine, standing on tiptoes to reach his lips.

I smile at his shock. He never saw that coming. Breathless by the time I draw back, I grin. "Aren't you sorry you've unleashed the monster?"

Soft throaty chuckles send delicious tingles through my body, making me want to kiss him again. "Not in the least. I'm quite taken with her."

If I weren't laughing so much, I would've claimed that second kiss, but since I am and all he'd get is teeth, I let it go. Although not without more than a twinge of regret. "Okay, so how am I not going to suffer the same fate as Sarissa and your sister? I mean, if what you've said is true, and the coercion serum eventually stops working, what if I become rebellious like they did?"

"You most likely will. The difference is you'll know to keep it hidden, under control. I'll help you work through all the other overly emotional stuff you're likely to experience, too."

Dubious, I eye him. "Really? You think you can help me fool them? What if I have a meltdown when you're not there?"

"We find some reason to blame it on you not eating their food because then there's no reason for them to up the dose. All they'll do is make you eat."

My expression is grim. "The same old excuse, then? My 'hypo-glycemia' is out of control? I still can't believe I fell for that lie. But what if Cygnus doesn't believe me? He'll send me for brainwashing, same as everyone else."

"No, he won't." Deran's voice is flat, unequivocal.

"You sound awfully certain, but I don't believe you."

Deran sighs. "I was hoping not to have to tell you this today, but since it's come up again, let's deal with it. You know the side project you were given?"

A vise clamping around my heart again. Hasn't this been a recent fear, that the projects I'm given aren't what they seem? I can't keep the quaver out of my voice. "Yes?"

"Remember why Cygnus asked you to work on it?"

"Because it would help people whose minds are murky—to 'cor-rect the clogged neural pathways from past exposure to toxic air.'" I quote the last words back to him, before stiffening.

Grim-faced, Deran prompts me. "And?"

"'A drug to retrain the minds of people affected by a particular ailment.' Those were his exact words. Aargh! A 'particular ailment?'" I want to hit something, break something, smash whatever is closest into a million pieces. Except that would be Deran, and I can't lose him. I buckle to a primal urge and release a long, loud screech, amused when Deran backs off a few paces. "Sorry! But that felt amazing!"

Humor is back in those gray eyes, glints of silver dancing across rippling waters. "It was worth the assault to my ears then."

"How did I not see it before?"

"You know the answer."

"Because I was drugged!" I hiss the reply, more tension seeping out with the effort. "And you think the drug I'm supposed to be working on for my 'side project' will take the place of the coercion serum for the people it stops working for?"

"I do. You have to give him credit."

"Him? You mean Cygnus? Why?"

"He's protecting his best asset. After all, he can't have you losing it and then subject you to something as barbarous as brainwashing. No way he wants to damage that brilliant mind. Instead, what better answer than having his go-to-girl solve it? That way, if she ever deviates from the planned path, he can use it on her."

Horror at this revelation sends fresh chills racing through me. "I hadn't thought it out that far."

"I have. No doubt, one day soon, you'll do the same. Once you start seeing the cracks in the system, another world opens, and you start guessing the reality of things before you confirm them." Deran's voice is ice, his eyes blue-gray chips to match.

"Deran?"

He glances my way, eyes warming again. "Yes?"

My voice trembles. "I think I've had enough truth for one day."

Before I can say more, Deran's at my side, arms gliding around my waist as he studies my face. "Yes, I think you have."

"Thank you for finally explaining why you were so opposed to me doing the side project, but I need time to process this, and the other truths you've told me."

"Understandable."

I lean into his arms, press my face against his chest, listen to that strong heart beating right next to my ear. The rhythmic sound is soothing, and soon, I feel more like myself. I raise my head. "What now?"

"Now, I collect my music player, and then we go eat dinner at *Little Italy*. Tomorrow, we return to work, I bring you food so you don't have to eat their tainted drivel, and we pick up where we left off—fixing the machine."

I lean back, surprised. "You think we should finish the machine?"

Laughter, but not the kind I'm used to, and certainly not the kind I love. "I didn't say that. I said we should 'fix' the machine, meaning we make it look like we're working on solving the problems, as Cygnus expects. My hope is this will reassure him enough to give us some leeway—leeway we'll use to find your brother and fix the system."

A snort bursts free. "You make it sound so easy."

"We both know it will be anything but. Dangers lurk everywhere, and we'll have to take precautions to ensure we have as much advance notice as possible should we be discovered poking into forbidden places." The grit in Deran's voice is an all too visceral reminder of the indisputable possibility: we may die in our attempts.

"Okay, but why *Little Italy?*"

Deran laughs. "I tell you matters of life and death, and you're worried about where we're eating?" I nod. "Because you love it there, and it's too late for us to go buy food and then still cook it. I'm not sure about you, but I'm ravenous!"

Night has snuck up on us, wrapping us in her dark cloak, sunset and twilight both passing unnoticed. Now that I'm aware how late it is, I'm also uncomfortably aware of that gnawing ache in my stomach. "Me too! Let's go!"

8

Dinner last night was wonderful. The best part? Definitely the goodnight kiss! No disappointing end to our dinner together like last time.

Still dreamy, I finish my shower and wander through to the bedroom. Only when I'm putting on my usual "uniform" of jeans and a t-shirt do I switch gears. I'm so *not* looking forward to being back at work. In itself, this is shocking—work is my refuge. But with everything I learned yesterday, I'm still overwhelmed. There's also a nagging fear I may have to hide this sudden deluge of new information from mindhunters.

The thought creates a tangential question. When did they start featuring more prominently in my life? After Sarissa died. Why then? Coincidence, or is there more? Unable to divine an immediate answer, I file the question for later pondering. A glance at the clock tells me I'm running later than usual, meaning I won't be in as early as I normally am. Perhaps not the best sign to give Cygnus on the first day back after he took my brother...

Eager to squash thoughts of my brother, sure to bring emotions I can't deal with today, I hurry toward the door. I make to grab my breakfast-to-go when I remember Deran's warnings. *Well, Astatine!*

What am I supposed to eat? I opt for an apple and a bag of nuts from my selection of snacks. Hoping they're acceptable, I vow to get Deran to define what foods are and aren't tainted by the serum.

But now I really will be late if I don't leave! I rush out of my apartment, running down to the trundle and hopping on just before the doors close. After plopping into a seat, I begin my morning ritual to focus on the day's work.

However, unsurprisingly, I arrive still preoccupied. Will my team notice there's something different about me today?

Then I remember telling them I'd had upsetting news, and I'd need time to adjust. Thankful for the ready answer, I'm more confident by the time the elevator dumps me onto the lab floor.

Seems I need not have fretted. Most of my team are still absent, so I sneak down the corridors between workbenches to my office, relieved when I only need minimal contact with the three team members already at work.

Better still, no mindhunters in sight! Remembering Deran's urging last night to behave as normally as possible, I set to work immediately: tapping my cube into wakefulness, entering my biometrics, and sending the data from the two tests we ran yesterday onto the holo-screen. This time, an anomaly in the data which escaped my attention yesterday draws me in immediately.

Such a tiny difference, but there's no doubt. Something definitely changed the second time. In the first test, the number of muons climbed from the outset, at an exponential rate. However, in the second, the one we ran for Cygnus despite my protests, the data paralleled the first test for only 6.231823 seconds.

As I dig into the other information gathered from the extensive sensors, I confirm in less than a hundredth of a second, muon production decreased by 32.478%. After that, the decline escalated, muon production non-existent 0.0254 seconds later.

We should've at least still have had *some* muon output. I lean back in my chair, contemplating what could've completely halted the process. A misaligned laser? Degradation of the electron beam? Problems with the pulse interval?

All feasible possibilities to explore. I'm not sure whether I listed the laser option first because it's the initial part of the cold fusion process or because I want to see Deran. Regardless, I leave my office and stroll to the workshop, still mulling possibilities.

But the closer I get to the workshop, the less I think of the machine and the more I think of the man. Remembering that kiss last night when he left me at my apartment door still make me giddy.

I never knew a kiss could touch every part of my soul. Like the sun rising and sending its rays of light and warmth over the land, so even dark corners thrive and grow. Is it like this for everyone? Or only when it's 'the one?' A snort escapes. I've never believed there's a perfect mate for everyone before, but it seems Deran is calling those beliefs into question.

"You know, snorting as you walk down a corridor could be construed in several ways."

I whirl, finding Deran right behind me. Grinning, I am about to launch myself into his arms, thoughts of another kiss like the one last night uppermost in my mind. Then I remember where I am. Since my momentum is already propelling me forward, I don't quite catch myself, and I stumble into him.

A throaty chuckle, betraying way too much knowledge of what I intended, leaves me breathless as Deran catches me. I glance up, finding that deliciously sexy smile on his face and mischief rippling silver ribbons through his eyes. How does he always look so yummy?

My fingers twitch, wanting to run through those silken spikes like they did last night. I clench them into a fist. I can't show any sign of affection here. Not with all the cameras.

Deran must agree because he sets me on my feet again and releases me reluctantly. Although releasing me physically, his gaze holds mine, the question there obvious. I dip my head as inconspicuously as possible, indicating I'm alright and have had no questionable run-ins this morning.

The usual mask he dons at work quickly replaces his momentary relief. "Falling over your feet again?"

My grin returns. "Only so I can have a strong, handsome man save me from myself." The words are whispered, for his ears alone, and I'm gratified when he laughs.

"As long as I'm the only one doing the saving, that's fine with me." Such simple words, yet they send a thrill of delight through me. His next words are at normal volume. "What was the snort for?"

I'd almost forgotten, but this is not the place to divulge the reason. "Wouldn't you love to know?"

"You women and your secrets!" Another quirk of those sensuous lips, but also the glint of understanding in his eyes. "Well, if you won't answer that, why were you in such a hurry to get to the workshop?"

"I didn't realize I was. I thought I was taking a nice, easy stroll."

"Honey, you were practically running."

I glance around, searching for cameras before remembering this isn't the first time he's called me that in this building. Perhaps it will be seen as just another term Deran uses with someone he's familiar with. Jealousy suddenly pinches. *He'd better not call anyone else that!*

"Okay, you really are going to have to explain that fierce expression!" Another whisper as delight crinkles the corners of Deran's eyes.

"Stop it! We can't do this here!" I want to be mad at him, but doesn't it take two to tango?

With a sigh, Deran straightens. I wasn't aware he'd been bending down to lean closer to my ear. A harsh reminder of why we must exercise more caution. "You didn't answer my question."

My mind replays our conversation, too addled to remember what his last question was without the playback. "Oh! I thought of a reason the second test may not have worked. Several, actually."

Interest sparks in those eyes now. "You did? So soon?"

Those last two words makes me wonder again how we'll pretend to "fix" the machine, without actually fixing it—at least, not until we know where Xanin is. Thoughts of my brother sober me right up, and Deran senses my altered mood. A raised eyebrow.

"Don't you know I'm on the clock? I want my brother back!"

"Noted."

As Deran turns and I take my place next to him so we can continue toward the workshop, I know he grasped both meanings of my answer. First, that I really do want Xanin back; second, that we're supposed to be making it look like we're working. Just because I've found a potential answer doesn't mean I'm going to apply the fix before we've found Xanin.

On the upside, at least I could supply an answer without further whispering. We really should discuss that—and how to deal with our obvious affection—soon. Too much of it and it won't go unnoticed for long.

We reach the workshop without further conversation meaning Deran's likely reached the same conclusions I just did. When we walk in, Deran's team all eye me warily.

I grin. "Relax. I've found my mind again. I'm not going to yell and act like a crazy woman."

Smiles as their concerns ease. To my amazement, Koni comments. "I'm glad to hear that because we didn't know the dragon lady who stormed in here yesterday."

A few chuckles and I accept the gentle jibe gracefully. "Sorry! I'll try not to incinerate you the next time I turn into a dragon."

More chuckles before Deran interjects. "Any reason you're all standing around instead of checking what I asked?"

"Yes, boss, we're done checking the lasers. Nothing wrong with their alignment."

My eyebrows shooting up, I face Deran. "You already thought to check them?"

Amusement sprays silver sparkles through those gray eyes. "It was the most obvious place to start."

I should've known Deran could come up with that solution as easily as I could. After all, he built the machine. He would know better than almost anyone else which mechanical aspects might be at fault.

Running a practiced eye over the machine, I take in the major components.

First, the complicated box housing the spectral beam combined fiber lasers. Then the special drum Deran and I designed to maximize the Wakefield acceleration of the electrons in their plasma. This piece generates an electron beam which is then directed onto the third key component, a tungsten target which produces first high-energy photons, then the muon pairs we're after. From here, the pairs enter the separation chamber, and finally, the coveted negative muons are channeled into the energy chamber. This last piece is where the magic happens. The muons replace the electrons in the frozen block of combined hydrogen isotopes, creating overlapping wave functions, and voilà! Cold fusion.

It all seems so simple, and yet, this is a complicated machine with countless moving parts. Any of which could be the problem. I turn back to Deran. "Are there any other likely suspects among the components?"

"Let's look and see, shall we?"

Deran strides back toward the table he and his team use for their meetings, then taps the cube there. Instantly, a 3-D holo image pops up, showing the details of the machine's design. His team crowd around. As Deran pulls the various components of the lasers out for inspection, his team explain what they checked.

An hour later, it's obvious neither the lasers themselves, nor anything controlling their directionality or intensity, are the issue. This leaves only one last element to explore. "What about the pulse interval?"

Deran's turn to frown. "Wouldn't that have shown up in the data? If I'm not mistaken, we built an alarm into the control panel."

"We did, and it should've worked. But if we're being methodical, we should check the interval manually and make sure it's correct. If it isn't, we can investigate why it didn't register on the control panel and repair the issue."

With a nod, Deran turns to his team. "You heard the lady. Start dismantling the outer casing, so we can get at those parts. I'll be with you shortly."

His team swarm a nearby tool cart, picking up what they need before jostling one another as they head for the machine. I turn to Deran, only to find him watching me. This time, his expression is guarded, that awful mask of neutrality in place once more. But I know why. Much as he trusts his team, that only goes so far. What a sad world we live in.

Taking my cue from him, I settle my own expression into cool efficiency. "Will you let me know what you find?"

"I will. You're not sticking around?"

"Thanks, and no. At least, not for as long as it'll take to dismantle that section and run the tests. I plan on drawing a sample of plasma and taking it back to the lab for analysis."

Deran nods. "I'll contact you later." Then he's off to join his team and I'm left admiring the view as he walks away. With a sigh, I realize it's time to get on with my own work.

9

The knock on the door of my personal lab startles me, and I almost drop my tablet. Glancing up, I peek through the small window. Deran's standing on the other side of the door, so I wave him in.

"Sorry, did you try to call? I had my comm muted."

Deran shakes his head before surveying the room. "I didn't realize you had your own lab."

"A perk that comes with being the boss."

"I see. Did you find anything in the plasma?"

"Not yet." I check the time on my comm link. "You're finished already?"

"No, we stopped for lunch."

Mention of food has my stomach growling, and I remember the paltry fare I called breakfast this morning. "About that—"

Deran interrupts. "I thought we might take a working lunch in the sunshine outside. Care to join me?"

Oh, so many things in two sentences. "Yes, I'd love that."

Deran leads the way as we head for the elevators, neither of us saying a word. I'm confused when he leads me to the cafeteria and then nudges me through the line. I collect my usual sandwich and fruit, wondering how this fits into not eating CC's food.

We continue the charade, through paying for our food and exiting CC HQ. Outside, we stroll across the extensive park surrounding CC HQ to a fountain on the very edge, bordering the trees I once used when on a covert mission to steal Sarissa's file.

Deran gestures for me to take a seat on the nearby bench before asking for my bagged lunch. Bemused, I hand it over, watching as he disappears into the trees, then returns still holding it less than a minute later.

Before sitting, he retrieves his handy music player from one of the many pockets in his overalls. He places it on the ledge of the nearby fountain, angling it so we're well within field range of the masking shield.

Finally, he sits, then hands my bag back. Curious, I look inside, and it all becomes clear. Inside the paper bag, on top of the cafeteria food, is another plastic bag of food. I grin, keeping my voice low despite the cloaking effects of water splashing in the fountain and the music player. "I get to sample your cooking?"

"Not exactly cooking. It's just a sandwich."

"Thank you!"

Eager, I dive in, careful not to remove the bag that would spoil the effort Deran spent switching the meal. One bite confirms the food is as delicious as it looks. "Yum!"

His sexy grin is ample reward. "I'm glad you approve."

I stuff my face, both because I'm famished and because it's so tasty. Deran's amused expression when I glance up has me pausing with the sandwich halfway to my mouth again. "What?"

"I don't know that I've ever seen a woman gobble up food the way you do."

I'm glad my mouth wasn't full, or I would've sprayed it all over him as I guffaw. "Why, Deran! You say the loveliest things."

The grin doesn't leave his face as he tucks into his own meal.

"Did you also switch your sandwich?"

Deran nods. "After learning the truth about what went into our food from those two buffoons in the processing center, I made it a permanent habit. Just wait—you won't believe how incredible you'll feel in a few days."

"I'll trust your judgement on that." Thoughtful, I chew a few more mouthfuls. "How are we going to do this every day without them noticing?"

Polishing off the last of his meal, Deran folds the brown bag and tucks it into another pocket on his overalls. "I thought about that last night after I left you. Without doubt, having lunch together every day would raise their suspicions, considering we could just stay in CC and discuss work-related issues there. But if we only have the occasional lunch outside like this, it should pass the acceptability test. Besides, occasional outdoor lunches make it easier to explain the music player, should they ask, because we can say it keeps the cold fusion project confidential."

"Huh, I hadn't considered that. You're ahead of me again."

"I'm sure the roles will be reversed soon. Right now, I only have the advantage because I've had more time to think about the issues we're facing without their drugs fogging my mind."

His last few words add another piece to an earlier puzzle I filed away. "This is why I've been struggling with breakthroughs on the machine, more so since my food trays switched from green to blue?"

A raised eyebrow. "You think they can make you more compliant without affecting your thought processes?"

Annoyed I hadn't put this together yet, (*Duh! How dense can I be?*), I'm about to snap a reply when Deran touches my hand.

"Chill. I know I keep repeating myself, but in a few days, you'll discover for yourself how much the drug has clouded your thinking. By then, you'll be reaching these conclusions on your own."

I huff. "I wish those effects would hurry and get here then."

Laughter from Deran makes me scowl again, but I'm soon laughing with him when he says, "Oh, I'm so sticking with calling you Miss Impatient."

All too soon, our mirth fades, and reality sets back in. "Since we're on the subject of concealing things from those dastardly cameras, um,

I think…" Why didn't I consider what I wanted to say before opening my big mouth?

But Deran's ahead of me again. "We should be careful about PDAs?"

Relieved he understands, I nod. "Yes! I know Cygnus, and if he even suspects how close we've become, he'll exploit that somehow."

"I understand and agree. After accidentally calling you 'Honey' this morning, I decided that was the last time I could do that at work. Or make it look like we were sharing secrets in the corridor."

His assessment is accurate, so I don't argue, but I can't resist one last tease. "And you'd better not call anyone else that."

Mirth dancing silver in those eyes again, Deran chuckles. "Oh, so that's what that murderous look was for."

Chagrined I let this slip, I can't let him think he guessed correctly. "If you say so."

More laughter as Deran shakes his head. "Fine. Keep your secrets. I'll pretend not to know."

My turn to laugh now before I remember what we were talking about. "You still haven't explained the food switches."

"We'll set up a dropbox."

"As in a place we both have access to, where you can leave food for me to collect?"

"Yes. We should also vary the dropbox's location and the pickup times, so we avoid a regular routine. This should make it more difficult for them to catch us should they figure out I'm your alternative food supplier."

I offer a quick grin, amused by his choice of words. "And once I've collected the food, I'll do the same as you did today? Replace what I bring from home with what you left for me at the dropbox?"

"Yes. Same goes for any cafeteria food you purchase. Unless you have to eat there for some reason. Then I suggest moving it around on your plate like you're not hungry before tossing it. If you must eat out, stick with *Little Italy.*"

Something in his tone catches, and I latch onto it. "That's the second time in as many days you've said I should go there. Why? And don't tell me again, it's because I like the food!"

Deran studies me before deciding to explain. "I think they don't add serum."

"What!" I'm sure my eyes will pop out of my head if I open them a fraction wider. "They'd blatantly disregard CC's edicts—assuming this is one if you're a restaurant owner?"

"You're asking the wrong question."

I give it some thought. "Oh! I should ask *why* they're not adding it!"

"Correct. If I'm right, they know what we do."

"But how? And what makes you think they're not tainting their food?"

"Answering the second question first, their food lacks that chemical taste pervading every morsel CC provides." At my dubious expression, he adds, "Again, I can only repeat you'll see for yourself shortly. For now, believe me when I say after a few weeks, you'll taste the serum."

"Is that why I think the food there is so delicious?"

"Probably. As for your first question, I don't know how they found out about the serum. Maybe because they're chefs and know about food composition? Or perhaps they don't know what the serum does, just that it makes the food taste terrible, so they thought there'd be no harm in not adding the 'nutrients.'"

"Or perhaps for a more sinister reason."

A sharp glance from Deran. "Meaning?"

I drop my voice to barely audible. "You once mentioned a resistance. Could they be part of it?"

Shock registers on Deran's face. "I never thought of that, but yes, it's possible." Another measuring glance. "You've barely skipped one meal, and already, you're making connections I would've taken far longer to make."

"Two meals. I skipped my usual to-go breakfast this morning in favor of fruit and nuts. I figured they couldn't add serum to those."

Deran grins. "An excellent solution, but just remember, from now on—"

"Yes, yes, I know. Make it look like I'm still eating their food in the same quantities and frequency as before."

"And Chiara?"

"Yes?"

"I mentioned it last night, but it's worth repeating. As the level of serum in your bloodstream decreases, you're going to find you're more… emotional. Make opportunities at least once a day where they don't *see* you eating. Then it'll be easier to sell the hypoglycemia angle we discussed."

I sigh. "Oh, joy! Just what I needed. Another thing to think about! As if mindhunters and conspiracies weren't enough!"

"Speaking of which, we should also brainstorm a few ways to mess with those cameras in the workshop."

Mindful I'm staring at Deran like he's grown horns, I still can't seem to curb the response. "Have you lost your mind?"

A cheeky grin. "Where there's a will, there's a way. Or so my mother always said."

"But Deran, not in this case! They're sure to notice."

"Only if we give them a reason to, which we won't, because we'll be selective about when those cameras fail."

"What do you mean?"

"We make sure the cameras only fail when we want to hide details about how we fix the machine from them."

I feel like I really have fallen through the looking glass. I can't believe what I'm hearing. Deran must sense my rising panic because he pats my hand reassuringly, the oddly impersonal reaction a reminder of where we are and who may be watching. "Don't worry. We don't have to work on that now; just something for you to consider. Also, we should come up with a way to combat the powers mindhunters possess more effectively should they start paying us more attention."

I battle the rising need to hyperventilate. Deran stops patting my hand and grips it instead. "Don't, Chiara! Don't freak out! I can't bear to see you distressed and not be able to do something about it."

I sense his desire to draw me in, hold me close, but also his resentment at having to resist that need. This makes me fight my panic, not wanting to upset him further. Resorting to some deep breathing, I calm my racing heart and note some of the tension drain from his face, although stress lines still mark the corners of his mouth and eyes.

"Thank you." His hand squeezes mine again. "To reiterate, we don't have to come up with all the answers today. But we should figure out what we need to factor into our plan and then focus on one thing at a time."

My laugh is shaky. "Not so daunting when you say it like that."

His smile reaches his eyes this time. "Glad we agree. Since we were discussing first things first, let's talk about possible locations for our dropbox and what sort of varied schedule we could apply to those locations."

10

By the time I get back to my office, both stomach and mind are full. Deran's sandwich hit all the right spots, and after eating the fruit (yes, they don't taint that!), I'm comfortably sated. If only my mind weren't whirling with all the dropbox locations and schedules we came up with, I might want a nap.

As I step off the elevator back onto the lab floor sans Deran, who took a detour back to main engineering for some parts, I curse inwardly. Our extended lunch didn't go unnoticed. I should've expected questions from Tandize.

She hovers in the corridor near her workbench. I should deal with this now. I march toward her, wanting to laugh when she sees me bearing down, on her toes like she wants to bolt. Her own fault. She was the one searching for me, wasn't she? Tandize suddenly straightens, then squares her shoulders, bracing for battle. But with whom— me or herself? I'd dearly love to know the answer.

"How may I help you, Tandize?" I'm impressed by my even tone. No sharp pieces to cut her.

Even she seems surprised when she blinks at me. Then, as if remembering I asked a question, she clears her throat. "I should've asked earlier, but how are you doing today?"

"If you mean 'am I better than yesterday,' I'm getting there. However, finding out something's happened to your brother takes more time to adjust to than most other things."

I don't know what to make of her reaction. Shock, then disbelief. "You have a brother?"

Too late, I remember the conversation with Deran. Most people don't have siblings. Nothing for it now, but to roll with the punches. At least this unexpected admission stopped her from asking more troublesome questions, like where I was or what took so long. "I do. But he's not the topic of conversation. Did you have a work-related question?"

Still stunned, Tandize pulls herself together. "Uh, yes, a few of us did. Do you have time?"

I sigh. As much as I want to get back to my work, I am head of this department and, as such, must carry out the duties expected of me.

An exhausting three hours and twenty-four minutes later, I'm finally free of their clutches, having answered all their queries and given directions on next steps to be taken for the other projects in the lab.

As I stagger back to my personal lab, I realize how tired I suddenly am. Is this another side effect of not getting the serum? A new lethargy instead of my normal boundless energy? Or is it simply an accumulation of the ravaging effects of the turbulent emotions I've endured over the past few days?

Beyond weary, I don't waste time divining an answer. I must finish analyzing the plasma I extracted this morning, then follow up with Deran on their findings regarding the pulse interval.

Another exhausting two hours and thirteen minutes later, I finally succumb to my fatigue. Neither the plasma nor the pulse interval are the culprits we were looking for, and there's no way I'm considering other possibilities now.

I drag myself out of CC HQ and onto the trundle, huddling almost comatose in my seat until my stop rolls up outside the window. With effort, I haul myself out of the uncomfortable plastic chair, battling to stay awake long enough to pass my building's biometric access points.

When I finally make it inside my apartment, I stagger to my bed and collapse into instant sleep.

I can't say how long I've slept when I eventually wake, but it's still dark outside, so I decide it hasn't been long enough. I roll over, half expecting I won't succeed. But, amazingly, the next time I come around, the sun streams through my privacy-filmed windows.

As I sit up in bed and stretch, I forgo checking the time. Who cares how late it is? All I know is I've had one of the best sleeps I've had in ages. Still marveling at being able to go back to sleep, I again wonder if this is related to the food. If so, the conglomerate is messing with more in the human body than they realize. Or do they know?

Suddenly irritated by the endless barrage of questions without answers, I bounce out of bed and into my shower. Its spa-like attentions always leave me feeling rejuvenated, and today is no exception. When I finally exit my bathroom, still rubbing in the lovely, jasmine-scented lotion, I feel more human. And hungry!

With a start, I realize I never ate dinner last night. Deliberately taking two meals out of my magic refrigerator (*Humph! Monstrous refrigerator!*), I dump them into my work bag. I'll dispose of both in the basement incinerator before I leave. Deran and I decided on several varied disposal locations, to be alternated like the dropbox sites.

Besides the incinerators in my building, I'll use others throughout the city, some in malls, some in backstreet alleys, and some in parks. As long as I don't use the same incinerator too many times, I should be good.

Reaching the basement incinerators without incident, I covertly add the food from my fridge to the bag of trash I brought down and toss the bag inside. When the burning food sends out a brief whiff of tantalizing aromas, my stomach growls, but I ignore it. I'll have food —*untainted* food—soon enough.

I exit the basement and sneak around the outer edge of my building to the rear entrances. Most people avoid this area, because unlike the front, this side is dirty and stinky. Delivery entrances weren't made to be pretty, but they serve their purpose. Or in this case, mine.

Fumbling around under the crates stacked to the one side, I find the small package Deran left for me. Relieved rodents didn't raid it during the night, I secret the bundle away into my bag, then hurry down to the trundle stop, heart still hammering in my chest.

Only after hopping onto the trundle and finding a seat do I look inside the package, reaching for food to accommodate my usual morning routine. My hand stills at the sight of two green trays. I expected a plastic bag, same as yesterday.

Are Cygnus or his mindhunters onto us? Have they played a cruel trick by switching out Deran's food with the poisoned junk they want me eating? However, as I lift the first tray, I spot the note tucked between. I'd know that handwriting anywhere.

C, don't fret! All good, I'll explain later. ~D

Deran expected I'd be worried. Grinning, I extract the first tray, eager to see what's inside and more than pleased I won't have to hide my food from any cameras keeping tabs on those in the trundle.

I mask my surprise. The meal inside looks exactly like anything else I might've pulled from my monstrous refrigerator, laid out in the same methodical fashion. All the pieces are neatly compartmentalized and covered with the familiar clear wrap keeping them fresh.

Mentally shrugging, I peel the wrap off, then bypass the grapes in favor of sampling the frittata with the supplied utensils. If I wasn't concentrating on not giving anything away, I would've rolled my eyes and groaned with pleasure as the blissful concoction hits my taste buds. Mouth suddenly watering, I dive in for another bite. Then I'm stuffing my face like there's no tomorrow. Without doubt, the man can cook!

I demolish the contents in minutes, then lean back, wishing I'd taken a little more time to chew. But it was so delectable; I couldn't get it down fast enough. Oddly, I'm not hungry for the fruit today. Another side effect of proper food, which actually fills you up instead of leaving you still feeling hollow after you've eaten?

Again, no doubt another answer I'll get in the next few days as my body adjusts and I can confirm my many suspicions one way or another. Time to get my brain geared for work.

Unfortunately, although my brain is fully in work-mode by the time I get there, the other solutions I come up with during the day don't pan out. I can't fathom whether it's because we just haven't hit on the right answer yet—or because needing to keep my distance from Deran when all I want to do is kiss him has me on a knife's edge and is hindering my thinking. Add to that the guilt I feel every time my mind wanders to Deran instead of focusing on finding a way to bring Xanin back, and it's no wonder I'm a mess.

My woes continue the next morning, with no success finding the answer and a rising frustration unrelated to the wretched machine. By the time late afternoon rolls around on Friday, I'm at my wit's end.

We've tested everything Deran and I could think of. I glance at Deran across the workshop bench, his team assembled around us as they wait for the next instruction. I grimace, although what I'd really like to do is smash a wrench against the metal sides of the machine.

Calm! I need to pretend I'm still in control of my emotions. I take a breath. "There's nothing for it but to dismantle the machine, go through everything from beginning to end, and see if perhaps one or more components were corrupted or thrown out of alignment by the vibrations from the initial test."

A collective groan, but we all knew this was an eventual possibility.

Deran glances at me, then his team, taking stock. "But we don't have to do it today. Right, Chiara?"

After the week I've had, I'm only too eager to agree. "Absolutely. Go home, enjoy your weekend, and we can start fresh on Monday."

Beams all around now as the team celebrates the decision. They're quick to collect their belongings, calling farewells as they hustle out. Deran and I are left sitting at the table alone.

"I know you're eager to nail this problem so you can get your brother back, so as a consolation prize for letting my team off the hook today, how about coming over to my place for dinner? We can use the time to brainstorm other possibilities."

Suddenly, I'm not so tired anymore. I can think of nothing better than time alone with Deran, away from the astatine all-seeing cameras. "Really? I get to see where you live?"

That throaty chuckle I cherish. "It's nothing special. My tier-three accommodations are less plush than your tier-four ones."

For some reason, this distinction rankles. I've never really paid tiers much attention before, but then why would I? They're just another fact of life here. The moment I think it, I recognize the flaw in the logic. As long as CC has everyone thinking this way, no one's ever likely to upset the applecart, are they?

The masses will leave the status quo as is, instead stomping on their neighbor's back if it will further their own cause, never stopping to wonder what could be possible if everyone worked together instead of against one another.

"What are you thinking now?"

Deran's watching me again, and I give the briefest shake of my head. "Nothing that can't wait until dinner. Want to send me your address and I'll meet you there in an hour?"

"Why wait? We may as well head directly there." I hesitate, and he laughs. "Really, there's nothing that needs to be cleaned up or put away before it's fit for your arrival."

"You must be a better housekeeper than I am. I'd never invite you over without feeling compelled to clean the entire apartment first."

Deran grins. "In case you forget, you already did."

About to refute his claim, I remember the one time he was inside my apartment—when he helped with Sarissa. "Ah, but then I didn't exactly invite you over for dinner, did I?"

A chuckle. "Doesn't change the fact that I saw the inside without you cleaning it first. If I were you, I wouldn't fuss. From what I saw, you're a decent housekeeper."

Abruptly aware of two things, I tense. First, we're openly discussing visiting each other's apartments. Is this something expected of work colleagues? Second, the particular escapade we're referencing so freely was meant to keep CC ignorant of Sarissa's "condition." Deran notices my sudden anxiety, and his gaze sharpens, keen eyes scanning the workshop for signs of trouble.

I offer a tepid smile. "Why don't we head out? I just realized I'm famished."

Taking the cue, Deran leads us towards the exit. He switches off the lights and sets the security force field before we head down the corridor and back to my office. After picking up my bag and briefcase, we head for the elevators and our two days of freedom from CC HQ.

11

As we board the trundle, anticipation swirls in my gut. Finally! Alone time with Deran! And no, I'm not going to feel guilty because we *will* spend time working on solutions and get closer to finding Xanin. Two birds, one stone… or so I tell myself.

As the trundle zooms away from the station, I wonder how much further Deran's home is from mine. His tier three status means he won't live as close to CC HQ as I do. Accordingly, I'm unprepared when he nudges me as the trundle pulls in at a station before even my own.

"This is our stop." I blink in surprise, prompting his laughter. "You're not wrong. This isn't where I live, but we have to make a pit stop to pick up supplies for dinner."

Fascinated, I follow as he exits the trundle. I don't recognize this station, and my eyes rove as I take in the fresh sights. Not that there's much different. Still the blocky apartments over the countless shops making up the malls beneath. Still the glitz and glamor of temptation. Still the same emptiness to it all. Only difference is the prices are higher here than they would be in my sector.

I turn inquiring eyes on Deran. "We're going to find supplies here?"

He notes my dubious tone and grins. "Not exactly." Deran leads me past the buildings flanking the station on either side for a decent-size city block, then down a narrow alley.

The smell is impossible to ignore. Stale body odor, rotting food, and something else I can't identify. Not that I want to. I tuck myself closer to Deran, grateful for his intimidating bulk.

Mercifully, our trip through the odious alley is brief. We exit into an open square, where I'm relieved to breathe fresher air, only to have Deran drag me down another alley, this one even dimmer and ranker than the last. After a while, I lose track of the number we traverse.

When Deran comes to an abrupt stop, I bump into him. He chuckles, silver streaks of amusement dancing in his eyes again. "I'll remember to slow down first next time."

Laughter is the only way to respond to his teasing. I shrug. "You did say you find my clumsiness cute, so I'm making the most of it."

With a full-on laugh now, he shakes his head before leading me into the square. I keep my mouth closed so I don't gawk as I take in the open-air market.

So much color and life and movement! Happy, open faces. Friendly eyes instead of suspicious ones. Brightly colored tents in azure, saffron, aquamarine and lemon defying the gloom of the surrounding buildings and defining each vendor's space, their tables makeshift stacked tinder blocks with boards tossed across the top.

Strange fruits (or vegetables?) I'm unfamiliar with, are arranged on several tables, grouped by type, and exude wonderfully earthy fragrances. Other tables display garments, woven from unusual fabrics, some decorated with beads or intricately stitched patterns. I'm absorbing the bottled goods, filled with fruits, thick amber-colored liquid that's slow to move when the bottles are turned (honey?) and pickled vegetables (maybe?) when a voice calls out.

"Deran!"

Smiling in recognition, Deran leads us toward the beaming vendor. My eyes feel like they'll pop out of my head as the two men give each other a heartfelt hug. I've never seen behavior like this between people who aren't family—at least, not since I was a child back in my old home.

The realization sets me at ease, and I smile at the man as Deran introduces me to Kaplan. He rewards me with the same warm hug, startling me.

Kaplan grins. "She's not from around here, is she?"

Deran shakes his head. "No, so be nice to her."

Kaplan nods assent before jerking his thumb over his shoulder toward his merchandise arrayed behind him. "I have fresh produce, just in from the farms this morning. What would you like?"

Deran picks up a few items, sniffing some, squeezing others, and turning some over in his hands like he's inspecting them. After making his selections, he and Kaplan haggle good-naturedly over the price, and my eyes widen again when I see Deran hand over some chards.

Deran catches me staring. "You know what these are?"

"Yes. How did you get them?" I've only ever received chards as payment from tier eights and above, and then only when I was fortunate (or unfortunate) enough to be asked to do a side project for them. Suffice to say, chards are tough to come by, considering you have to know someone in those tiers to get the work, then hope they pay you with chards so your extracurricular activities can't be monitored by the conglomerate.

Scratch that last part. Hope has nothing to do with it. Most tier eights who want us lesser mortals doing work for them also want the conglomerate oblivious, so chards are their *only* payment option.

Deran merely gives an enigmatic smile. "Another thing I'll have to share with you one day."

His guarded response makes me realize that while I thought everyone here was a friend, it's possible there may be spies among them. Instantly, my guard is back up again, Deran's only acknowledgement a grim smile.

We say our farewells to Kaplan, then meander through the market. Deran hunts down two other vendors, one for meat and another for fizzy liquid in a bottle, before leading me back to the trundle, me eyeing the way they wrapped his purchases in brown bags, implying he'd purchased the items from one of the chain stores found in every mall.

"Where do they get the bags?"

"From their customers. Usually, I bring several with to pass along."

"Do they give you something in exchange?"

"No, because there are times like today when I need bags, but haven't brought any. The vendors share so there are enough to go around. Your question also tells me you've realized there's a bartering system we can use when we don't have chards for payment."

I nod. "While you were paying for the meat, I noticed a lady at another stall paying for her scarf with a pair of gloves." I give it a minute before adding, "Will the store sell those gloves to someone else?"

"Impossible to say. From what I've observed, bartered items don't always make it onto the shelves."

"So maybe it depends on whether the store owner needs the item for themselves?"

"Either that, or they already know someone who wants it and who they can barter with in turn."

As I digest Deran's words, we exit the maze of alleys, then walk the short distance back to the station. We hop on the trundle as soon as it arrives. I count the number of stops past mine before we reach Deran's station. Four. Not too bad. An extra seven minutes and thirteen seconds.

Deran's apartment is also not as close to the station as mine. We walk at least three blocks more before he stops in front of a building behind those flanking the trundle's tracks.

Not nearly as flashy as those buildings, this block also lacks any stores on the lower levels. Just a plain entry into an apartment complex. Intrigued, I follow Deran, almost disappointed when further access to the building requires most of the same biometric scans as my building.

The elevator creaks as it grinds upward. Deran's apartment is nearly on the top floor. The higher your floor, the greater your prestige—or so CC always led me to believe.

I itch to ask, but wait until we're inside Deran's apartment. "Is it true that the closer you live to CC or the higher your living floor, the more important you are to the conglomerate?"

Clearly bewildered, Deran nods. "Yes. You didn't know that?"

"I did, but I wanted to check this wasn't another lie I'd been fed."

The grim lines around Deran's mouth remind me I've yet to uncover plenty of lies. But there's time. I'm far more interested in exploring the space he calls home.

As Deran leads me down the short entry corridor to his living room, I note the layout of our apartments is almost identical The rooms are smaller and the fixtures more outdated than my own.

"Make yourself at home. I need to change out of these overalls."

I do, my interest homing in on the walls in his living room. Assorted pieces decorate the walls, all shapes and colors and styles. From professional photographs of the long-since-destroyed rainforests, to abstract paintings, to music band posters, it's an eclectic collection. The guitar on a stand in the room's corner is no surprise.

A sound makes me turn—Deran walks back in from the bedroom beyond. *Al-Li and Astatine!* He looks good enough to eat: soft gray t-shirt straining against his broad shoulders and playing up the color of his eyes, denim hugging his hips and highlighting those long legs. *Hmm... Chiara, get a grip!*

I swallow, clearing my throat, then gesture toward the guitar. "You play?"

Deran grins. "Don't sound so surprised."

"I've never known anyone who could." The awe I feel must come through in my voice because Deran suddenly looks uncomfortable.

His hand rubs the back of his neck. "I said I play, not that I'm good at it."

"Still," I run my hand over the warm wood of the guitar, then gingerly touch the strings, "an accomplishment few achieve."

Deran's eyes sharpen. "You didn't know musicians at your academy?"

"No." I turn and face him. "They kept the musically gifted in a separate part of the school. No interaction between them and us."

This time, Deran doesn't answer, but he's obviously thinking as he unpacks our purchases and sets them on the counter.

I have to ask, so I sidle closer, then lean in so I can whisper. "Is it safe for us to talk here, or do you need to get your music player out?"

"We're good," Deran replies at normal volume, but he's still distracted.

"What's on your mind?"

Suddenly shaking his head as if he's decided whatever was bothering him isn't worth spending more time on, he smiles. "Nothing important. Here." He offers me a bag.

I grin when I recognize the gummy worms. "You're feeding me candy for dinner?"

"No. Just something to snack on while we make dinner." After I've popped one into my mouth, he hands me the lettuce. "Want to wash this and break it into pieces for our salad?"

I raise an eyebrow. "You do know I have no clue what I'm doing."

He flashes me a wicked grin. My insides turn to goo again; heat rushes through my body, flushing my face. "I'm sure you'll muddle through."

"You'd better hope so. I wouldn't want to give either of us food poisoning."

This time, the throaty chuckle reaches all the way down into my core. "Oh, I don't think that's likely. Not with this food. Here, use this to rinse the lettuce."

Deran hands me the oddest bowl I've ever seen, with holes all around the outside.

"A colander," he explains. "It will allow you to run the water over the lettuce and drain it away, leaving the rinsed produce behind."

"Ah!" I follow his indirect instructions, surprised when I spot the small clumps of dirt washing away. No wonder the market had that earthy smell. "Where does Kaplan get his produce?"

Deran shrugs. "I don't know, and it's best not to ask. The less you know, the less you can give away if you're ever cornered by a mind-hunter bent on getting answers."

12

Deran's answer sobers us both, and we lapse into silence which lasts only until I can't resist asking another question.

"Thank you for my food the last couple of days. Where did you get the trays?"

A mischievous grin. "I stole them from the very place they keep them."

By now, I'm sure my eyes are going to roll out of my head from surprise. "You didn't!"

"I did. Took them right out from under the noses of the food distribution center."

Abruptly, I'm angry. "What's wrong with you? There's no need to take such unnecessary risks!"

"Don't worry—no one saw, and there were no cameras to capture my theft."

I can't tell if he's annoyed or just being flippant. "Are you sure?"

"Yes, I took them from the discard pile they send to the incinerators."

"Why? Were they used?"

"No, they were defective. I'm not sure why because I couldn't see anything wrong with them."

I go motionless. "You don't think they coat the insides of the container with the serum before adding the food, do you? I mean, if they did that, then tested them, that's a reason they could be 'defective,' isn't it?"

Deran stills. "What made you say that?"

I shrug. "I suppose now I'm learning truths, I'm paranoid. Answer the question."

"It's possible. But then why were they using that massive injector on Pegrow's trays?"

"Could it be they only use it to increase the dose on a container already lined or pre-sprayed with the correct amount of serum?"

Abruptly, Deran's face drains of color. "Chiara, I'm sorry! I didn't consider that." He looks ashamed. "Suddenly, I don't feel so clever anymore."

I give him a playful shove on his arm, resisting the urge to suck in a sharp breath when my hand meets bare, firm muscle just below his t-shirt. *No, don't go there!* I struggle to remember what I wanted to say. Finally, my brain latches onto the straw pulling the rest of the memory with it.

"Don't beat yourself up. First, we aren't certain my suspicions are correct. Second, if they do, we've learned something new, and no knowledge is ever wasted. Third, if it makes you feel any better, I could've just as easily come up with other reasons they were 'defective,' like not being perfectly symmetrical or leaky or some other equally flimsy reason."

A burst of incredulous laughter makes me grin; I savor the carefree expression on his face. "Not perfectly symmetrical?"

I giggle. "Well, this is the conglomerate we're talking about. You never know what insignificant detail will set them off."

By now we're both laughing. Still giggling, we resume our tasks. Another idea brings another question. "Deran, do you have more trays?"

"I do. Why?"

"Let me take one back to the lab. I'll test the lining and see if I find anything."

Deran's face clouds. "Now who's being careless?"

My turn to grin. "My personal lab isn't monitored. I've checked. Too many sensitive things I've had to work on over the years for Cygnus to allow anyone to witness what I'm doing."

"Ah!" A dangerous glint in those eyes. "You're feeling rather pleased with yourself. Cygnus gave you something you can now use against him without his knowledge."

"More than a Cheshire Cat who just polished off the cream."

Deran grins while shaking his head. "Again, remind me to never get on your bad side."

"Meaning?"

"Just that the mettle running through you isn't obvious at a super-ficial level."

"You don't know how I hope Cygnus has remained oblivious!"

"I'll bet! If he doesn't know it's there, or even suspect it, he won't see your punch coming."

We lapse into thoughtful silence, returning to our respective tasks. Shredding the lettuce with my bare hands is surprisingly satisfying, and I take comfort in the action. When I'm done, Deran hands me tomatoes, cucumbers, and a red onion (with a warning to use only a quarter) to chop and add to the salad.

In the time I take to perfect a more efficient way of cutting up the produce, Deran's cooked the meat and made a sauce with mushrooms to go with it. My mouth waters as the savory aromas fill the air, making my stomach grumble.

Smiling knowingly, Deran slides the salad closer to his place beside me at the counter, adding feta cheese and olives, before shaking a bottle of homemade dressing, then pouring it over the salad.

"Voila! Time to eat." Deran ushers me to the table, already set with plates and utensils. He drops the salad down before nipping back to the kitchen for the plate with the meat and jug with the sauce—or is it gravy?

Too hungry to care about terminology, I twitch in my seat, barely able to wait for him to sit.

Deran laughs as he eyes me. "No need to stand on ceremony. Tuck in!"

I need no second invitation. The first bite of the steak smothered in sauce has me groaning with pleasure. When this produces more laughter from Deran, I sigh.

"Laugh all you want, but this is the best food I've ever tasted."

Deran's laughter settles into a quiet smile as he dishes up salad for himself then digs into his own meal. Realizing I was too eager to get to the tantalizing steak, I add salad to my plate and sample a forkful. "I can't add to what I've already said about the quality of this food, so all I'll say is thank you! I would never have believed food could taste this marvelous!"

Another grin from Deran, but he resists the laughter teasing the corners of his lips. "Better than *Little Italy*?"

"Ah, now you're just fishing for more compliments! But I won't begrudge you. You deserve every little bit of praise I can give. The food truly is amazing. And yes, better than *Little Italy*."

Smile turning satisfied, Deran settles down to his own meal.

"Where did you learn to cook like this?"

"My mom."

The simple reply reinforces Deran's close ties with his family, which only reminds me of mine. Loathe to destroy the lovely atmosphere Deran's created for our meal, I suppress the worry. The clinks of our cutlery on the china are the only sounds breaking the silence.

I make it halfway through the steak before I realize if I eat another mouthful, I'll explode. "Deran, is it my imagination, or is food without the serum more satisfying? Delicious as this dinner was, I couldn't stuff another bite in."

"No, you're not imagining things. Untainted food is more filling, or else I'd have to doubt your claims about how fantastic the meal was."

I gently kick his shin under the table, sparking bright mischief in those gray eyes. I doubt I'll ever tire of the constantly changing tides there. Then the sparkly silver dulls to gray slate. "What?"

Sighing, Deran nudges his empty plate aside. "Let's discuss how we're going to circumvent all those cameras at CC HQ."

"I thought you said we'd do that on an as-needed basis."

"I said we'd pick our times so as not to make it obvious."

Deran doesn't ordinarily nitpick. "Okay, I think we can agree we're saying the same thing. You said we should be selective about when the cameras fail, so those times coincide with keeping details about how we fix the machine from them. Care to elaborate?"

A hand raking through his hair tells me where he's at. "You sure know how to home in on the key parts to a discussion when you put your mind to it."

I bide my time, aware he's considering how best to approach this. Then why was he so sensitive to my first response on circumventing the cameras?

"Chiara, you're the expert on this machine." He holds up a hand to forestall my objections. "Yes, I know I built it—or my team and I did—but according to *your* specs. And while I've been able to give input on some possible mechanical issues related to the second test failure, I don't understand the machine's intricacies. Certainly not the science of the plasma or the muons or what you do with them."

"Really? You sound like you grasp a lot more than you're just now admitting to."

"Yes, really. I've excelled at this job because as long as I understand the end goal and what's required of me and my team, we can get the work done. But grasping big-picture concepts enough to build the machinery is not the same as understanding the minutia of the science."

"Fair enough. So what are you suggesting regarding the cameras and me being the expert?"

Deran hesitates before answering. "Chiara, have you thought about why Cygnus wants cold fusion technology?"

Though I'm initially thrown by the abrupt change in topic, the question, so carefully phrased, reminds me of my own doubts about the reasons Cygnus supplied.

My gaze never leaves Deran's. "I may have been drugged and

oblivious for most of the last decade, but even before you told me about the true purpose for my 'side project,' I had serious, similar misgivings about my other inventions."

Surprise flickers in those eyes. "You did?"

"Let's just say after that meeting with Cygnus, where he was clearly looking for an answer to a question I didn't know had been asked—"

"The one where you forgot his greeting?"

"Yes. I did a lot of thinking. I realized many of the projects Cygnus has assigned could've been used for alternate purposes."

A long, low whistle. "You clearly were beginning to think for yourself. You must've had Cygnus all sorts of worried what you'd figure out with that brilliant mind of yours if the serum was failing!"

I grimace. "Worried enough for him to up my dose." Deran bites his lip; I guess the question he's suppressing, not wanting to ask. Not wanting to test the level of trust between us. His caution almost makes me want to tell him. Almost.

"No, I won't tell you what the projects were or their alternative uses, but only because it's not relevant. What is relevant is these suspicions *did* make me wonder why he truly wants this cold fusion machine."

Deran leans back in his chair, and his face falls into shadow, making it difficult to read him. Did he do that on purpose, or because he was relieved I'd already come to this conclusion on my own? "In that case, have you decided on his true purpose?"

I can't even detect anything in Deran's tone. A little alarmed at his apparent withdrawal, I know now is not the time to hold back. I need him to feel the same trust he's given me. "I'm convinced he wants the endless energy it will provide at little to no cost. However, Cygnus's assertion that we need the power because the population's grown isn't corroborated mathematically. So what is he truly planning on using all that abundant energy for? The only thing I know for sure is it will further his agenda alone, and no one else's."

Deran leans forward, his face illuminated by the overhead light again. I can finally read his expression. Earnest, imploring. "Which is exactly why we can never give it to him. At least, not until we get your brother—and not until we have a plan in place to stop him from using it for his own evil ends."

"I agree. Cygnus doesn't get the machine until we have Xanin and certainly not until we've worked out his true purpose for it."

Deran licks his lips. What's he so nervous about now? "Chiara, can I ask one more thing?"

"Sure."

"Can we agree if we don't meet both those objectives, we destroy the machine?"

I blink. Did I hear wrong? "Destroy it?"

Deran nods, studying me intently. "I know it's your baby and all, and from what I've gathered, it was miraculous you got it to work, but—"

I wave a hand. "You don't have to explain. I wouldn't want Cygnus having that much power either, now that I know what he's capable of."

Relief washes over Deran's face. For the first time tonight, the strain leaves his body. I hadn't even realized it was there until I saw it drain away. He suddenly looks exhausted.

"Hey!" I grip his hand. "It's okay! I'm not upset. In fact, I'm thrilled we're thinking along the same lines."

Deran moves so fast I don't register he's left his chair, lifting me from mine and into his arms. Shrieking with laughter, I snuggle into him as he draws me close. Then he tilts my chin up, dropping his head so our lips meet, and more powerful emotions sweep away the mirth.

Giddy and needing air by the time we finally pull apart, I manage a grin. "If I'd known such a small thing would make you so happy, I'd have told you sooner."

A devilish smile from Deran. "I'm an easy man to please." Instead of letting me go, we both indulge in the pleasure of a second kiss.

This time, when he ends it without warning, I'm left feeling hot and bothered. I reach for him as he takes a step back, his breathing uneven. I've never seen his eyes this way. Wild, turbulent seas.

Then it clicks, and I blush. I had my hands all over him. My fingers twitch, eager to feel those powerful back muscles moving under them again.

"Sorry," I mumble, mortified. No need to ask myself what I was thinking because clearly I wasn't.

Sensing my distress, Deran closes the gap between us again and cradles me against his chest. His voice is rough. "You don't have to apologize. Ever."

I tuck my head into his shoulder, glad for a place to hide. I'm not sure how long we stand like this, but when Deran finally pulls away, we're both in a better place.

"Do you have dessert?" Almost as soon as I blurt it out, I regret the words. Color rises in my cheeks again, and I curse my porcelain skin.

Deran chuckles, the sound low and rich, knowing exactly where my mind went, but he's considerate enough not to tease me about it. Instead, he ambles over to the refrigerator and pulls out a cake.

"Chocolate?" I'm already reaching when I remember I can't eat just anything anymore, and I pull my hand back.

"It's okay. My mom's recipe. It's safe."

"I think I love your mother already."

Deran laughs, but am I imagining sorrow lurking in his eyes? Deran traces my lips with tender fingers, wiping away my thoughts. "That's better. I don't like it when you have no reason to smile."

Somehow, this touches a raw chord, that's love and family and my missing brother. The tears slip out.

Deran grimaces. "I didn't mean to make you think about Xanin."

His understanding why I'm crying without asking only makes the tears roll faster, followed by those horrid, hiccupping sobs. To his credit, Deran doesn't shy away, taking it all in stride the same way he did last time.

Drawing comfort from him, I don't hold back, allowing the grief and worry and stress of the last week to flow out of me. By the time the sobbing subsides, I'm spent but feel better for letting it all go.

"Up for some cake now?"

I giggle, then sniffle. "A tissue first would probably be advisable. Okay if I use your bathroom?"

"Sure. You know where it is."

In his bathroom, I blow my nose, then wash my face, taking in my wan skin and topaz eyes, more aquamarine and startling today after my crying jag. I finger-comb my hair, trying to settle the unruly mass, but give up after a few minutes. Deran's probably wondering what's taking so long.

Not wanting him to wonder what I might be inspecting while in his bathroom (and don't I itch to open his cabinets?), I hurry back to the living room.

However, there's no sign he was worried. As I return to the room, he grins, angling the knife over the cake in wedges of varying sizes. "How big?"

"About there." He cuts the slice and slides it onto a plate, grinning wider. Did I ask for too much? I decide I don't care. Chocolate in any form is essential right now, and more is better.

I take my seat at the table, and Deran brings our dessert over before sitting, too. He hands me a spoon. "You're going to love this."

I do. I've never tasted chocolate so creamy before, or cake so decadent. Using my fingers to snatch the last remaining crumbs and pop them into my mouth, I glance up to find Deran grinning.

Spotting my indignation, he raises his hands. "I'm not saying anything."

"Smart man. But you were right—I loved your mom's cake. If I could cook, I'd ask for the recipe."

"Maybe we'll make a chef out of you yet." Deran pauses, warning me we're getting back to business.

I wait, but he still seems uncertain, either about what to say or how to say it. "Alright, spit it out. No point tiptoeing around things. I'm a big girl. If I don't like what you're saying, I'll tell you."

A broad grin replaces Deran's initial surprise. "Like I said—mettle."

"Go with it. If I freak when you first tell me something, just give me a moment to absorb the information. You only need to panic if I pass out."

Laughter now. "Okay, okay."

I take the initiative. "You didn't answer my earlier question. How do the cameras and me, being the expert on the cold fusion device, tie together?"

"I asked about your intentions because I needed to know where you stood before I made my proposals."

"And?"

"First, don't take this the wrong way, but I think it's better if you're the only one who knows how we fix the cold-fusion device, assuming we eventually get it working again."

"Oh, we'll succeed—it's just a matter of tracking down the problem. Help me understand better, though, why you don't want to know how I solve it."

A heavy sigh. "I think you're the person least likely to suffer—interrogation—should something go south with Cygnus."

I snort. "That's a really polite way of saying he won't torture me for information. But you're wrong."

"He'd never hurt you! You're too valuable."

"You don't understand. He may not lay a finger on me, but he'd make me suffer by hurting you, your team, or mine. If none of those worked, or if he was desperate enough to get the information faster, he'd start with my family." Bitterly, I remember what Cygnus once did. How I refused him. How he left my family to starve. How he made me watch.

Understanding turns Deran's eyes dark. That familiar muscle in his jaw tics, and his broad shoulders tense. "Of course! Coward wouldn't touch anyone who could actually fight back. The rat bas—" Deran breaks off mid-curse.

Inexplicably, hearing him swear when he's normally so well-mannered is funny. Or perhaps it's the sudden horror on his face at cursing of all things. Laughter burbles out. Pressure release for my emotions? I only know it feels right.

Suddenly, Deran's chuckling too. "You know, I can never guess how you're going to react to things."

"Well," I manage between giggles, "I think it was your expression more than anything else, but it doesn't matter. I needed the laugh."

"Me too. Alright, where were we?"

Deran obviously won't finish whatever he planned on saying about Cygnus, and I'm eager to move on. "You'd made first point—I'm the only one who knows how we fix the problem and get the machine working."

Deran nods. "Second, while we're selling doing all we can to fix the machine, we'll confuse them. I propose that after breaking the machine down next week, we purposefully put it back together incorrectly."

Now I know I've misheard. "Pardon?"

"Think about it. Until now, whatever we've done in that workshop, whatever we've discussed there or in your office or in the corridors… hell! Anywhere in HQ! It's all been recorded by those damn cameras."

"Oh!" I sit for a moment, digesting the ramifications. "Meaning that at any point in time, they could yank us off the project and rebuild it on their own."

"Precisely. Cygnus knows we already had the machine working properly once, either because those mindhunters told him or because the goons monitoring the cameras did."

"More likely, Cygnus himself was watching those feeds. I doubt he'll let anyone else observe in case someone steals 'his idea' and uses it to usurp him."

Deran chuckles. "You're really getting with the program here! No wonder Cygnus was worried about the serum's effectiveness."

I grin. "Anything to pay the man back for all the years he's had me under his thumb. I mean, I'm not dumb, but seriously? It took all this time to realize he was hiding things from me. One more injustice of living in this world, I guess, drugs to deceive you into cooperating."

"Someone not only woke the bear, but poked it!"

Deran's delight breaks me free of thoughts of the narcissist. "Let's get back to the cameras. What's the plan?"

"What I said earlier—we put the machine back together incorrectly when those cameras are watching."

"Ah!" I say, catching on, "and we turn them off when we do the real work? Use the correct parts or add pieces we may have left out."

"Exactly. Nice idea, leaving some pieces out. It'll be a handy excuse for any failures when we finish 'repairing' it."

"Okay, so we only use proper parts or add them when testing the machine. And I'm the only one who'll know what those are. How do we ensure the cameras are only looking when we want them to?"

"I've thought of a few possibilities. Putting the recordings on a loop, knocking the cameras off-angle with ladders or tools or equipment, using our bodies to hide what we're doing. Some of these may even allow us to leave the lab without them noticing, giving us a head start to get out of the building should we ever need to evade them."

"You really think we'll be able to sneak past all those cameras without one of them picking us up?"

"If I plan it right, we should be able to get in or out of the building when there are convenient 'transmission or power failures.' Also, now that I know your personal lab is camera-free, I'm adding a bullet point to make sure it stays that way."

"Similar to what you did with your apartment?"

Deran nods. "Some of these will take longer to implement than others, but they're all possible."

"So what if they realize we may be working on something important out of their view, so they send mindhunters?"

"That's more problematic. We'll have to make ourselves scarce when they appear. Get out of the workshop or lab, escape to the cafeteria for a break or somewhere else."

"Like the gym," I muse.

"The gym?"

"My favorite place to get thinking done."

A smile from Deran. "Is that where you disappear to when I can't find you in your office?"

"Usually. Okay, so we'll have to come up with some better solutions for the minus men, especially if they decide to be persistent and stick around until we can't avoid getting back to work."

Deran sputters, his eyes watering. "Minus men? Where do you come up with these names?"

I grin. "You like it? In their case, it was the only thing I could think of when they were in the workshop and I was trying not to think of what they're really called."

"Right, because you're not supposed to know."

I nod, then ask the real question. "How much time do you think all this subterfuge will give us before Cygnus starts whining?"

Another bark of surprised laughter from Deran. "Whining? I can't say I've ever thought about his demands that way, but that's pretty funny."

"Glad you like it. Think of it next time you're mad at him."

Another snigger before Deran picks up the thread again. "So we have fake parts and missing parts; what about a different configuration? Could we pretend this machine doesn't work and we have to start all over again?"

I consider the possibilities before answering. "No, I don't think so. When I originally gave Cygnus potential solutions after he demanded the cold fusion device, I could only come up with three viable options. I could conjure something else given enough time, but it's unlikely, even for me. That said, this may be useful as a last resort if we really, desperately need more time to meet our objectives. Otherwise, I think we'd be going too far."

"Returning to your earlier question, you know Cygnus better than I do. How long do you think we have before he starts 'whining?'"

That last word in air quotes has a smile touching my lips, even as my mind factors in previous projects and timelines. "Difficult to say. For whatever reason, I believe this project is by far the most time-sensitive of all those he's given me. So, I'd estimate we have a month at most. To be safe, let's say two weeks."

The moment I name the timeframe, fear is a suffocating vise. Is it possible to find Xanin and determine why Cygnus really wants the energy, not to mention also discovering and fixing the problem?

Warm hands envelop my own, and I glance at Deran, his worry evident.

"I know that doesn't give us a lot of time. But we have no choice. It's literally do or die. We have to make it work."

"Easy for you to say. You don't have to figure out the flaw in the machine!"

"But at least you know it does work. You've seen it. It's not like before our successful test—floundering around in the dark, running endless permutations, trying different configurations, switching out parts and chemicals."

Deran's point makes me feel more optimistic. "You're right! I'm not back at the beginning. All I have to do is figure out what made the second test fail." I sigh. "So, we have a loose plan. Now what?" As the last word slips out, so does a yawn. "Oh, sorry!"

"Now I get you home." Deran rises, offering me his hand.

I blink up at him. "What? No, why? It was only a yawn."

"Right, and those little slits you call eyes are only that way because the light in here is too bright, not because you can barely keep your eyes open."

Realizing he won't back down, I yield. "Fine. We can pick this up tomorrow."

Deran shakes his head. "Sorry, no can do. Not only do I have to stick to my usual routines, but so do you. Also, we can't make it look like we're spending too much time together. Besides, I must devise a way to get our diversions in place to keep them invisible should anyone look for them."

I deflate. "You mean I won't see you until Monday?"

Deran smiles. "Now, who's the one whining?"

I smack his arm, harder than usual this time, because… *Astatine! I don't want to wait until Monday to see him again.*

Instead of striking back, he kisses me again. And why would I want to say no to that, let alone think past it?

14

Hours after Deran's delivered me safely to my apartment, I'm still awake. I toss and turn in my bed despite the exhaustion dogging me. One phrase runs through my head, over and over, insistent, impossible to ignore. *He deserves payback. He deserves payback. He deserves payback.*

Growling, I flip onto my back. I must reset: get up, move around, then return to bed. This routine usually helps when I'm having trouble sleeping, so I rise and pad through to the kitchen. I plan to warm some milk and add honey, but then I remember the food restrictions. Are the milk and honey really spiked?

Aargh! Now what? I open and close cupboards, taking stock until I find an old box of chamomile tea at the very back of a shelf. Not exactly inspiring after thinking I'd have warm milk and honey. But better than nothing, I remind myself, remembering those long-ago days as a child when there was never enough to either eat or drink, let alone a choice.

After heating water in the blitz, I lean against the counter sipping my tea, trying to quell that stupid phrase running on a never-ending loop. The accumulation of revealed lies over the past four days prompted it, and now it's front and center, demanding attention. Because, yes, Cygnus deserves payback. But acknowledging what my subconscious mind wanted me to recognize doesn't quiet the repetitive phrase, which only gets more emphatic. Finally, instead of avoiding it, I face it.

First, it's never a good idea to plan revenge. It usually gets you into trouble. Second, I'm not that sort of person. *Am I?* Third, what could payback even look like?

Just like that, the idea pops into my head. I try to smother it, really I do, but the more I shove it away, the more it invades conscious thought.

I sigh. Best to face this too. Convince myself it can't be done and move on. I focus on the ridiculous "side project" which is now front and center. So, Cygnus wants something to "help" those "poor people afflicted" by some ailment preventing them from following simple instructions, making their lives "miserable." How about I give him what he wants, with a nasty surprise he won't expect?

Because now that I've wised up, I know what he's really after. Or at least, I think I know. What if Deran's right, and Cygnus uses my side project solution to ensnare those no longer responding to the coercion serum, making them slaves to the conglomerate's dictates for the rest of their lives?

Wouldn't it be payback if I turned the tables on him? Came up with a new adult version of the coercion serum which made it look like people were now obedient and pliable, but after a set time, the body's own defenses took over and not only nullified it, but allowed the "subject" to remember every detail of what they were made to do while under its influence?

Thoughts swarming, my body remains frozen in place. Could I do that to people, let them be subjected to that, even for only a short time? Resentment for all Cygnus has hidden from me since my kidnapping seizes me, turning to anger and a fierce, burning passion. Wouldn't it serve him right if these people suddenly turned on him? Made it known to all and sundry what the conglomerate had done to them—*made* them do?

Rational thought is completely beyond me now. Can I make a drug that will behave as I want it to? But if I do, then they discover what I've done, can they then use my version as a basis for a further iteration compelling permanent compliance?

The last thought finally makes it through the red haze of hate. *No, I cannot make this drug. I shouldn't even try.* Deran doesn't want me working on it. Too many things could go wrong. Besides, what if someone figured out I created this new "adult serum," and they came after me or, worse, my family?

Still giving myself reasons why this plan is a terrible idea, I drag myself off to my shower. I won't sleep with my mind in this state, but I can't exactly go for a run at this time of night either. Even though tomorrow's Saturday, I have trouble sleeping in.

As the hot water hits my skin, I shut all thoughts down to focus on a single image. The daylily's petals are maroon this time, the throat bright yellow, the midrib in each petal delicately marked in a soft shade of gray. The color of Deran's eyes. *No, focus!* I bring the image back and study it, concentrating on the details.

In under ten minutes, lethargy drags at my limbs, and I tap the buttons that will end the shower. Still keeping the solitary image in mind, I sleepwalk through the drying and nourishing cycle before bumbling back to bed. This time, I have no problem falling asleep.

To my utter incredulity, I wake around lunchtime on Saturday. As I wallow in the comfort of my bed, enjoying being lazy for once, I mull the strange truth. I've only ever slept this late before after extended weeks of snatched sleep in my office while on deadline for a project. Once again, my only explanation has occurred to me before: the lack of coercion serum in my food.

I might have the means to investigate this idea further now. Deran's given me one of the unused food trays he nicked from the food distribution center, mistakenly thinking they would be perfect for my substitute meals. What if I went into the lab and tested the tray's lining for the serum?

This kickstarts another rabbit trail. Deran said we should stick to our usual weekend routines. Well, mine are totally random now without Sarissa around.

Sarissa! I'm a little perplexed by the pang of loss. I'll admit I miss our Saturday mornings together, where she'd give me makeup lessons or we'd go shopping. I didn't enjoy the shopping as much as the time together, the shared coffees or lunches. Carefree times I can look back on with fondness only because they were so innocent. Free of deceit and betrayal. *And dare I say it?* Filled with friendship.

For the first time since Sarissa's death, I replay mental images of our time together, analyzing each interaction, every nuance, the tiniest microexpressions. Anything that could've warned me she wasn't my friend, and Cygnus's spy.

When I find nothing to support the theory her careless words about my family set in motion, I can't accept it. I run more memories through my mental projector, the images flashing faster and faster until all I can see are her lovely brown eyes, milk chocolate swirled through with cream, and the trust and the affection in them.

I shove the images aside and flop back against the pillow, closing my eyes. *No, I refuse to believe it. I must be missing something.* The Sarissa I knew would never have been so callous about my family's welfare or my concerns for them.

A tiny voice I've forced myself to ignore raises its volume, the words still mere whispers, but whispers I hear. *She only changed after they took her away. After they brainwashed her.*

Abruptly, I bounce off the bed, unable to lie there for a second longer. As I walk toward the closet, reaching for jeans and a t-shirt, I can't stop the compunction, the sudden driving fervor.

I have to know what happens to people after they're dragged into that room, the one they took Sarissa and Carys through. It's the only way I'll ever know for certain whether Sarissa was the friend I thought she was.

Although, the truth may not be something I want to know. Will I survive the devastation I'll feel if it turns out Sarissa never betrayed me?

I block further thoughts as I finish dressing, then pick out a random meal from my monstrous fridge. Dumping the meal into my bag, along with the pristine, standard food tray and dinner leftovers Deran gave me last night, I head out of the door, thoughts firmly fixed on the tasks at hand. Destroy CC's food, head to the lab, and test the tray.

The first two are accomplished with ease; the third proves more challenging. When I walk onto the lab floor, instead of darkness, I find the lights blazing. Then I spot Tandize.

She's at her workstation, peering into her microscope. *Why? Surely the holo image it projects would be so much easier to study?* But now's not the time to wonder about trivia. I must escape, flee before she sees me.

I'm backing out when her head whips toward me. Her eyes widen, panic on her face. "Chiara! What are you doing here?"

Surprised by her reaction (wasn't I the one trying not to be noticed?), I stick with my best defense: offense. "I could ask you the same thing. What brings you into work on a Saturday?" Tandize snaps the microscope's light off. Curious, I amble closer. "What are you working on?"

"Nothing." Mumbling, Tandize angles her body, trying to hide the microscope behind her.

Undaunted, I sidestep her attempt, flipping the light back on as I peek through the lens. With one glance, I take in the complex protein structure, the tiny molecules… this isn't what Tandize was assigned! "Why are you looking at poly-dipeptides?"

For a moment, I think Tandize will make a run for it. Then she calms. The transformation from scared rabbit to serene scientist is fascinating to watch. "I have a rat problem at home."

While the words are innocent enough, she's clearly saying something else. I analyze the sentence. Rats? Okay, typically vermin, which could also mean undesirable people. Home? *Hmm, that's a little trickier.*

I pull up her employment application from memory, scan through it, but there's not much about where she lives. So does she really mean "home" as in where she lives, or "home," as in where she works?

Out of the corner of my eye, I catch movement, and my head automatically turns to follow it. *A min—minus man!* In a flash, I understand her warning. Mindhunters in the lab. But how is this connected to these toxic molecules?

Warning myself not to think dangerous things that could be "overheard" by the mindhunters, I run mental mathematical problems, trying to allow backstage thoughts to figure out Tandize's scheme.

When she starts singing, so softly I strain to hear it, I'm momentarily flummoxed. I've never heard her even hum at work before. As I gape, she lifts her chin ever so slightly toward the invaders. Slowly, I turn my head so as not to make it obvious I'm watching them.

The most curious thing is happening. The minus men's faces turn lax, their eyes becoming more distant than usual. Even their postures relax, like the rods holding them in those stiff, unyielding positions a second before have turned to mush. They seem to be in some sort of trance. I try not to gawk.

Tandize moves her hand ever so slightly, keeping it under the workbench, out of sight, but where I can still see it (does she know about the cameras?), gesturing we should leave.

When I glance at her, suppressing my shock with difficulty, she turns imploring eyes on me. Her quiet singing stops as abruptly as it began. As my eyes flicker toward the mindhunters, still not paying us any attention, I can only guess she's silently urging me for a reason for us to leave. Before the mindhunters regain alertness.

All too aware of the ever-present cameras, I'm careful with my words. "Ugh! I hate rats! How about I take you out for a late lunch and we can discuss your solution?"

Tandize is too smart not to understand. Despite her desperation to leave, her reluctance to explain herself is obvious. "No, it's fine, really. I shouldn't bother you with my problems."

My gaze is steel, my tone unyielding. *"I insist."*

Looking like she wants to be anywhere but here, Tandize wrings her hands, her eyes skittering around the lab.

Still trying to find an escape. This won't do. "Tandize, you're part of my team. Let me help." I turn her microscope off, then remove the slide. Her eyes follow the slide all the way into my jeans' pocket.

She reaches for it before realizing I'm not giving it back until she accepts my "invitation." After another worried glance toward the mindhunters, Tandize huffs. "Fine."

"I know just the place. Follow me."

15

I lead us out of CC HQ and along the paths to the mall and *Little Italy.* This time, instead of asking the hostess for a table, I request our food to-go. She hands us menus and offers us seats near the door, showing us the personal kiosks in the far corner. "Order when you're ready."

I don't even look at my menu, already knowing what I want. Instead, I run the scene in the lab through my mental projector. No doubt about it. Tandize's singing caused the mindhunter's discomfort. Itching to ask her questions, I remind myself I don't know how trustworthy she is or where she stands.

Admittedly, this isn't the first time she's given me an indirect warning, though. Weren't Deran and I just talking about this in the park the day they took Xanin? Deran's caution then rings clearly now. Blindly believing her would be a mistake because the incident with Sarissa, as well as what just happened in the lab, could both be ploys to earn my trust.

I sigh, and Tandize glances up. "Sorry, am I taking too long?"

"No, I'm just thinking about work." I almost blink at how easily the lie slipped out. This is becoming a bad habit!

Tandize wisely refrains from asking further lab questions in a public setting. Instead, she gestures toward the menu. "Do you have any recommendations?"

"Go with your first choice. If you don't have one, pick anything. I haven't had a meal here I didn't like."

A slight widening of Tandize's eyes. "You eat here often?"

Again, the double meaning. Although this time it doesn't sound like a warning. Then realization hits, and I curse myself. *Really? Did I have to bring her somewhere so expensive?*

"No. But just so you know, in case it wasn't clear before, your meal is on me." Her discomfort at the idea doesn't go unnoticed. "Don't worry—I said I wanted to help and I do. But as you know, I have to eat regularly, and our little chat coincides with when I should have a meal."

Relief flutters across her face before her mask settles back in place. "Thanks. I'm ready to order."

We stroll over to the kiosks, placing our orders and allowing the biometric scanners to code our meals for our "nutrients." Or, hopefully, lack of them, if what Deran suspects is true.

While we wait, we stay silent. Tandize fidgets, worried about what I'm going to ask. Perhaps I shouldn't have given her time to come up with plausible explanations. But my mind has its own puzzles to unravel.

By the time our food arrives, I've made my decisions. We thank the hostess, then leave. When we head back toward CC HQ, I sense Tandize's rising anxiety. She relaxes as I steer her off the main path and toward the secluded bench near the woods Deran and I used the other day.

Tandize eyes the water spraying in the fountain with approval. Speculation in her eyes, she takes her seat, then opens the bag containing her food.

"Thanks for the meal." The tinkling water easily covers Tandize's soft words.

"You're welcome." I decide to eat first, hungry because I haven't eaten. Although I would normally eat on the trundle on the way into work, I didn't today. I only had the leftovers Deran gave me and no way to disguise them. Never mind. His leftovers will make for excellent dinner tonight.

I gobble up my spaghetti bolognaise, exquisite as always. I'm too absorbed in my own food to notice Tandize is only picking at hers until I'm finished. Clearly, Tandize is more worried about my questions and how she'll respond than with the delicious fare. "You don't like it?"

Startled eyes fly up to meet mine. "Oh, no, it's wonderful. I'm just not that hungry."

I put a hand on her arm, trying to reassure her. "Relax, eat the food. It's good. You'll feel better afterward."

"If it's all the same to you, I'd rather talk first."

"If that's your preference. Want to tell me why you were really looking at poly-dipeptides?"

Not missing a beat, Tandize answers and I wonder again if I gave her too much time to come up with lies. "I genuinely have trouble at home, but not rats. My mom has frontotemporal dementia. I'd heard poly-GR peptides might help."

"So you thought you'd come in on your day off and use the lab for some research of your own?"

Tandize nods, but doesn't meet my eyes. "I know I'm not supposed to work on personal projects, but—"

"When did your mom first display symptoms?" While I only understand the dementia part of that diagnosis, I suspect something else.

Obviously expecting retribution, not an inquiry, Tandize stammers a reply. "Um, er, oh, about, um, fifteen years ago?"

This means Tandize would've been around ten when her mom was diagnosed, making her mom thirty-three, give or take, based on the average age of conception. A little old for the serum to wear off, but the brain *is* still one of science's biggest mysteries.

"What were her symptoms?"

Another blink. I would laugh at her confusion if this weren't so serious. "I don't know exactly. I was just a kid."

"What do you remember?"

"Well, she went away to visit my Aunt Molly, and when she came home, she just wasn't the same."

She just wasn't the same. Weren't those almost the identical words I used this morning when I was thinking about Sarissa pre- and post-brainwashing?

"What are her symptoms now?"

"She can't do anything for herself or even follow simple directions. It's like our roles have been reversed, and I'm the mom and she's the kid. I have to take care of all her needs."

The second one on the list is what I was looking for. So, Cygnus has been busy. How many others suffering from failed brainwashing attempts have been diagnosed with dementia? More disturbingly, how long has this been going on? Do these procedures precede Cygnus, or were they his idea?

Chilled despite the sun warming my skin, I nod. "I'm sorry to hear that. Do you want to tell me what you've found concerning a cure?"

This time, Tandize swallows her surprise, eager to get input from someone with my "reputation." Should I tell her I'm not a pharmacist and thus unlikely to help her? Or do I remain quiet and glean what information I can to aid my own rogue agenda?

The latter wins out as Tandize babbles on, not giving me a chance to interrupt and enlighten her. I gain one useful piece of information: if the toxic merger of poly (GR) and ribosomal proteins found in the brain tissue of people with dementia can be broken down, a cure, or at least an abatement of the disease, is possible. The extent of Tandize's research and the depth of her knowledge on the subject impress me.

When she finally runs out of things to say, I nod. "Thanks, I appreciate the input. If I think of anything which might help once I've had a chance to digest the information, I'll let you know."

I make to rise, but she puts a hand on my arm, eyes furtively scanning our surroundings before she whispers, "You're not going to ask about the singing?"

"Why should I?"

Apparently flummoxed, I give her the silent treatment, waiting to see what she'll come up with. Besides, I decided I couldn't ask. My questions might reveal too much of what I really know about mind-hunters and their abilities, information which would be dangerous should Tandize be a spy for Cygnus.

"Uh, no reason." Tandize drops her head as she gathers her food, preparing for our departure. A convenient way to hide her true feelings on the subject?

The trip back to the lab is also silent, but I'm too wrapped up in my own thoughts to wonder what she's thinking. There's no way to know whether her story about her mother is true. Considering her depth of knowledge on poly-dipeptides, I'm thinking the reasons she gave for her research are legit, but a few things still bother me.

First, that incredible transformation that happened right in front of my eyes, from terror to serenity. Surely you can only pull such a stunt off if you suddenly remember you have a handy explanation to justify your actions?

Next, the warning she gave me about the mindhunters. Was that to stop me from asking about her unsanctioned project in front of them, or just because she wanted me aware of their presence?

Then the way her singing somehow neutralized them. How did she know it would do that? I've already filed the tune away in my eidetic memory for later analysis.

Finally, there's her mother. If that happened to my mother, I'd have more than questions if I checked into the diagnosis and found it lacking.

Is this simply what happened here, or am I seeing conspiracies in every situation? I suppose it's possible her mother has genuine frontotemporal dementia, nothing more sinister. I need to research whether it could produce the symptoms Tandize listed.

We're almost all the way back to the lab before Tandize thinks to ask the question I've been waiting for. "Are you okay with me continuing my research in the lab?"

"As long as you do it on your own time and don't use an excessive amount of lab resources. But," I give her a stern glare, "if you need anything expensive, you run it by me first."

"Absolutely! Thank you!"

Her gratitude is a little unsettling, considering I just picked her brain without her knowledge—and discovered something useful about mindhunters.

But more on that later. Right now, I have a sample of my own to analyze. I'm thankful when we reach the lab and find it free of the dreaded mindhunters. After accepting Tandize's thanks again for the lunch, I hurry off to my personal lab.

Finding no cameras have made a sudden appearance since yesterday, I set to work. Not long after, I've isolated the tray's coating.

When the NMR spectrometer beeps, I toss the results over to my holoscreen, eager to inspect them. The gasp escapes as soon as I recognize what I'm looking at.

Hands shaking, I collect another sample from the tray, prep it, and then slip it under my microscope, just to be sure. I'm looking at the polymer Tandize had on her microscope not even two hours ago.

When the mass spectrometer dings, I almost leap out of my chair, still in a tailspin. I grab the results, adding the information to what I've already extracted from the NMR spectrometer.

Frenzied, my brain speeds. I didn't ask Tandize about her sample, so how did she get the serum? Correction: I'm assuming this is the serum. But if it's not, then what is it? And why was Tandize studying it? Are the serum and brainwashing process related? Did her research truly have something to do with her mother, or was the whole shebang she fed me utter hogwash? It wouldn't be the first time someone on my team deceived me.

Sudden urgency fills me. I should clean this up. Now! Before someone pokes their head through that tiny obnoxious window and sees what I'm up to. Making a mental note to get maintenance to add privacy film to the glass, I void the spec machines' results, erasing their memory, then incinerating all evidence of my work here today, grateful for my infallible mind. Paper copies are never necessary.

Not that this is the most important thing right now. No, what's more important is that there are cameras in the lab. Not to mention those mindhunters when I first arrived. Were they here to take

Tandize away, to interrogate her, or did they just happen to be patrolling?

I think of how she got rid of them, and paralyzing fear fills me. If they didn't think she was up to something before, surely she raised their suspicions? And not only about her.

Because there's no doubt those insidious cameras caught me looking at Tandize's slides, then doing nothing to stop Tandize from messing with the mindhunters. If those weren't enough, I followed up by escorting her out of CC HQ. To anyone watching, it could appear as though I was colluding with Tandize. What trouble have I just unleashed?

16

I spend the rest of the weekend terrified, expecting mindhunters to crash through my door at any second, but no one comes to abduct me. I only hope the same is true for Tandize. After my final revelation on Saturday, I ran out into the lab to check on her, only to find her already gone, the main lab dark.

By the time Monday rolls around, I'm a nervous wreck. Perhaps this is part of their plan, making the condemned wait for judgment, so when they ultimately collect you, you're falling over yourself to confess to anything they want.

I procrastinate, finding arbitrary things to do, dreading going into work. Then I remember Deran. I've avoided thinking about him all weekend, not wanting to run to him for safety. He can't protect me from the mindhunters, but at least I won't be alone anymore if I'm at work.

Once seated on the trundle for the ride to CC HQ, I run through my arguments again, the reasons for my actions on Saturday. I'm as prepared as I can be for the questions I'm expecting.

I didn't foresee Tandize's absence. My mind spins, shifting gears. I've been so consumed by how best to defend myself, I was blinded to everything else. Did Tandize really leave the lab on her own on Saturday? Or was it staged to look that way?

Barely able to walk I'm shaking so much, I totter to my office, confirming it's empty through the windows before entering. I collapse into my chair, sickened, my mind unable to move past Saturday.

While I was playing spy in my personal lab, did mindhunters scoop Tandize up and subject her to some agonizing procedure? Has this been going on all weekend?

Unable to face the horrific images my mind conjures, I stagger back to my feet. There must be something I can do. I'm exiting my office when mindhunters storm the lab en masse, shouting, blocking the exits, waving weapons. Weapons!

They've come for me!

Too terrified to move, my eyes follow them as they work their way toward my office, questioning every member of my team. Adrenaline kicks my "flight" response in, and I'm about to bolt when their guttural shouts suddenly become words my brain processes. *Tandize! They're looking for Tandize, not me!*

At first, I can't make sense of it. Surely, they took her? Then another answer blindsides me. What if Tandize realized the trouble she was in and has run somewhere, tucked herself away in some hidey-hole?

Before I can fully process the idea, I saturate my mind with the usual formulas to shield my thoughts. I can't have one of these minus men reading my thoughts and suspecting I may know where Tandize is.

Saliva turns metallic in my mouth as the intruders move inexorably closer, I observe their progress. No polite requests, no clearing their invasion of my lab with me, just an assumption they can do whatever they please. I won't have it.

I storm out of my office and onto the lab floor. "What is the meaning of this?" My voice cuts through the chaos; my team all draws in sharp, shocked breaths.

Fortified by thoughts of my own importance, I press the issue. "I asked a question, and I expect an answer. This is a restricted area, and unless you have written authorization, you will all leave. At once!"

Stunned expressions and openmouthed disbelief from my team contrast with the minus men's complete lack of reaction. One of them finally takes the lead and marches toward me. I stand my ground, although, honestly, I'm quaking in my sneakers.

"Morning, ma'am. We're looking for Tandize DeMott."

I wave a hand over the lab. "As you can clearly see, she's not here."

"Where is she?"

Although I'd dearly love to tell the man to find her, I dare not exercise more snark. "I have no idea. Obviously not at work, and she hasn't called in sick either."

The man stands there, face blank. Then his eyes snap back to me in that eerie way of these people, as though he just received his next instruction. "You will notify Mrs. Jacobs as soon as Miss DeMott arrives."

"May I ask why?" Another combined sucking sound as my team inhale sharply.

But the man doesn't answer. Instead, he turns and leaves, following the rest of the minus men out of the lab. I glare at their retreating forms, wanting to chase after them and demand explanations, but that would be foolish.

I'm about to return to my office when someone calls my name. I turn, searching for the source. Benita, not only the oldest member of my team but also here the longest, sidles over. "Chiara, I don't mean to tell you what to do, but may I give you some advice?"

Interesting choice of words, but she's been this way ever since Cygnus made me head of this department. Most likely because everyone, including her, thought she was the shoe-in candidate when the previous incumbent retired unexpectedly. "Of course." I'm satisfied I've kept the rage riding me out of my voice.

"It's not the wisest choice to question upper-level security."

Her decision to use that phrase, the one they all use around me instead of what minus men are actually called, slips the reins off my anger. "Really? And why is that? Do they have special permissions I don't know about? Oh, yes!" I snap my fingers. "That's right. When I asked you about these ULS people, you couldn't wait to get away from me. And you weren't the only one!" I glare at my team. "Not one of you would enlighten me."

Lowered heads, gazes slinking away, guilty expressions. But I'm too mad to care. "If you were all so worried about the ULSs, the least you could've done was warn me before I ranted at them today."

I march back into my office, slamming the door behind me. I'm in there for less than two seconds before I realize I need space. Snatching the door open again, I stomp back down the corridors between the lab benches. The silence turns to buzzing murmurs as I barrel out of the lab.

The gym is empty when I get there. Perfect, I have the place to myself. No need for small talk because at this rate, I'm likely to bite someone's head off if they're using equipment I want.

When Deran enters, I've been on the treadmill for twenty-three minutes and fifteen seconds. I'm so astounded to see him in the gym, I almost miss my footing and trip. Quickly recovering, I slow the pace to a walk, then dab at my sweaty forehead with the towel hanging on the nearby rail.

Deran ambles over, his serious expression confirming someone blabbed about what happened in the lab. I raise an eyebrow. "Are you here to lecture me, too?"

For a moment, he says nothing, taking in my appearance. His appraising gaze makes me self-conscious, sure my face must be beet-red, and my hair is no doubt escaping its elastic band. My hand goes there, finding it the mess I expected.

As I step off the treadmill, I yank the band out, then sweep my hair back into a tighter tail with agitated hands before securing the band again. When I confront Deran again, I'm no more at peace.

Deran's hands lift in a placating gesture. "Whoa! I haven't come to fight." His tone is quiet, his eyes calm. "I wanted to see if you were okay."

The wind goes out of my sails. I wasn't prepared to fight his care and concern. "It's been a rough few days."

"I understand. Want some fresh air?"

Belatedly, I remember the cameras. "I'd love nothing more. But I need a quick shower. Can I find you in the workshop when I'm finished?"

Deran nods, eyes still grave. "Don't think this lets you off the hook. If you fail to show up in thirty minutes, I'm coming to find you."

I can't resist the grin finally creeping onto my face. "Thanks, I won't be late."

Twenty-one minutes later, Deran and I walk out the front doors of CC HQ, and I realize I'm famished. "Have you eaten?"

"Lunch?"

A quick check on my comm link tells me it's probably a little early, but I don't care. "Yes, lunch."

"Not yet, but I'm up for a snack."

No words are necessary as we follow the familiar path to the mall and *Little Italy.* When we arrive, they're only just opening, and we have to wait a few minutes to be seated, the hostess offering apologies.

After what feels like forever, we're in a booth, our food ordered, sipping on glasses of lemon water. Deran's fingers slide over to "accidentally" touch mine ever so briefly before they retract.

I sigh. "Yes, I'll be fine. I have a lot to catch you up on." I suddenly realize this may not be the best place to share that knowledge. "Do you have your music player with you?" Deran nods. "Then how about we ask if we can make our order to-go instead?"

"Sounds like a plan. I'd prefer the fresh air and sunshine, anyway."

We slide out of the booth, making our request known to the hostess, who's happy to oblige. As we wait for the food, Deran and I keep our conversation superficial. When we finally get outside, Deran leads us to a different part of the HQ park.

He discerns my unspoken question. "I live for changing scenery."

Apparently, the dropbox locations for the food he leaves me aren't the only places I should vary. Hopefully, using the same bench Deran and I once used for my chat with Tandize on Saturday wasn't a poor choice. Too late to change that now.

How Deran finds these magnificently secluded spots, I don't know, but the little alcove he ushers me into, almost right in the middle of massive grounds surrounding CC HQ, is delightful. Formed partially by tall, well-manicured hedge walls on one side, and a line of fountains on the other, the spot is tranquil. Tension from the last few days leeches away as we plop down on the grass, pulling our meals from the brown bags.

Deran sets his music player up. "You know, we should probably also make it look like we dine at places other than *Little Italy*."

I almost choke on my mouthful, coughing to clear my throat. When I succeed, I frown. "I thought you said that if I eat out, it should be there."

"It should, but don't you think it will look suspicious if that's the only place we frequent?"

Although I accept his point, I'm not happy. "So, we'll have to waste money on food we won't eat."

"Sorry, it's unavoidable. I don't like being wasteful either, but do you want to risk losing our one safe restaurant?"

Grumbling, I shake my head. "No."

Deran's grin is a ray of sunshine touching icy fields, and the chill that's enveloped me since Saturday melts. I smile. "How are you always able to lift my spirits?"

His grin widens, touching every part of his face and taking my breath away. "It's what I live for."

A simple answer, but there's no doubting the truth of it. Feeling insanely special, I touch his hand, careful to keep the contact friendly for any watching eyes. "Thanks."

Unable to hold Saturday's events to myself for a second longer, I fill Deran in.

17

Deran listens, not interrupting until I've caught him up. His *Little Italy* food tray is empty when he sets it aside. So much for a snack! I can't resist the grin that creeps onto my face.

"What are you smiling at?"

"I thought you weren't hungry."

With a wry smile, Deran glances at his tray. "I suppose I was hungrier than I thought—or your story was more absorbing than I expected. Either way, as you suspected, there's more to Tandize than we realized."

"Yes, but the question remains. Whose side is she really on?"

Deran shrugs. "Only time will tell. I'd love to find her and ask what that sample was, if not the serum, as well as where she got it."

"Me too."

"You think she'll be back?"

"I don't know. Does she suspect she may be in danger, or is she simply ill and didn't bother calling in? She's known for not following office protocol."

Deran looks thoughtful. "Any idea why her singing affected the mindhunters?"

"No, but I plan on finding out."

With a sigh, Deran nods. "Excellent. I can't say my weekend was any less exciting."

Only then do I remember his plans for the weekend. "Were you able to find 'solutions?'" I keep the question deliberately vague.

"Yes, but not without a few challenges of my own. I needed parts for a particular piece, so I went against my own advice and slipped into HQ, which I never do on weekends. My gamble didn't pay off because I had to come up with a reason for the unexplained visit. The SerSents from the front desk stopped me at the elevators."

Fear claws me. They never stop anyone who has access to the building via the chips we all have in our arms. "What did you say?"

"I made some excuse about checking on the availability of a specialized part in Engineering that I'd need for work on Monday."

"They accepted that?"

"Oh, no! They wanted to know why I couldn't wait until Monday. Told me I didn't have clearance to be at work over the weekends."

"What did you do?"

"I played the 'Chiara card.'"

"The Chiara card?"

Amusement lights his eyes, allaying some of my fears. "Yes, the one where you tell people you're working on a project for Chiara Baschet, and if there are any delays, they can explain it to you or the director."

I blink. "That worked? I didn't know that was a thing."

Laughing, Deran sneaks a gentle hand squeeze. "I'm not the first person to use it, and I doubt I'll be the last."

Now I'm intrigued. "Really? Who else has used it?"

"Sarissa for one."

I can't believe I'm only hearing about this now. But then, why am I surprised? I haven't exactly been observant. I catch Deran's concern. "Yes, I know, I shouldn't blame myself. There was a reason I didn't see it before. Anything else exciting happen after the SerSents let you in?"

I meant the question as a joke, but Deran's grim smile tells me this wasn't the last of his unusual experiences.

"The head of engineering was waiting for me at the elevator."

The icy plains, melted only seconds ago, freeze over again. I can't resist gripping Deran's hand now and maintaining the hold. I keep my voice low, my eyes skating past him to take in our surroundings. "Deran! Are we on their radar?"

"Possibly, but before we jump to conclusions, let me say I asked around discreetly this morning, and my boss comes into work every weekend. Also, he wasn't really waiting for me. He was actually on the way down to the cafeteria for something from the vending machine."

I shake my head. "I don't believe in coincidences anymore."

"Neither do I. But I will say his interest was cursory. To the point he asked a single question, nodded absently at my answer and then went on his merry way."

"Did you run the inventory check for the part you told the SerSents about?"

A pained expression crosses Deran's face. "I'm not an idiot."

"Sorry, I didn't mean to imply you were. I suppose you've been doing this longer than I have, so you would've known they might check up on you."

"Indeed. Anyway, after those two run-ins, I decided installing my 'solutions' could wait until the workweek once I'd finished them."

"Smart decision. Let me know when you've placed them, and we can work on the machine accordingly afterward."

"Will do. I would've already set some up today, but then I heard what happened in the lab."

"So, you came to find me." My insides warm, touched. "Thanks!"

A sideways glance. "Are you feeling any better?"

Allowing the smile I know he's looking for to wreath my face, I nod. "I am, thanks. Divine food and sunshine and fresh air didn't hurt either."

"I thought you were going to say it was my sterling company."

"I shouldn't have to. That goes without saying."

Deran squeezes my hand before reluctantly letting it go. "I suppose we should return before we raise even more questions."

Grim-faced, I nod. "Time to pretend the only thing we've been discussing is work."

On our way back to the lab, Deran fills me on the specialized part and his plans. Once back at HQ, we head directly for the workshop.

His team have just finished dismantling the section of the machine where this supposed part will fit. When they arrived this morning, Deran told them this piece was the essential element we were missing all along, leaving them none the wiser about the deception.

After they spend all afternoon trying to make the part work, I can see how believable Deran made this solution sound. His team's disappointment matches his own, and he "complains" that he can't understand how this wasn't the key. Wrapping up his rant, Deran informs the team they'll begin dismantling the rest of the machine first thing tomorrow. Then we troop out of the workshop as a group. Deran and his team head for the elevators, while I detour to my office, wanting to check on things before making my departure.

Silence greets me, the quiet workstations and dim lighting evidence of my own team's punctual departure. I can't blame them. If they're as scared of the mindhunters as Tandize was, they would've wanted to leave the instant the clock hit five.

Relieved I don't have to face them, I gather my belongings and head for home. Only when I'm on the trundle, do I realize my terrible error. I blatantly allowed my emotions to get the better of me. Will my trays change color again?

The thought nags at me all evening until I come up with a way to remind myself to keep my emotions curbed when those cameras have their eyes on me. An old trick my mother used when she had to remember something. As I enter the lab the next day, I think of her, trying not to touch the rubber band chafing against my skin under my long-sleeve t-shirt.

How did my mom keep it on her wrist for more than five minutes? I've worn it for less than an hour, and it's already driving me nuts! Deciding my mom must've had a band that didn't kill her circulation, I resolve to find a looser one as soon as I've taken care of an essential task: correcting what I messed up.

After much thought, I decided apologizing to my team would only make my outburst look worse. Besides, I don't want to be the boss constantly expressing regret—that sort of behavior will only lead to a loss of respect.

Instead, I march onto the lab floor, a forced expression of joy on my face (doesn't my work make me happy?), greeting those already present cheerfully, even stopping to ask if they've resolved some problems they had.

My usual demeanor immediately sets my team at ease, and odd smiles slip onto faces as they pick up their work again. No one, including me, comments on Tandize's continued absence, but it's a bitter reminder of another absence.

Xanin's been missing for a week today, which gives me an excuse if anyone questions yesterday's outburst, but I'm glad I don't have to use it. Thoughts of him—and how my mom and sisters are doing without him—will only upset me again. I stop at my office to drop my things before heading for the workshop, eager to forget the anguish rubbing me raw.

A hive of activity greets me. Deran and his team have already dismantled a third of the machine, and when he spots me, Deran strides over, wiping greasy hands on a cloth.

"Morning. Did you need something?"

I grin, taking in those muscles on his bared forearms, and keep my voice low. "I doubt you could give me what I want here, but it's nice of you to ask."

His shock frees the laughter I've held back, but the sound stills at the wicked gleam in his eyes. His voice is equally low. "You're playing a dangerous game."

I swallow. Maybe this wasn't the best way to get his attention. When he suddenly grins, I'm relieved, but it doesn't stop the color already rising up my neck from reaching my cheeks.

"Is the boss being mean to you again?" Silvan strolls up to join us.

Clearly, he didn't miss my heightened color. "Yes, please tell him to stop, or I'll have to sentence all of you to working without meals or snacks."

Silvan chuckles. "Boss, you'd better listen. You know how cranky we get without our food."

Deran only shakes his head. His laughter joins ours as the rest of the team glance our way. "Did you have a question?"

At first, I think he's addressing Silvan; then I realize he meant me. "No, I came to check if there was anything you needed. I won't be available for the next few hours."

The question in Deran's eyes is plainly visible, but Silvan is oblivious because his head is bent over the holo-image displaying blueprints for the machine.

I shake my head the smallest fraction, and Deran understands, asking no further questions. "I doubt we'll need anything from you. We have our work cut out here. It will take us the best part of two days to pull everything apart."

"That long?" I ask because I should be disappointed, but secretly, I hope they take all week. Deran and I need all the time we can get.

Deran's glib explanation slips out like the most logical thing in the world, betraying his agreement. "Unfortunately, but it may take longer, considering we have to be careful with the components there aren't replacements for."

"Do your best. You can leave a message on my comm if you have questions in the interim."

Deran nods. As I leave the workshop, I pretend it's all business between us, but my hands itch to have at least touched his.

Fifteen minutes later, those thoughts the furthest thing from my mind, I experiment with Tandize's song in my private lab. After mentally replaying her exact words, I found a recording. Unfortunately, it sounds nothing like Tandize's version. I'm unsure how it's different, so I fiddle with frequency and tempo, trying to get everything exactly as I heard it from Tandize's mouth.

However, there are limitations to the human ear. Or, rather, mine. Perhaps those trained in music could discern the slight nuances which would fine-tune the music, so it matches Tandize's rendition, but not me.

Persisting, I keep working on the problem, until I eventually realize it's futile. I can't get the right balance, and by now, what I'm attempting to recreate is messing with what I heard.

Exhausted, I lean back in my chair, pondering the problem. Is the song the key or the tempo or rhythm or frequency of the sound? Perhaps the song is part of the solution, providing the right backdrop for all the other elements to come together correctly. If so, why wouldn't *everyone* sing it when the mindhunters were near?

Because not everyone knows. Tandize acquired this knowledge specifically, but from where? Who would know this precise combination of sounds could mute the mindhunter's abilities?

18

After some thought, I come up with only two answers: either Tandize stumbled upon it accidentally, or someone gave it to her.

The first option is unlikely. Who would think of singing when mindhunters were near? More likely, you'd be too terrified to make a sound in case it got you noticed.

This leaves the second option, one with two possibilities, and I'm not sure either is good. The first and most obvious: she really is spying for Cygnus, and he gave her the information. Although this is more feasible, it doesn't explain Tandize's panic every time the mindhunters were near. Surely, if they were both on Cygnus's side, she wouldn't fear them?

All this leads to the last solution, and the one I'm most worried about. Could Tandize be part of the elusive resistance? It makes sense such an organization would've come up with a way to nullify the mindhunters' abilities. If Tandize is a member, but has now been marked as such for further investigation by the mindhunters, where does that leave me, someone who appears to have colluded with her to get her out of the lab when the mindhunters were there?

While I'd love to trash this last option, regrettably, it's the most viable. I'm even more aware now of potential danger. Much as I want to avoid the thought, Tandize is likely safe with her cohorts, leaving me the only target for the mindhunters.

I sigh. Sitting here coming up with scary scenarios I can't prove one way or the other is not a prudent use of my time. Especially considering I've made zero progress on finding out where my brother may be. My hearts aches as I think of his grim smile at the end of our second-to-last meeting, how he said he'd protect the rest of our family with everything in him.

Always. As long as I have breath. Those were his exact words. And now, where is he? Does he still have breath in his lungs? I suck in a shallow, painful gasp. I hadn't meant to let myself go there, but it's an all-too-real possibility, and avoiding it won't make it less true.

Time to face the truth, head on. I can't work blind anymore. I know better. Cygnus may have fooled me for over a decade, but no more. Somehow, I must get confirmation of whether my brother's still alive. There's only one card I can play—a dangerous one. A gamble I'm not sure I'm ready to take. I'll need to give it careful thought, weigh the pros and cons. Once I've ventured down that path, there'll be no turning back.

Unable to face how helpless I am a second longer, how futile my lone defiance may ultimately be, I return to a task I can do something about. But hours later, I'm fuming, still no closer to recreating Tandize's song.

What I need is a recording. This would be the best way to duplicate the exact specifics. If only I could access the recordings the conglomerate keep of the lab.

My laugh is bitter. *If only!* I can imagine marching into Cygnus's office, voice dripping with honey as I ask if he'll hand them over.

No, that will never happen. Besides, I'd be confessing I'm aware of the cameras. I'm about to resume my attempts when another alternative pops into my head.

Is it possible?

After clearing the song's information from the cube in my personal lab, then making sure it's fully erased, I hurry out, back to the workshop. The room is in chaos, machine pieces scattered everywhere, but not a soul in sight. Where is everyone? I glance at my comm link, stunned to find it's past seven in the evening.

The day has run away from me. Still, would Deran leave without saying goodbye? "Deran?" My voice echoes in the empty workshop; no welcome reply returns to me. Pursing my lips, I traipse back to my office, only then noticing the lab floor is dark.

My team have also all left for the day. Careless! I should be more vigilant about time and my surroundings. Otherwise, a mindhunter could sneak up on me, and I'd be oblivious. The disturbing thought makes me set a few alarms on my comm link, reminders to check on the outside world. I have to keep up appearances, check on my projects and my team, and eat my "meals."

Food! My stomach growls. I totally missed lunch. Irresponsible if I'm supposed to be eating the tainted stuff Cygnus wants me stuffing down my throat. Then again, this would be a useful "missed meal" if I get overly emotional anytime soon.

I have to get out of here, escape those watching eyes!

Halfway home, I change my mind. I need a question answered. Will Deran mind me arriving at his door unannounced? Before I can talk myself out of it, I allow the trundle to carry me past my station.

As I exit the trundle at Deran's stop, my heart flutters in my chest. *Is this wise?* I've come this far. I may as well see it through. When I reach Deran's building and press the external buzzer for his apartment, I get no answer. I repeat my mental question.

Maybe he went out with his team. Maybe he's at the market. Maybe he's reporting to Cygnus. Where did that last thought come from? I guess I still have subconscious doubts.

No! Time to make a stand. I'm setting all doubts aside, believing Deran is exactly who he appears to be. Because, if I'm brutally honest, if it turns out I'm wrong, I don't think I could live with it.

Disappointed he's not home, I make it halfway back to the trundle when a familiar face approaches. "Deran!" My relief that he's here, that nothing's happened to him, manifests in a spurt of energy. I run to him, not caring who may see, only to stop short of hurling myself into his arms. There could be drone surveillance.

The welcoming grin on Deran's face is a balm, but evidently, he understands the need for caution as much as I do. "Hello, stranger. I came to find you in your office, only to find it dark and you nowhere in sight."

I knew he'd come to say goodbye! Grinning with sheer joy, I shrug. "Seems like we missed each other. I went to the workshop and found the same thing. I thought you'd left without giving me an update." Hopefully, the excuse he would've given for the benefit of any cameras.

"Well, seems you were desperate enough for answers to track me down at home. Why don't you come up and I'll tell you how things went today?"

Our conversation seems perfectly normal on the surface. Pulling one over on Cygnus or his mindhunters fills me with glee. But if Cygnus has always been as suspicious as I've recently become, maybe we're not as smart as we think we are.

Deran must pick up on my sudden tension because his eyes scan the area. Despite finding nothing, he remains vigilant, saying nothing. Only when we're inside his apartment, and he's checked on his own surveillance system, does he ask the question. "What spooked you?"

"Maybe Cygnus knows we're playing games."

A raised eyebrow. "What makes you think that?"

No alarm in his voice, just a quiet, steady calm, settling me. "Nothing I have any proof of."

Deran nods, those gray eyes grave. "I know you're newly 'enlightened,' but I promise, if you overthink things, you'll start seeing monsters in every shadow."

My laugh is shaky. "Don't think I haven't already told myself that!"

"Yeah, but knowing it and trying not to get hung up about it are two different things, right?"

Relieved he understands, I tuck myself against his chest, wrapping my arms around his waist. My hands touch those rippling back muscles that have tempted me all day. As I inhale his familiar scent, I relax, the world landing back on its axis.

Deran is in no hurry to end our embrace. His arms slide around my shoulders, pressing me closer, holding me there. Seems I'm not the only one drawing solace from our contact. But as we breathe each other in, another emotion takes over.

I lift my head, and Deran's mouth comes down to meet mine, eyes blazing with an intensity that turns them bright silver. His lips are no less gentle, and he kisses me with a passion he's held back on until now. When we finally part, I'm breathless, my cheeks heated.

Deran gives a satisfied sigh. "I've wanted to do that all day."

"Me too!"

Eyes glinting with mischief, Deran kisses me again. This time, the kiss is short, but oh! So sweet! I want to melt into him. When he pulls away too soon, I groan my displeasure.

"That's enough for you. Much as I could kiss you all night, we have work to do."

I sigh. "Don't remind me."

Deran leans back against the counter, putting space between us.

I'm not sure if that's for his benefit or mine, but it's irrelevant. The mood's broken, and I came here to ask him a question. "Do you have any cameras in my lab?"

Immediately, Deran's eyes are guarded. "Why?"

A frisson of alarm ripples through me. But it's time to follow through with my decision about his trustworthiness and hope I'm not wrong. "Why did you answer my question with a question?"

This catches Deran off-guard.

I can see him thinking about how best to answer, so I cut him off. "Deran, I've told you before and I'll remind you again: just give it to me straight. Time is too short for us to still be working out if we can trust one another. We either do and accomplish our goals, or we don't and part ways now."

At my challenge, Deran raises an eyebrow. "I already told you I trusted you. Seems like you're the one who still had to make up her mind."

His tone is light, holding only the merest hint of rebuke, and I sigh. "You're right. I'm sorry. Will you forgive me for accusing you of things you're not doing?"

Deran chuckles. "Another one of your convoluted sentences, but I understand. Yes, I forgive you. Before you ask again, I only installed those cameras last week. With hindsight, it would've been simpler for me to just explain."

I wave away his explanation. "Last week, as in before Saturday?"

"Yes. Where are you going with… Oh!" His eyes widen. "You want to see if my cameras recorded Tandize singing on Saturday?"

I nod, looking at him expectantly.

"They should've, but I'm sorry—I don't have access to those recordings here at home. I'll have to go into work to get them, and you know how touchy they are about me being there after hours."

Although disappointed I won't get an answer tonight, I understand. "I do, and agreed, we should try to draw as little attention to ourselves as we can. I'll just have to wait."

The flash of a grin as Deran detects my defeat. "I take it that means you worked on it today and couldn't figure it out?"

Frustration wells anew. "I just can't define the sounds."

"Why are you trying to? Can't you simply use the recording?"

"Perhaps. Do you think the quality will be good enough to duplicate the effect?"

A shrug. "We won't know unless we try."

Deran's answer leaves me discontented. If we can't use the recording, we're back to where I am now. I realize something. "You play music! Maybe you can tell me what I was missing?"

His laugh holds genuine amusement. "I told you I play. Also that I wasn't necessarily good at it."

I bounce on my toes. "But can you at least try? Please?"

Still grinning as he shakes his head, Deran lopes over to collect his guitar and flicks a holoscreen up. "What's the song?"

"'Don't Stop Believin'' by Journey."

Deran searches for the music, then tosses the instructions onto the holoscreen. In another window, he opens the song itself, listening to the melody. "I like it!"

I remember something else that may be important. "Tandize only sang the first two verses."

"Interesting."

"Why?"

"They only have five chords. And I bet if I had a piano, I could get away with four notes for a basic version: C, D, E, and G."

I stare at him like he's from another planet. "I thought you said you weren't good."

He shakes his head ruefully. "Reading music is easy; playing it well isn't." After a brief pause, he asks, "Do you think Tandize deliberately stopped singing at the end of the second verse, or was it merely convenient?"

"I'd have to say deliberate. After singing the first two verses, she repeated the first and got partway through the second before stopping. Why?"

"There would be only minor variation in the sound with four notes. Could be nothing, but then again, maybe it's the key you were looking for."

"Meaning?"

Deran rubs his chin thoughtfully, "I'm not sure." Then he shakes his head and puts his guitar in place.

When he plays the first chords, I sit entranced, watching those strong fingers glide across the strings. Hearing him play the music I've been listening to all day is surreal. If I was entranced by his playing, I'm captivated when he sings, voice deep and resonant.

"What?" Deran's question coincides with the end of the music, and I'm bewitched no longer.

I blink. "Uh, pardon?"

"You're ogling me like you've never heard music before."

Instantly, I realize I've made him uncomfortable. I avert my gaze, sure I'll keep staring if I don't. "Sorry. I didn't mean to 'ogle.'" I use his word, putting air quotes around it. Daring to peek, I see the shadow of a smile twitching his lips. "You said you weren't good, but you obviously haven't heard yourself."

His scowl is perfect. "Ugh, Chiara! Did you have to?"

I grin. "I did. But if it makes you feel any better, I already discovered earlier today I don't have an ear for music."

Voice dripping with sarcasm, Deran gives me a sideways glance. "Yes, I feel so much better. Seriously, though, now that I've played the piece, I think I was onto something earlier."

"You mean only four notes?" Deran nods. "But what does a limited sound range mean?"

A shrug. "I'll leave it to the person with the big brain to figure that out."

"Gee, thanks!"

"I have every faith you'll find the answer."

"You'll get me those recordings tomorrow?" Deran nods, but suddenly, it's as if he's another person. He withdraws; the channel of intimacy flowing between us closes. Apprehensive, I scan his apartment, spotting nothing amiss. But something's definitely up. "What?"

"Chiara, there's something else you must know. One last, great truth that's been kept from you." He studies me intently, gauging my reaction.

I can't help immediately feeling guarded again. "Okay." I tell myself not to overreact, to allow him to finish before letting my emotions run wild. "I'm ready."

"I doubt you'll ever be ready for this, but if I don't tell you now, you may never forgive me." Deran swallows, eyes never leaving mine. Whatever's coming must be momentous.

I steel myself anew. "Just get it over with!"

Although he wanted to put distance between us moments ago, now he clasps my hands, linking his fingers with mine. Sudden anxiety paints tiny lines between his eyes, thins his lips, and tightens his jaw. "Please don't hate me for not telling you sooner. I couldn't risk it until you started believing at least some of the things I said. Because this," one hand releases mine momentarily, raking his hair into spikes that stand on end, "this is something you'll find almost impossible to accept."

He takes a deep breath. "Our world isn't fixed. It's still broken."

19

I frown. "I don't understand. We have clean air and ample food and water, don't we?"

"Sure, *here* we do!" When my frown deepens, he tries again. "This world we live in, the world you and I live in... it's artificial."

Panic swells inside, wanting out, but I leash it. I'm careful to keep my tone neutral. "Artificial how?"

"Chiara, we live in a bubble."

I laugh, the statement completely absurd. "Don't we all?"

"No, you don't understand. I mean, we literally live in a bubble. There's a giant dome over this entire city. Outside, the world is still the same as it was when you were a kid. Probably worse."

For a moment, the words make no sense. Then my legs buckle, and only Deran's muscular arms stop me from crashing to the floor.

"What?" The word is so soft, so strangled, I'm not sure Deran heard.

Then he picks me up and carries me to the sofa, depositing me carefully. He darts back to the kitchen for a glass of water, which he puts to my lips. "Drink!"

My body obeys, mind still too numb to resist. The water slides down unnoticed, but it must do something because clarity returns, whooshing in like sound after a vacuum's removed. "Impossible! This city's too big!"

Deran's face is bleak, his eyes serious. "Believe me, they've perfected these domes. I think some of your inventions may've helped."

My crazed thoughts careen back to that evening only weeks ago, where I listed alternative uses for my projects. Specifically, my greenhouse, with its designer glass. Hadn't I written the glass was strong enough for a cage; *a glass cage that could serve as a prison?*

I even remember berating myself for thinking anyone would use a glass prison.

A hysterical laugh escapes. Apparently, I was right.

What else was I right about?

Nausea roils, and I shove Deran aside. Leaping up, I run to the bathroom, making it just in time to purge the water into the toilet and not all over the floor.

Hunched over the bowl, I hug its wonderfully cool sides, still trembling. How could I have been so stupid? Another round of queasiness boils in my stomach, coming up and spewing out. Bile, bitter as my regret, coats my tongue. I've hardly eaten today. My stomach churns again. I groan and lean over the bowl a third time.

Tender hands pull my hair away and rub my back, prompting the tears. How does Deran always knows what to do? I feel better just having him next to me. His touch was all I needed to settle my stomach, because as he soothes, the nausea fades. After wiping off the worst of the gunk with some toilet paper, I lean away to rest against Deran instead.

His arms wrap around me as I wait for the jitters to calm. When I feel somewhat normal again, I suck in deep breaths. Despite this, I still can't wrap my mind around a dome covering this city. Is this really true? Much as I hate to admit it, Deran was right to hold off. And yet...

Sensing I'm over the worst of it, Deran grabs a washcloth. Afraid to dwell on the revelations further in case the retching returns, I watch the steam rising from the stream of hot water Deran runs over the cloth. As I offer the ghost of a smile, he pulls me up off the floor, then sits on the edge of the tub. He tucks me into his lap before wiping my face with the warmed cloth.

Incredible what a difference a kind touch and a clean face make. Deran is watching me, a question in his eyes. "What?"

"Maybe I should wait."

I understand where he's coming from. "I think I'm done throwing up."

A small smile tweaks his lips. "Well, at least it wasn't all over the floor because I know that would've totally stressed you out!"

I roll my eyes. "You know me too well." I wait a beat. "So, your question?"

"I'm sure news of the dome was a shock, but I think something else set off the hurling. Care to tell me what?"

"You're far too observant, you know that? But you're right." I explain about my greenhouse project, how I'd guessed the answer without realizing it.

Deran gives a long, low whistle. "You may be right."

"You've seen the dome?"

"I have."

No details, just the confirmation. "Well, don't keep me in suspense!"

A grin. "There you go again, Miss Impatient."

Although I swat his arm, I'm also smiling. "I'm never going to lose that name, am I?"

"I doubt it."

Desperate to repeat my question, I resist the urge, well aware he's waiting for me to ask. When he chuckles, I throw my hands up. "Fine! I give up! Tell me."

Deran plants a soft kiss on my lips before running his knuckles gently up my jawline. "Never lose that tenacity."

The extreme emotion in his eyes has silvered them again, bright waters blinding under a summer sun. I'm totally out of my depth. Before I drown, he releases my gaze, either sensing I'm floundering or because he's uncomfortable.

His wriggling reminds me he's sitting on the narrow shelf of the tub, supporting my weight on his lap. "Oh!" I leap up. "Sorry! You should've told me to move sooner."

With a wicked smile, he shakes his head. "Why would I want a beautiful woman off my lap?"

And I'm back in the ocean, the waves relentless, water buffeting me on all sides. In the blink of an eye, Deran rises, wrapping his arms around my shoulders as he rocks me. "Hey! It's okay. I'm sorry. I was just teasing."

Do I tell him I know, but that I didn't want him to be? Suddenly, the stress of the past days wears on me. Fatigue creeps over me like a shade drawn to hide the light. And how could he kiss me after I threw up? *Ew!*

Finding the excuse I need, I pat his chest, offering a tepid smile before slipping away. "Sorry! I need to rinse my mouth." I thoroughly wash my mouth out at the sink, cleaning the basin when I'm done.

When I rise, Deran is still standing where I left him, arms crossed, that muscle in his jaw ticking. "Did you hope I'd leave and you could hide?"

The dangerous glint in his eyes reminds me how much he hates it when I run away from him. "Seriously, Deran, all this is too much! I have nothing left. Today marks a week since Cygnus took Xanin, and we've made no progress on finding my brother, let alone establishing whether he's even still alive! Finding the key to the song's been a bust, and I'm stumped on what could be wrong with the machine. Not to mention Cygnus's true intentions." Tears well a second time, and I'm too tired to care when they spill, fat drops dribbling down my cheeks.

Then Deran's arms enfold me, and the tears run faster. I lean into the closeness, his support, snuffling into his shoulder. I'm messing up his shirt. "Ugh! Sorry!" I pat at the wet spot, eyes and nose still streaming.

"Don't worry. Here." Without letting go, Deran maneuvers us closer to the vanity for the tissues before handing me one.

Unabashed (he's already seen me at my worst, hasn't he?), I blow my nose loudly, then blubber into his shoulder again. Finally, reality sets in. Leaning back from Deran's totally ruined shirt, I stare at the blob of goo. "I owe you a shirt."

Deran's laughter, that familiar warm blanket, wraps around me, offering more solace. "Nothing a little detergent won't get rid of. But if it's all the same to you, I'll change into a clean one."

"Sure—sorry I had the POMs there."

"The POMs?"

"The poor-old-mes."

Amusement flits across his handsome face. "Interesting acronym. Don't worry—we're all prone to feeling sorry for ourselves occasionally. If it's any consolation, I think you were more than entitled to them today."

"Thanks." My smile wry, I wave him off. "Now go change." By the time Deran returns to the living room, I've realized something. "There was a reason you told me about the dome tonight, wasn't there?"

Deran grunts, surprise evident. "What gave it away?"

"You rarely change subject so abruptly."

"All your talk of what hadn't gone right today made me realize I might be able to help."

"I'm still waiting to hear how these dots connect."

"I think Cygnus is keeping your family in the zone."

"The zone?"

"The area beyond the dome."

Air whooshes out of my body, and I sink into the couch behind me. "You really were telling the truth?"

Deran nods, eyes grave. "I know—it's a lot to take in."

"People really still live there?"

"Yes. They reserve domes for those the conglomerate deem worthy, those who have proven their loyalty."

Panic rises again, and I feel lightheaded. "Domes? There's more than one?"

"Oh yes, one in the heart of every major manufacturing area, meant to taunt those living in the surrounding zone."

The bitterness in Deran's voice doesn't surprise me. I think of how my family and I ended up here, and I understand. "The domes are only for the people in power, and those who can serve the conglomerate's purposes at a higher level than just a worker bee?"

"Precisely."

Overwhelmed, I squeeze my eyes shut, flopping against the couch. Suddenly, Deran's assertion that our world remains broken is all too unbelievable again. I need to see it for myself. "Can you take me to the zone?"

"Yes, I had planned to. Although, admittedly, at the time, I wanted to prove to you why you shouldn't give Cygnus the machine. Since we agree, that's no longer necessary, but there's still reason to go. I'm hoping people there may know where your family are."

"People?"

There goes that hand again. *Poor spikes! They certainly don't need any help today.* Deran considers me for a moment before he answers, voice flat. "People who used to be friends with my parents."

Pieces I hadn't realized I'd stashed away fall into place. Him telling me he wasn't from here. "You're not from another city! You're from the zone."

An incredulous shake of his head. "Well, that didn't take you long."

"Puzzle pieces, remember? That's why when you came here, your family had more than one child?"

"Yes."

I want to ask, but I'm not sure if I'll offend him. Deran raises an eyebrow, inviting the question. "How did your family end up in the dome? Or should I call it what it is—an artificial biosphere?"

"Yes, that's more accurate, but everyone just calls it a dome. To answer your question, our family got here by chance. My parents' names were chosen by ballot as the next 'lucky' recipients of dome life. Even the conglomerate doesn't have enough power to use droids for everything. They still need people for most of the menial tasks."

I think of Sam. How loathe he was to reveal his existence, how fearful he was he'd be discovered talking to me, because, in his words, cleaners were meant to remain invisible. "They conscripted your parents here to clean?"

"They did. After my parents worked themselves to the bone to move us up from basement dwellers to the first tier, the conglomerate suppressed further promotions, kept them there until the day they were no longer useful."

Deran's face turns hard, his eyes dull chips of unpolished steel. "The day they murdered them."

20

By now, I should be accustomed to feeling inadequate. But what do you say when the man who means so much to you tells you his parents were murdered?

Words simply aren't enough. I wrap my arms around him, press in close, find his body tense against mine.

As I hold him, rubbing his back, he gradually relaxes. To my surprise, I realize I'm also not nearly as perturbed with emotional distress as usual. I'm getting better at this comforting thing.

When Deran leans a little away to look down at me, I angle my face toward his. His expression is unfathomable, eyes flat pools of gray, still water on a lake pre-dawn. "Do you want to talk about it some more?" I ask.

Deran sighs, then nods, tugging me back toward the couch and pulling me down to sit beside him. I turn sideways, folding my legs under me, smiling a little when he realizes what I'm after.

"I guess this is the way we talk." Deran turns to face me and sits cross-legged like I am, moving so that our knees touch. He grips my hands. "Where do I start?"

"The beginning is usually a good place."

"Smartypants!" A smile teases his lips before shadows return to his eyes. "I was only a year old when my folks 'won' their place here. Carys was five. The only reason we could both join my parents was because of the Glamboski's."

"Friends of your parents?"

"Not initially. They 'won' their place here at the same time, but had no children."

"Oh." I remember Deran's explanation. "They offered you the place of any children they might have?"

"Yes. After suffering through the death of both their children in the zone because of the hazardous living conditions, they knew they'd never survive the loss of another. Their sacrifice, their kindness, allowed me to come here with my family."

"I can see how they meant more to you than simply being fellow immigrants."

The sharp bark of laughter, mirthless, makes me blink. "Yes, I suppose that's exactly what we all are: immigrants. After all, aren't immigrants typically given the most menial tasks, kept on the border-line of starvation, made to beg and scrape for every scrap?"

His bitterness is a slap. "I'm sorry. I didn't realize things were so bad."

Shaking his head, Deran squeezes my hands, shrugging off the despair cloaking him. "It's not your fault. You were in the same posi-tion as us."

"I doubt that. I came here as a child of privilege compared to you."

"But no less free."

"I won't argue that."

"Well, bless the Glamboski's. Without them my parents would've had to choose between me and my sister."

Appalled, I stare at Deran. "They wouldn't really have made your parents choose, right?"

"They would've, and they did; it happened to other people we knew. But, at least back then, our parents were allowed the chance to bring their other children. Cygnus isn't as benevolent as his predecessor."

Goosebumps run up my arm as I'm once again reminded of the

monster masquerading as my benefactor all these years. "Cygnus allows no mercy, ever?"

"No. Although, his predecessor probably wouldn't have either, if there wasn't unrest in the zone when he was director. I think he was worried if he didn't provide a way for the families conscripted to bring multiple children, they would rebel and bring the conglomerate's precious production to a screaming halt."

"And they couldn't allow that, could they? Still, it must've been nice to grow up with your family." I can't keep the longing out of my voice. How many times did I wish for that? Instead, I believed Cygnus's lies. I thought they were pursuing their own dreams and requesting more time with them would be selfish of me.

Deran squeezes my hand, drawing my attention back, but his expression is somber. "It is wonderful growing up with your family. But when they're all murdered, with you helpless to do anything about it, you wonder whether it would've been better being alone."

I'm not sure I agree. "Can you tell me... how do you know..." I fumble for words, not sure how to ask about the manner of their deaths. Maybe because I'm not sure I should.

Voice sharp as flint, Deran answers the question I couldn't formulate. "I didn't. Not at first. I went to visit them one day, and strangers answered their door. Imagine my shock when those strangers told me my parents had moved, and they had no additional information. They'd disappeared without a trace. None of their stuff was even in their room anymore."

"Their room?"

"Yes, and they were lucky to even get that. I mentioned earlier we were basement dwellers." My confusion must show. "You've never heard the term?"

"No."

"It means you're a nobody—you have no tier. You literally live in the basement of the building you're assigned to work in. Below the basement, in fact."

"There's a basement below the basement?" My tone is dubious, with good reason. I've seen nothing to indicate these spaces exist. *Is this where Sam lives?*

"You wouldn't know it was there unless you knew how to reach it, using paths darker than the tunnels to Hades. There's no natural light at all, and you live in perpetual gloom. We endured the hell for almost five years, until they made both my parents supervisors. Just like that, we became tier ones. We got a room to share, with our own kitchen in the one corner and bathroom—"

"You didn't have that previously?"

"No. Basement dwellers live crammed together in one large room, no privacy, no separation. No kitchen facilities. The only bathrooms are communal, not even separated for gender."

Outraged, my anger spikes. "You mean, not only are they cruel enough to deprive the people they bring here of sunlight, but basic human decencies?"

Deran's smile is wry. "No need to get upset. It's quite cozy when you get used to it." His face turns serious. "Although, if we can change that, turn the tables on Cygnus and the conglomerate by not giving him this machine, and give it to the masses instead, perhaps we can make a difference."

"Why, Deran! You sound positively revolutionary!"

"If I could find the rebels, I'd join them!"

Although my comment was in jest, Deran's admission shocks me. "You would?"

"Yes. They're changing the status quo, and I want to be a part of that."

Uneasiness slithers through me. "Weren't you the one warning me about them? And shouldn't you be careful what you wish for? After all, we both know Cygnus somehow always ends up with information he shouldn't have."

A cheeky grin. "Only because Cygnus relies on the technology that made CC what it is today. All those cameras and drones, the software in the machines, spying, gathering data so CC can use it to manipulate people when they want something."

I stiffen, realizing something. "I forgot!"

"What?"

"The software CC used to blackmail and destroy their way to the top."

"How's that relevant?"

"What if Cygnus hasn't only been watching us on those cameras? What if there's spyware on our cubes, so he knows every little keystroke we've made, has recorded every idea I've ever written, has stored every test result from the machine, every diagram on its design?"

Deran's face pales. "You're saying he could recreate the machine without us if he wanted?"

I nod slowly. "It's possible."

We contemplate the ramifications.

When I smile, Deran eyes me warily. "What does that smile mean?"

"I think we can beat Cygnus at his own game."

"Meaning?"

"I have work to do. Files to corrupt, data to alter, records to purge."

Deran gapes. "You're going to destroy everything you have on the machine? But how will you get it to work? How will you get your brother back?"

This time, my smile wreaths my face. "Have you forgotten my eidetic memory? I don't need computers."

Laughter suddenly spills from Deran. "If only we got to see Cygnus's face when he finds all his precious information isn't what it seems!"

My laughter joins his. At the thought of turning the tables on Cygnus, pure delight fills me. "I'll get started tomorrow." I pause. "You never finished telling me about your parents." The words are halting, hesitant. *Should I have asked?*

Deran dispels my qualms, gripping my hands again, face earnest. "You can always ask questions. Whether I choose to answer is my prerogative. But never hold back because you're afraid you might offend me."

"Thanks."

"My parents remained tier ones until their disappearance. They never moved out of that room. I wouldn't have moved either if Carys hadn't died."

"That was why you didn't know they'd disappeared?"

"Yes. Only one child ever gets to move into a place of their own, and then only if they prove they're worthy. But when I graduated—after having the opportunity to even attend school, something not offered in the zone, they moved me up to tier two—and I earned my own apartment. When I became team lead, I was promoted to tier three. Interesting that happened only a few weeks after they assigned me to your lab full-time as a mechanic."

"You don't think it was coincidence?"

"No. I'm sure it's all related, although how, I've yet to figure out. Regardless, my first promotion helped me support my parents. After Carys died, their bodies were no longer up to the rigorous demands of their work. They aged overnight, and as a result, their duties suffered."

Before he says it, I know what's coming, and I want to shrink back, tell him to stop. I shift, but Deran grips my hands tighter, his eyes steel, holding my mine with an unbreakable tether.

"You need to hear this. My parents were no longer productive citizens—at least, not as productive as CC wanted them to be. Why keep them around as mouths to feed, bodies to clothe, when there were plenty of younger people to take their place? So they terminated them."

The words are a blow, brutal, bruising. I can barely speak. "You're sure?"

"Yes. After their sudden disappearance, I approached my supervisor, demanding answers, telling him I needed to find them if he wanted any profitable hours out of me. He put his neck on the line, asking the higher-ups, and I was summoned to Cygnus's office."

Shock widens my eyes. Cygnus seldom interacts with anyone other than the Board or the various division heads of CC. For him to speak to someone without rank, let alone a lowly tier three, is unheard of. "Cygnus spoke with you himself?"

"I know, right? I couldn't believe it either. But the whole time he had me in his office, I felt like he was weighing me. Like he was thinking of some other use, deciding how best I could serve some objective of his I couldn't fathom."

"I know the feeling."

"Yes, you do."

"Did you figure out what he was after?"

"No. But that meeting was right before they assigned me to the labs, before my promotion, so I'm guessing it had something to do with you."

Apprehension grips me anew, making me shiver. "What game is he playing now?"

"I don't know, but we'd better figure it out before he reaches the endgame."

I nod. "What else happened in that meeting?"

A disgusted grunt. "He gave me some story about my parents being promoted, moved to another dome, then said I wouldn't be able to contact them there because it would be a security breach for comm links to cross domes."

I latch onto the snippet. "You think the comm link bit is true?"

"I don't know. Inter-dome communication must be possible. Otherwise, how would Cygnus know what was going on outside of Cirrian?"

"Yes, but maybe they don't use comm links because they aren't secure. Or they don't have the range. Have you ever heard of another way of communicating?"

"No, not even with all my snooping." Deran pauses, returning to the past. "After my promotion, when I discovered I could learn things crawling around in the ducts... I saw a termination procedure. What they do to people they no longer find useful."

His words cut deep, and I shudder. How awful for him! Finding an inner reserve, a strength, I grip his hands and capture his shimmering gaze with my own. "I'm sorry you had to see that."

Deran swallows, then nods. "Thanks. At least it's quick. I know my parents didn't suffer. Just closed their eyes and slumped over, if what happened to those people happened to them."

The desperation in his voice shreds my heart. "I'm sure it was. CC isn't very creative in changing their methods."

My words may've been blunt, but Deran needed them. His smile is taut, his face set. "I'm choosing to believe that. And in all honesty, knowing what probably happened to my parents, what CC did to Carys, those played into my decision to help you. I couldn't bear to see you experience the same things."

Overcome, unable to speak, I simply nod, thankful when Deran nods. I know he understands my gratitude. We sit like that for a long time: knees touching, holding hands.

21

Finally, Deran stirs. "I should probably get you home. It's been a long night for both of us."

I don't want to leave Deran's apartment. I don't want to be alone. But I can't stay. However, I do have an excuse to linger. "Do you have any food I could eat?" Deran's startled glance makes me laugh. "What?"

"I'm sorry—I should've thought to offer you something sooner."

"I wasn't feeling up to it then." Even the oblique reference to my vomiting makes my stomach twinge. But no food for hours might be part of the problem.

"I have just the thing." Deran moves to the kitchen, and soon, I smell the comforting aroma of toast.

Before I'm conscious of moving, I find myself in the kitchen. "Yum! May I have some?"

Deran pushes two slices toward me. "Don't eat too fast, and no more honey than I've already put on."

As I sink my teeth in, I sigh. So good! I finish four slices in short order, then barely catch the yawn slipping out right after I take my last bite.

Deran grins. "Time to get you home."

Reluctantly, I allow him to pull me to my feet. At least we'll still have time together on the trundle ride home.

The journey home is far too short, and I'm not the only one dawdling as we head for my apartment. Chivalrous as ever, Deran rides the elevator up to my apartment with me. When we reach the door, I'm loathe to say goodbye. "I would offer you some hot chocolate, except…" I don't finish the sentence, but he can fill in the blanks. No point mentioning tainted food and drink in a monitored hallway.

A brilliant flash of teeth as he grins. "A glass of water will do."

With a matching grin, I wand my arm over the access panel and step inside. As soon as my foot connects with something that shouldn't be there, I know something's wrong. "Lights!"

The lights blaze, and I stand, frozen. Deran inhales sharply behind me as he takes in the sight. The bathroom, visible from here, looks like a bombshell hit it. The carnage continues into the bedroom, clothes littering the floor. But the destruction ends there. From my bedroom door back to where we stand, the only sign of disturbance is an upended drawer in the coffee table. Otherwise, the kitchen is completely untouched. Confused, I glance down, realizing it was a tube of toothpaste my foot encountered. Still, how it made its way here…

Heart thumping, my mind races as I try to work out what they could've been looking for. *And who the heck are 'they?'* There's only one suspicious thing I own, but with the kitchen unscathed, I'm hoping Ferret's still secure in his hiding spot.

Deran brushes past. Keeping me firmly behind him, he scans the living area. Nothing stirs. Even the air holds its breath. Cautiously, Deran slinks toward my bedroom. I scamper after him, not wanting to be left alone.

The bedroom is empty. No one hides in the shadows to pounce on us. With the worry out of the way, I take in the scene. Worse than I thought. My linens were ripped from the bed, and my nightstand is in pieces. In the bathroom, every bottle I own was opened, and the contents gouged through.

Amidst the chaos, my upended laundry basket draws my attention.

The jeans lying on top of the pile of dirty clothes niggle. "Oh!" I dash past Deran, snatching up the jeans and searching the pockets. *It's gone!* Eyes wild, I stare at Deran. Before I can utter a syllable, he gives the faintest shake of his head.

Instantly, I tense, wary of a new unseen threat. When Deran pulls his hand from his pocket, I expect a weapon, but he holds nothing. Ever so casually, he slides up to me, pretending he wants water with one hand while nudging my side with the other. Attempting to keep the act inconspicuous, I glance down, noticing the small device concealed in the palm of his hand.

Although questions burn, I keep my expression neutral, allowing Deran to step back unchallenged. He lifts the glass to his lips and sips the water. Then he strolls away, still holding the glass as though he's just inspecting my apartment. But he surreptitiously moves the device around the bathroom before taking it into the bedroom and then the living area.

At last, he lowers his arms and faces me. "No listening or recording devices. You're free to speak."

Horrified I could've said something to implicate us, I swallow. "You sure?"

"Yes." He taps the device. "This takes care of that. What did you realize in the bathroom?"

"It's gone!"

Perplexed, he studies me. "What's gone?"

"The slide! The one Tandize was looking at in the lab on Saturday."

Deran stills. "You mean the serum sample—or what we think was the serum sample?" I nod. "We're in trouble."

"Understatement of the century! Who do you think came looking for it?"

"First guess would be mindhunters. Second would be Tandize."

"Tandize? She's missing. Or I suppose she could be hiding. Why her?"

"If it was serum, she knows she's in trouble if you recognize it. Or rat her out. Remember, Tandize doesn't know if she can trust us any more than we know if we can trust her."

"But why risk coming here? She couldn't have known I wouldn't be home. And with all the cameras in the malls, she would be broadcasting her position to the mindhunters, asking them to catch her."

Deran shrugs. "Maybe she felt it was worth it."

"Or mindhunters did this."

Worried gray eyes find mine. "If so, we need to get you out of here, away from the dome."

I lift my chin. "Not before I've sabotaged the data."

"You don't have time!"

"I disagree. Think about it. If they really wanted me, wouldn't they just have nabbed me already? Why waste time making it look like someone ransacked my apartment? Because why would I remember the slide? After all, I left it in my jeans. Clearly, I didn't think it was worth putting in a safe place."

This makes Deran pause. "You really think they believe you don't know what it is?"

"If they didn't, I wouldn't be standing here talking to you. I'd be in some sort of cell with mindhunters probing every memory I had."

Obviously unhappy, Deran runs his hand through his hair. "I don't like making assumptions."

"We're making educated guesses. Safer than assumptions and much safer than going off half-cocked because we think they're onto us. Perhaps that was their plan. Retrieve the slide and then see what we do. Our actions, once we discover it's missing, will dictate what they do next."

Huffing out air, Deran paces. Finally, he stops and faces me. "How can we be sure?"

"We play their game. Pretend we think it's robbery. Report it like any good citizen would. Then, if asked, act as if we didn't even realize the slide was taken."

Deran still looks troubled, but I'm getting through to him. "Okay, we report it."

An hour later, the SerSents have come and gone, their questions bland, interest lackluster. When the door closes behind them, I sigh with relief. I'd been worried they'd want to conduct their own search, but as soon as I told them I thought nothing was missing, they couldn't leave fast enough.

Deran stares at the closed door. "Think they bought our story?"

"I think the only thing that could've shaken them out of their apathy was telling them aliens did it. They weren't terribly thorough."

"Makes you wonder how many burglaries there are if they're so disinterested."

"Agreed. Now what?"

"Now, you give me some blankets and a pillow and I sleep on your couch tonight."

I gawk at Deran. "You're not serious?" But even as I ask, I'm relieved he's staying.

"I am. We still don't know who really took the slide. I would never forgive myself if I left you here alone, and mindhunters spirited you away in the night."

"Thank you." I curl into him, and he cocoons me in his powerful arms. Accepting the reassurance, I lean against his chest, soothed by the steady beat of his heart. When I totter unsteadily on my feet, I realize how tired I am.

"Sorry." I lean back from his embrace, a yawn slipping out. "I need sleep."

"You and me both. How about that bedding?"

Strange as it is to wake the next morning with Deran in my apartment, it's wildly comforting. I sit up in bed, stretching, gratified I'm not alone, then race through a quick shower before venturing into the living room. I expect to find Deran still asleep, but he's picking through my kitchen fruit bowl.

Deran lifts an apple in salute. "Morning. Sleep well?"

I kiss him because I can—and because I know I won't be able to touch him for the rest of the day, I take my time, breathless when I pull back.

Bright silver ripples in those eyes. "Now that's a good morning kiss!"

My grin matches his. "Just making sure I get my affection for the day. You asked if I slept well. I did. You?"

"Yes! You have an exceptionally comfortable couch there."

I grin. "I'm aware and thus thrilled that whoever broke in didn't slice into it! It's a recent acquisition and one I'm pleased I finally made."

Deran cocks his head. "Sounds like there's a story, but it will have to wait for another day. I'm going to be late for work. Want to travel in with me?"

"Why not? If they've been watching us, they'll know you spent the night here." I pause, suddenly realizing the implications. "Oh, no —you don't think they'll think you 'spent the night' spent the night?"

Instead of teasing me, Deran shrugs. "A little late for us to be worrying now." Sensing my anxiety, he hurries to reassure me. "But if we don't have another sleepover again soon, they'll probably write last night off to exactly what it was—me staying to make sure you were safe."

He's right—or at least, I hope he is. I don't want to dwell on the implications if he isn't. "In that case," I grab my work bags, "let's go."

Our ride into work is quiet, and when we reach CC HQ, we go our separate ways as though it's business as usual. At least, that's what I strive for. But my carefully placed mask slips the moment I walk into the lab and spot Tandize.

I gape. My surprise has already been caught by any watching cameras, so I may as well play this out. Marching over to Tandize's workstation, I sense rather than see the way the rest of the team quiets, watching me.

Restraining my emotions (do I even know what I'm feeling?), I stop at Tandize's desk. She glances up, then stumbles to her feet. "Chiara! I'm sorry! I can explain."

"Let's continue this in my office." I turn on my heel, expecting her to follow. My team's disappointed faces make me want to smile. Were they expecting me to ream Tandize out in front of them? Not an invalid assumption, given my emotional outbursts lately.

This reminder only makes me more determined to keep things with Tandize beyond prying ears and eyes. Deran's warning is more appropriate now than ever: trust no one. Surreptitiously, I snap the elastic band encasing my wrist.

But, as I march into my office, something else occurs to me. Why would the rest of my team want Tandize in trouble? Isn't she their spokesperson? Is it perhaps a role she assigned herself, not one the others are happy about? The idea bears further consideration. But later.

After setting my bags down, I face Tandize. She hovers by the doorway, like she wants to be anywhere but here. "Come in and close the door behind you."

Tandize swallows, but complies, remaining just inside, face wan, hands twisting in front of her.

"Please, sit." My cordial tone surprises her, widening her eyes which are red-rimmed and puffy. Obviously, she's been crying. When she's perched on the edge of the chair on the other side of my desk (really? I'm not going to eat her!), I wave a hand. "Now, explain your unsanctioned absence."

"Remember I told you about my mom's dementia?" I nod. "When I got home on Sunday afternoon after doing our weekly grocery run, she'd disappeared."

Thwack! Only I hear my rubber band hit my wrist, but the sound grounds me. Because oh! So many ideas flooding my head right now! I shelve them, keeping my face neutral, telling myself to hear her out. Warning myself to watch for signs she was subjected to the same "treatment" Sarissa was.

When I give no response, Tandize's agitation ramps up. "Do you know what it's like to have to watch a person every minute of every day, to make sure they don't walk off not knowing who they are or where they're going?"

"No, I'm sorry. I don't."

Tears roll down Tandize's cheeks, and I wonder how I should respond. She either doesn't notice or care. "I'll tell you: it's a living nightmare. So when you get back home and your dementia-afflicted mother isn't there, the nightmare's come to life. I spent the last two days searching for her."

"You didn't think to at least let us know you were alright? Or ask for that time off?"

Her wail is unexpected, and I jump in my chair. "You don't understand! The worry is all-consuming! There's no space in your head when you're trying to find someone you love, someone who's lost and alone and probably walking into danger without being aware of it!"

At her outburst, heads turn toward my office. I aim for a pacifying tone. "Alright, calm down. I clearly don't understand how distressing it was for you. But you're an adult, and I expect you to behave like one. You can't disappear for days without letting me know where you are, or if you even intend on returning."

More sniffles. "You just don't know what it's like."

I grab the box of tissues from the cabinet behind me and rise. Offering them to Tandize, I perch on the edge of my desk next to her. "Look, perhaps it's best if you take some time off and address the situation."

Tandize pauses in the middle of blowing her nose, eyes wide with horror. "No! I can't do that. I have to work."

The sheer desperation in her voice reminds me of something else. I glance down. Her shoes are in no better condition than those of most of her coworkers. "You need the work so you can support your mother?"

Tandize flushes, then nods before dropping her head. Or did she drop it so I couldn't see any gleam of triumph in her eyes? Getting to keep the job that will allow her to continue to spy on me for Cygnus?

Ugh! All this cloak-and-dagger stuff is exhausting! I stroll back around my desk, mulling options, keeping my face averted from both Tandize and the camera in the corner. *Was* Tandize looking for her mother? Did her mother go off on some dementia-walk, or did mindhunters subject Tandize to some sort of "conditioning?" Worse, could they be holding her mother hostage, so Tandize will do whatever they ask? After all, it happened to me.

I make a decision. Despite the risk, there are reasons to keep Tandize here. I need to know where she got the serum sample, whether she knew it was the serum, and how she learned to sing that song. My only hope of getting answers is to keep her where I can watch her. Rather, where Deran's cameras can watch her. Because I can't ignore another glaring fact: Tandize returning to work the day after my apartment was ransacked, the slide stolen, is a little too convenient.

"Fine. You can stay. While I may not understand what you're dealing with, I understand wanting to take care of your mother. There's no need to apologize for that or feel embarrassed. However, I want you to promise you'll let me know next time you have to be out of the office because you're having problems with her."

Tandize nods. While I examine her for signs of duress, somehow been altered, I find only relief and gratitude. "Thank you, Chiara! Yes, I promise. I truly appreciate the second chance."

"Don't make me regret it." A quick nod. "Okay, lecture's over. Time to get back to work."

Tandize leaps up, eager to please. "Absolutely! Thanks again." Then she's out the door.

I'm left staring after her, wondering if I've just made the biggest mistake yet.

22

I settle into my chair, activating my cube and prioritizing my tasks. Two of the lab's other projects have fallen behind schedule, so I must check on those first before I can focus on my personal agenda today.

Time shrinks as I address the problems for each of the lagging projects with the appropriate team members. One requires additional resources I'll have to requisition (didn't Cygnus promise to send me another assistant?), and the other contained a flawed calculation skewing the results. Unfortunately, finding that error took far longer than expected.

By the time we finish, it's past lunchtime, and I hurry to my office, eager to attack my own tasks. I'm barely seated at my desk when a familiar shadow graces my doorway. I can't help but smile at him. "Hello, stranger. Imagine seeing you again so soon!"

Deran grins, his cheeky smile warming my insides. "I thought you would've been in the workshop by now to see how we were doing."

"I would've, except I had things to deal with here first. How's dismantling the machine going?"

"About as well as can be expected. I wish we were further along, but you can only move so quickly with some of those components."

I hear what he doesn't say: we can only stall for so long before

Cygnus notices. "I trust you'll do your best. Do you need anything from me?"

"Yes, actually. Want to pull up the schematics here, or should we go to the workshop?"

Deran's tone tells me I have no choice. "Workshop—we can deal with it more effectively there."

Deran leans aside, allowing me to step out of my office ahead of him. As soon as I'm out, I turn and wait for him to step up beside me. Another cheeky grin confirms he knew I guessed what he was up to.

"No leering at my behind today," I mutter under my breath, so only he can hear.

His grin morphs into that wonderful laugh, making me smile. About halfway to the workshop, my stomach growls. A sideways glance from Deran I can't fathom. "I'm guessing you haven't had lunch yet?"

His tone holds slight accusation, and I'm immediately defensive. "It's been a busy morning."

"Not an excuse. You know you should eat."

I'm about to bite his head off for repeating Cygnus's words when I register the subtext. *Oh!* The briefest hint of a smile is the only indication Deran's pleased he's finally gotten through to me. "You're right. Perhaps I should eat first. Then I'll join you in the workshop afterward?"

"Sure. My questions will hold for a while."

"Alright, I'll see you in a bit."

Turning, I retrace my path back to the lab, then hurry down to the cafeteria. I select and pay for food, then take the bagged lunch and head for the exit. Five minutes later, I'm free of CC HQ and glorying in the sunshine as I make for today's dropbox.

After Deran's oblique reference, I'm eager to see what's there— besides the food. I grin to think of his deceit. All anyone watching those cameras in the hallway would've seen was a concerned friend reinforcing what everyone knows to remind me of. Not a partner in crime urging me to collect whatever else is in that bag as soon as possible.

Soon, I'm trotting through the small glade of trees leading to a bench on the other side. Except I pause in the trees and root around in the bushes, beside the twisted tree Deran described when we set up the dropbox locations. My hand brushes against the bag, masterfully concealed, and I extract it.

When did Deran have time to put this here? He was at my place last night, and I doubt he went all the way home between us getting to work. Does he have a way to get untainted food at CC HQ?

But I'm more curious about what else the bag holds, so I peer inside. Just as well Deran warned me to expect something extra. If I wasn't looking, I might've missed the tiny data chip taped neatly to the inner rim of the food tray's lid.

Carefully, I work it free, placing it securely in an inside pocket of my lab coat. Then I stuff Deran's bag inside the cafeteria bag before exiting the glade. I plop onto the bench, my supposed destination, and extract Deran's sandwich.

Yum! My mouth waters at the first scrumptious bite, and I can't gorge the food fast enough. I'm licking my fingers, wishing there was more, when I remember the chip. Hustling back to CC HQ, I dump the cafeteria bag (with Deran's still hidden inside) in the incinerator, then hurry to the R&D floor.

No one accosts me with questions as I make my way across the lab to my personal workspace. As soon as I've checked the lab is still without surveillance, I remove the tiny chip and drop it into the carrier tray, allowing me to access it via the cube here. Since this cube is air-gapped, I've no reason to worry what I do here will be accessed by strangers without my knowledge.

The software loads, and an image appears on my holoscreen. *Yes! Deran found it!* Impatiently, I watch Saturday's replay, eager to get to the singing. Quickly, I snip the song, then slide it over to the audio mixer I worked with yesterday. Now that I have the music, capturing the frequencies is a simple matter.

As the numbers come up on screen, I'm hardly surprised to find Deran was right. There are indeed only minor variations in the notes.

In fact, the song can be played in the range D4-D5, so the frequency ranges from 293.665 to 587.33Hz.

Sticking with the first two verses (because surely Tandize did for a reason!), I focus on the notes. To replicate the sound, I adjust the key, using F4, G4, A4, and C5 instead of the middle C group of notes Deran suggested.

Once updated, I find the frequency range reduced to 349.225Hz through 523.25Hz. Satisfied I've finally isolated them, I record the tune, repeating it on a loop onto the dictation device I keep with me almost all the time. *Nothing new here to raise your suspicions, Cygnus!* Then, remembering Deran's advice, I copy Tandize's rendition onto the device too, also on a loop. Can't hurt to have that handy, just in case.

Done, I lean back, exhausted. More from the constant worry someone would walk in on me or spy through that ridiculous little window than because the work itself was difficult. I really must follow up with maintenance about that security film!

Before leaving, I scrub the history from my personal lab's cube, remove the chip, and check the volume on my dictation device. Satisfied only someone standing right next to me could hear, I exit my personal lab and stroll back to my office.

Several heads go up on the lab floor, and I can see the questions before they ask them. *Thwack!* The rubber band hits the soft flesh on the inside of my wrist. Instead of wincing, I paste a smile onto my face. *Yes, I love my work and yes, I'm thrilled to be here, and yes, I'll answer all your silly questions until the cows come home, as though you're all the smartest people in the world!*

I must maintain appearances for those wretched cameras. Resisting the sigh that wants out because all I want to do is cross my next task off my list, I smile at the expectant faces. "Who's first?"

Despite my initial resentment, my genuine joy in the wonder of science soon takes over, and I lose myself in the intricacies of the problems. I move from one team member to the next, until they can all continue without me.

Naturally, the entire afternoon has slipped past. I remember I promised Deran I'd go see him. As I hurry along the corridor to the workshop, I hope I'll still catch him.

He and his team are packing up, setting their tools in the spots assigned for them, accounting for all the pieces to make sure they haven't lost anything. One glance tells me they're about halfway. They'll no doubt be done by the end of the workweek. *So little time! But time might be running out for my brother, too.*

I offer Deran an apologetic smile. "Sorry, I got wrapped up in some other work and forgot I was supposed to meet you."

Deran grins, not looking the slightest bit upset. "I figured."

"Was it anything important?"

"No, I would've come to find you if it was. But since you're here, can you answer my questions so we can get started on that section of the machine in the morning?"

"Need us to stick around too, boss?" Silvan asks.

"Thanks, but no. You're free to leave. I'll catch you up tomorrow."

Nods accompany farewells. Then Deran and I are alone in the workshop. He turns to me. "Here, let me show you the pieces we had questions on."

Deran leads me to a part of the machine tall enough to hide us from the cameras on the opposite wall. Then he bends down, getting us low and taking us out of the line of sight of the cameras on this side. He touches a part, as though pointing something out. "Did you find it?"

"Yes!"

A devilish grin. "From your glee, I gather you were successful?"

My face falls. "Well, I have it ready to go, if that's what you mean. Whether it will work remains to be seen. We need test subjects."

Deran laughs. "I don't think they'd like to hear you calling them that!"

"I don't care what they like. I just need them to test these versions. They're never around when you need them."

My attempt at humor falls flat, and Deran sobers. "I'd rather have it that way."

"Me too." I point at the machine. "Was there really something you wanted to ask?"

"Actually, yes."

Deran leads me to a different area, clearly in range of multiple cameras. No wonder he didn't bring me here first. He asks several questions about the minuscule components, confirming which ones should be preserved and which are easily replaceable.

"You can't save them all?"

"I'll try, but with the enormous pressure these joints were under when we ran the machine, I can't promise some won't shatter when we remove the mechanisms holding them in place. I just need to work out the best way of approaching the problem, so the most essential take the least strain when we pull everything apart. Then we can keep them intact. Or try to."

"I hope you succeed. If this piece here breaks," I point it out, "we're in trouble. I'm not sure we can get another in a hurry."

Deran understands the inference. If we want delays, this is exactly the piece to break. He nods. "We'll do our best."

"Anything else?"

"No, that covers it."

Disappointment lances through me. I've barely seen him all day, and now we have to go our separate ways. His hand brushes mine, his head turning away from the cameras and voice low. "I know. I wish we could spend more time together, too. But you know why we can't."

"I do." With a sigh, I paste an artificially bright smile on my face, returning my voice to its usual volume. "See you tomorrow then." Before I can change my mind, I raise my hand in a quick wave, then turn and hurry out of the workshop, not looking back.

23

I reach my office. The only thing to counteract my moping is work. Just as well I have a mission then. Touching my cube to bring it back to life, I toss the data from the two cold-fusion tests I've been staring at for days onto the holoscreens.

Before I mess with what's real, I take one last look at the data. *I know, I know!* No doubt a vain attempt at trying to divine the problem. I've looked at it from all angles already. No reason the machine worked as it should in the test on the left of my screen, but failed miserably when we ran it the second time for Cygnus in the results on the right.

I scroll through the data on both sides simultaneously, trying to pinpoint the exact moment things went south. All I do is confirm my earlier conclusion, the graph showing the variation between energy input and output veering violently into negative territory at 6.231823 seconds.

With a flick of my wrist, I pause the results comparison, then pull up the mass of data from the various gauges on the machine. Comparing the readings, from laser intensity to heat generated to plasma concentration levels to countless others, I still find no glaring discrepancies. It's like the results just magically became negative

164

instead of positive. If only I had another set of data... *Oh no! How could I? Why didn't I run a third test?*

I can't believe I was that stupid! Every scientist knows you don't compare data from only two sources. You have a third set to act as a control, like sailors of old taking three depth readings, allowing the third to confirm which of the first two was more accurate.

And now it's too late! A primal scream erupts. I barely stop myself from throwing something. I take to pacing instead. The machine's already halfway dismantled. No way to run that third test and still have the exact variables we had in the first two.

Why, oh why, didn't I remember? My brain was still fogged from the serum, but surely that's not the only reason? As I consider this, I realize there were plenty of other factors at play. The traumatic meeting with my mom, and Tavi, and Frankie. Xanin's abduction. Deran's silence. My stressful confrontation with Cygnus. Everything I learned from Deran. Oh yes—let's not forget trying to escape the mindhunters to even get to that meeting. Then everything that's happened since.

The list goes on. I can hardly be shocked I forgot something so basic.

But Cygnus can never learn about my failure. He'd know I was off my game.

Or... can I use it to my advantage? He did increase my serum dose. Perhaps I can pretend I'm more addled than usual?

Yes, that might work. Deran and I already discussed the issue when he told me about my "hypoglycemia."

The threat of Cygnus discovering my mistake resolved, I ponder what I might've found. Would the cold fusion device have worked or failed miserably again? A sigh. I'll never know now. The obvious turning point in the results should define the cause. Unless...

Oh, no! Really? I can't take much more of this. I've never been this inept in my life before! Then again, doesn't Occam's Razor exist for a reason—the simplest explanation is usually the right one? In this case, so simple I hadn't even considered it until now. But it's the only solution that makes sense. If I can get the footage I need of the tests without raising Cygnus's suspicions—or letting him know I realize there are cameras in the workshop—I can confirm my theory.

Surely, though, he must suspect I'm aware of the cameras? I scour my memory for anything he might've seen in the last few weeks to tip him off. Although I've been careful to hide my newfound knowledge of the cameras, my actions may have given me away.

The way I "disappeared" in the mall the night I broke into CC HQ. My subversive tactics to get to the picnic with Deran. Most recently, the way I circumvented the mindhunters when meeting Deran after that awful family reunion, minus Xanin.

Xanin! How am I going to find him? Where could they possibly have taken him? I don't want to think about what they might be doing to him.

I shut those terrifying images down in the blink of an eye. Frazzled, my pacing turns frenetic. Now that I've opened the door to family, I can't stop worrying about them. Not only Xanin, but my mom and other siblings. Are they safe? I was so consumed with Xanin's kidnapping—I didn't stop to think what might've happened to them after the SerSents crashed in and dragged them away.

What was Cygnus so worried I might learn? He was right to be concerned. The last time I saw my mother this distraught was when Cygnus took me. The day she learned my father was… what? Dead? Captured? Never coming home again? In that state, who knows what information desperation may have led to her to reveal, consequences be damned.

Harrowing thought after harrowing thought slices into my conscious mind, each cut more acute than the last. I can bear it no longer. *I have to get out! Go! Move!*

Snatching my bags, I sprint out of my office, then down the stairs, not wanting to wait for the elevator. I burst through the doors at the stairwell's end into the lobby of CC HQ, banging the door against the wall and startling the SerSents on duty.

They're too slow or don't care to stop me because, in a flash, I'm outside, beyond their reach and racing for the trundle. At the station, one has yet to arrive, and I bounce anxiously from foot to foot. *Come on, come on!*

Then the rails vibrate and a glaring headlight appears down the track, the telltale whoosh of air rushing ahead of the trundle. I barge through the barely open doors, not caring about banging my elbow, and slump into the nearest seat. If only I could stand for the trip… well, why not? I've seen it done before. Granted, it's not advisable given the speeds at which the trundle travels, but who cares? I need something to challenge my mind, to stop the torturous thoughts.

I rise, wrapping a hand around the leather strap secured to the overhead rail. I'm almost thrown off my feet when the trundle takes off, and I gasp, righting myself, before grinning like a loon. *Yes! This is more like it!*

With a wild abandon filling me, I negotiate the twists and turns as the trundle streaks down the tracks. Staying on my feet takes all my concentration. When we reach the next stop, I feel like I may be getting my "sea legs." Or would that be "trundle legs?"

Who gives a flying fig? The trundle whizzes off again, almost sending me sprawling a second time. But I hang onto the leather strap for dear life, wanting to shriek with delight, riding the vicious turns with absolute focus.

By the time we near my stop, I'm quivering from the exertion. While I'd love to do this all night, I'm forced to accept my limitations. Frail human body! Betrayed, I hang on for the bracing stop. I'm almost catapulted through the back end of the trundle. Recovering, my hands let go of the strap as the trundle settles on its mag-lev tracks.

Legs wobbly, I stagger to the exit, supporting myself using the steel frames backing each of the chairs, then lurch through the open doors. Suddenly outside with nothing to help keep me upright, I almost fall flat on my face. I catch myself, but not before my knees hit the pavement—painfully.

Groaning, I remain where I landed, scared even the slightest movement will topple me. Several ragged breaths do nothing to help me regain control of my limbs. I'm not sure whether I'm relieved or distraught no one is here to witness this. Finally, using one hand to steady myself, I push back to my feet. My legs are still cooked spaghetti.

I shuffle over to a nearby station bench and sink onto it. Flopping my head back against the wall, I wait for the shaking to stop. I didn't realize that ride would take so much out of me. When my stomach gurgles, I understand. It's close to midnight, and the only thing I've eaten all day is the lunch Deran provided and a piece of fruit for breakfast.

Unable to face trekking to the dropbox for the food Deran left for my dinner, I remain in place. But sitting motionless does me no favors. The thoughts assail me once more, driving me to my feet, pushing me on, giving me strength I didn't know I had.

In a daze, I collect the food, then force myself onward, collapsing just inside the door of my apartment the moment I get inside. Yes, I should wash my hands before I eat, should get utensils, heat the food, but I'm exhausted. Like a starved man finding a cache on a desert island, I tear into the meal with my bare hands, shoveling it into my mouth.

The first few mouthfuls go unnoticed, my body still too worn out to pay attention to anything. Then gradually, I taste the food. My rabid fingers stop scrabbling in the tray, and I take more measured bites. After scraping out the last morsel, I lick my fingers contentedly. A yawn slips out, and I yearn for sleep. Isn't that what Mom always used to say? *Maagies vol, oogies toe?* An expression passed down from her grandmother's grandmother, roughly translated to, "Tummies full, eyes closed."

I'm not sure whether it's thinking about the saying, or the sheer physical and mental exertion of the last few hours, but my bed beckons. I drag my weary bones up off the floor, stumbling to the bedroom and flopping onto the bed. Blissful, all-consuming sleep claims me.

Sun warms my face, and I squint, shrinking away from intense light. Blearily, I move my head away, then struggle up into a sitting position, taking stock.

Teeth furry? Check. Eyes scratchy? Check. Body aching all over? Check. *Ugh! I need to get clean!* I lurch out of bed, heading for my shower. Under the steaming, stinging spray, I let my mind wander. There must be some scientific reason for always getting your best thinking done in a shower. After less than two minutes, the thoughts I tried suppressing yesterday return. However, instead of the overwhelming deluge, they come in an orderly flow. This time, I don't chase them away, facing them, analyzing each as it surfaces.

First, I'm almost positive I know why the machine stopped working. Second, I need to confirm those suspicions. Third, it would be better to ask Deran for help with this than Cygnus. That would raise another whole complication that's best left untouched.

Fourth, my family. Deran said knows people in the zone who may know where they're hidden. The sooner he takes me there for answers, the better. Especially if I'm right about what blew up the machine's second test.

Fifth, I need to work on what I'm going to say to Cygnus. This is the part I've avoided for too long. I didn't want to give Cygnus an ultimatum in case he did something to my mom, or Tavi, or Frankie. But he's already taken Xanin. There's nothing to say he hasn't already done something to the rest of my family, too. I have to get proof they're all okay *and* work out how best to present my ultimatum: my family for his machine.

Which brings me to the last few points. No point figuring out why Cygnus wants cold fusion technology. He's not getting it, and it's as simple as that.

So, sabotage the machine, corrupt the data, get myself and my family out of here. Away from this dome with its rules and regulations, its ever-present cameras, and those dreaded mindhunters. There must be somewhere my family and I can go. A place where we can be safe, live in peace. I need to work on answers for that, too. And hope Deran will come with us when we finally make a run for it.

Did I miss anything? I don't think so. I touch the button, switching the shower from water spray to air dry. My fingers are pruned. At least they're clean, the food still under my nails from last night washed away.

When I step out of my shower a few minutes later, refreshed and rubbing in my pear-scented lotion, there's only one thought left in my head. Time to put my plans into motion.

24

Nothing like a plan to put extra pep in your step. An excellent breakfast doesn't hurt either. I made a point of collecting Deran's meal this morning so I wouldn't be running on empty again. Once I reach work, I implement my strategy for attacking my problems.

First stop: the workshop. Deran and his team are already swarming the machine, tools whirring as they pull it apart. Deran spots me from his perch high on the far side of the plasma drum and waves. "Give me a sec. I'll be right down."

I wait, watching Deran's team's easy camaraderie. They pass tools between themselves, working together to solve the problem. Could any of them be working for Cygnus? It would be awful, but I remind myself again: trust is dangerous, something I can't allow, no matter how much I may like them.

Deran taps my shoulder. "Earth to Chiara!"

I turn, grinning up at him. "Sorry. I was thinking about something else."

"Clearly." He waits, but when I don't elaborate, he gets the hint. "Did you need me?"

"Yes. Do you have time to walk with me for a bit? I'd like a sounding board. Sarissa used to help with that, but..." I trail off, strangely reluctant to finish the sentence.

Dubious, Deran scratches his chin. "And what does a sounding board do, exactly?"

"You listen. No need to understand the science. You just have to hear the words coming out of my mouth." I shrug. "I know—it sounds ridiculous. But somehow, when I did this with Sarissa, it helped me work through problems."

"Sounds easy enough. Let me first check the team are all squared away, and then we can go."

I nod, and he clambers back up the ladder. I don't hear the conversation, but I see the gestures, the nodding heads. Then Deran's on his way back down to me.

He jumps off the last rung, feet landing with a soft thud. "Ready?"

"Yes. Let's walk outside. The change of scenery also used to help."

A gleam of understanding enters those gray eyes, but Deran's careful to keep his expression neutral. "Whatever aids the process."

We make it out of CC HQ without incident, and I inhale deeply. The air is fresh, the sweet yet sharp scent of freshly mowed grass mixing with the earthy overtones of damp moss and tree trunks still wet from the sprinklers.

I glance at Deran. "Why don't you pick a place?"

A charming smile that makes me wonder what he's thinking. "Sure. This way."

When he leads us to yet another secluded spot, I'm astounded. "How do you find these places?"

"I actively search for them. Surprising how many you can find." Reaching into his pocket, Deran pulls out his personally modified music player and sets it up. Serious gray eyes find mine as soon as he's seated. "What's up?"

"I've figured out why the machine didn't work the second time around. Or, at least, I'm 99 percent sure."

A soft whistle. "Seriously?"

"Yes. But I need your help to confirm it. Any chance you have cameras in the workshop?"

Disappointment clouds his face. "No, not at the time we ran the tests. I've added a few since then, but I'm guessing that won't help?"

"No, it won't. Any chance you can access the conglomerate's recordings?"

"Sure. I'll stroll into their control room and ask."

I grimace. "Okay, you can skip the sarcasm. I just thought you might have a way to piggyback off their cameras and get into the system that way."

Sudden interest streaks his eyes with silver again. "That's not a half-bad idea. I doubt it's possible, but then, I haven't seriously considered the concept before either."

A solution occurs to me, and I offer it before I can change my mind. "I may have something."

"Something?"

"Yes, he's called Ferret."

Genuine amusement as Deran chuckles. "Ferret? You come up with the funniest names."

"I prefer to think of them as apt. In his case, he ferrets out information I need. Breaking codes and hacking systems are his specialties."

"You are talking about a device, aren't you? Not a real person?"

I giggle. "Yes. I'd be foolish to trust another human with that knowledge."

"I'm relieved you understand. So, where's Ferret?"

"In a safe place that's not here. You could come over to my place this evening, and I'll have him there for you?"

A quick shake of his head. "We're running behind schedule with the machine. My team and I will need to put in extra hours if we want everything dismantled before the weekend."

"You could finish on Monday."

"We could, but do you think that's wise? Aren't we supposed to be making it look like we're going as fast as we can?"

I sigh. "I suppose. But I really need that footage."

"Why?"

"So I can confirm what else was happening in the workshop when we ran that second test."

Deran grasps the implications. "You think external factors skewed the result?"

"You're a smart man." Deran's quiet as he considers what those factors might be. "Don't think too hard. I thought you didn't want to know how I solved the problem."

"I don't, but still." Deran runs a hand through his hair, making his spikes stand more on end than usual. "Tough to resist the desire to know what screwed us."

I grin, giving him a playful shove on the arm. "You hate problems without solutions as much as I do!"

"Guilty as charged." Deran flashes a wicked grin. "Can I say that's partly what drew me to you?"

Huffing out a laugh, I give him an incredulous stare. "I'm not a problem without a solution!"

"Maybe not in the way you think. But when I first met you, you were oblivious to how wrong this world was. Can you blame me for wanting to enlighten you? For wanting to save your family so I'd feel I hadn't lost mine for no reason?"

My hand brushes his with a feather-light touch. I want more than this fleeing contact, but there may be unseen drones overhead, recording our interactions even though they can't hear what we're saying. Deran's eyes soften, the pale grey of an early morning sky before it's shot through with the first streaks of sunlight. I smile. "Thanks for helping me find answers."

"Always."

I sigh. This was not where I thought our conversation would go, but I should get us back on track. Although how to transition to business when all I want to do is hug him, have him close, and give him the comfort he's given me so many times is a dilemma I don't know how to address.

"I doubt you dragged me out here for only one reason."

Deran's statement reminds me how observant he is. Also, how often he saves me from myself. Relieved, I pick up the earlier thread.

"Correct. I didn't only want to see if I could get the footage of the workshop when we ran those tests. I also wanted to know when you'd take me to the zone. We need to find Xanin."

His lips twitch.

I scowl. "Oh, don't say it!"

"Why? Now that you've figured out how to fix the machine, isn't it accurate to say you're impatient to get on with finding your brother?"

At least he didn't call me *Miss Impatient*. "So? When can you take me?"

Deran chuckles. "How about Saturday? We're not expected at work, and we'll have the whole day."

I want to go now, but his suggestion is more logical. No point raising suspicions by going when they'd expect to find us at work, or when we won't have as much time as we might need to find the people with answers. Assuming we can find them at all.

"Do you know who we're looking for when we get there? And where they are?"

"I do."

"How?"

"My parents. We went back there after Carys died. We needed a place to mourn her properly, people who knew her, who could relate to our struggles without someone reporting us for anti-conglomerate sentiment."

"You haven't been back since?"

"I have. Recently, in fact. I needed to test something I designed which will allow us to leave the dome undetected."

A chill runs through me. "They monitor who leaves?"

"Yes. We learned that when we did our little day trip. SerSents were waiting for us when we returned."

"And?"

"Fortunately, something else had their attention that day. They warned us never to leave again or face deportation back to the zone, and that was the end of it. But they made a mistake."

"How so?"

"If they hadn't waited to deliver that warning, I never would've known I'd need to find a way to pass unseen."

I cross my arms, eyeing him. "So, you've been working on this for a while already?"

"I have. Better to be prepared in case of emergency."

I hear the subtext. "Because you weren't sure you could trust me with what you told me and needed a quick escape ready, just in case?" Deran runs his hand through his hair again. He opens his mouth, but I place a hand on his arm. "No need to explain. I understand. Thanks for trusting me with the information, despite your reservations. I appreciate you taking the risk."

Relief washes over his face, erasing the tiny lines furrowing his brow. "Thanks."

We sit on the bench for a few minutes, simply enjoying each other's company, the sun warming our skin, and the soothing scents and sounds of nature.

Finally, Deran turns to me. "Was there anything else?"

"Not right now."

"There's more?"

"Yes, but nothing actionable yet. Not until I've confirmed my suspicions about the failed test or found out what we need from your contacts in the zone."

"Fair enough. Ready to head back? I should check on my people."

Reluctantly, I nod. Deran rises, then offers me his hand. I greedily accept the chance to touch him for more than a millisecond. His hand is warm, his eyes more so as he watches me.

"It will be good to be out of here, be in a place where we don't have to be so careful." Deran's words are murmured, but his eyes shine with promise.

"I'll hold you to that, Mr. Thomas!"

That wonderfully rich laugh rewards me. "I look forward to it."

We stroll back to CC HQ, taking our time, then part ways when we enter. Deran aims for the workshop, me for the lab. After checking on the other R&D projects my team are handling, I'm satisfied we're back on track. With no questions, it's time to tackle the last item on my list.

Focused, I work steadily through the afternoon, late into evening. My growling stomach is the only reason I finally pause. Strange how I never felt hungry with the conglomerate's slop, but with proper food, I can't get enough. Deciding I can't afford to leave work, I call *Little Italy* and ask if they deliver.

Pleasantly surprised by their confirmation, I order, thrilled I can get decent food more efficiently when the need arises. So immersed am I back in my work, mere seconds seem to pass before the SerSents send a message informing me of my food's arrival, and I dart downstairs to grab it.

Back at my desk, I tear open the container with the bruschetta. I went all in, ordering appetizer, entrée, and dessert. After all, I can keep leftovers for later, right?

Mouth already watering, I tuck in while studying the coding on my holoscreen. Although it took a fair amount of time initially, it was worth every second I spent calculating how I wanted to alter the data. Because not only must the manipulated data look like the real deal, but I must also keep track of what I've altered.

Add to this manipulating the data without the cameras noticing, and it was an excellent puzzle. Although I'm not sure how to fool Cygnus's spyware, if I make enough changes, erase and re-record enough times, the initial data may end up corrupted. Assuming he can't just rewind the changes.

My fork leaves my mouth. I've nearly finished my main meal, barely having tasted the delicious food. With a quick push, I swivel my chair away from the all-consuming numbers and gaze mindlessly out onto the empty lab floor, taking time to savor the remaining bites. Exquisite! I sigh contentedly as I pop the last tidbit of tiramisu into my mouth. Heaven on a spoon!

Groaning, I touch my full stomach. I shouldn't have eaten so much! The creeping lethargy of an excellent meal steals over me, and my eyelids droop. I should've ordered some espresso as well. I glance at the clock. Too late now. Well past midnight.

Although I want to retire for the night too, I can't. Stopping in the middle means they might remove the data from my cube to prevent me from making further changes or block me some other way. Better if I finish this in one sitting, before anyone gets wise to what I'm doing or, worse, alerts Cygnus.

I slog through the night, press on through the morning, and into mid-afternoon before I'm satisfied. Enough minute adjustments to bamboozle anyone trying to duplicate what we did initially. An emphatic yawn slips out. I don't bother covering my mouth, allowing my eyes to close for a second.

"Wow, hippopotamus!"

My eyes snap open. Deran stands on the other side of my desk, his grin stretching from one ear to the other.

"Don't judge. I was here all night."

Immediate concern shows on his face. "You were? You didn't go home?"

"No, I didn't even grab an hour to nap on my couch here."

"Why, what were you doing?"

"Updating the data based on some new assumptions."

Deran's radar detects the nonsense I just spouted. "Did you at least finish?"

An inane question I take to mean was I successful in changing the data. "Yes. But I'm absolutely shot now. I need sleep. Did you have questions before I head home?"

"No, I just came to give you an update. After some extra hours last night, we're on track to finish dismantling the machine today. We can start rebuilding Monday."

I raise a weary hand. "Excellent, thank you. Please tell the team I appreciate the sterling effort. Also, send apologies because I'm not conveying my thanks in person."

"Will do."

"Thanks. Now, if it's all the same to you, I'm off. Call me if anything urgent comes up."

25

A soft, yet persistent buzzing wakes me. I'm so out of it, it takes a while to realize it's my comm link. Blearily, I order the connection.

"Hey, sleepyhead. Time to rise and shine!" Deran's cheery face greets me.

Glancing at the time, I come fully awake in an instant. "It's nine o'clock!"

The grin on Deran's handsome face makes my heart skip a beat. How is he always so enticing? "Yes, and here I thought you were a morning person. I didn't expect to find you still sleeping. Buzz me in, so I can bring these up." He waves a bakery bag and two cups in a carrier.

"Coffee?"

"If you let me in, you can find out."

"Okay, okay, give me a minute." I throw on a pair of jeans and a t-shirt, then stumble to the access panel next to the front door, tapping the buttons.

Two minutes later, he's striding in, scrumptious aromas wafting ahead of him, the unmistakable, pungent bite of coffee mingling with the sweet pastries a heady combination. I reach for a cup. "May I?"

Deran grins, the devilish glint in his eyes making my heart beat even faster. "Not before I get compensation."

In one fluid motion, he sets his gifts down on the counter and sweeps me into his arms. Dazed, I stumble against his chest, thankful for his powerful arms wrapping around to steady me. Before I've caught my breath, he's kissing me.

My head swims, my senses heighten, and euphoria fills me. I relax into the kiss, indulging the desire I've had all week for this contact. Deran deepens the kiss, and my arms tighten around him in response, wanting him even closer. All thoughts leave my head, and sensation takes over.

By the time we break apart, I'm gasping for air. "Well!" I swipe a stray curl off my face. "Good morning to you too!"

Deran's grin is lazy, his eyes ribboned with silver. "Good morning. How do you like your coffee?"

"Sweet and creamy."

The grin widens. "Ah! Just like you!"

As he hands me a cup, I giggle. "If you say so."

"Here's to a successful day." Deran touches his paper cup to mine, and we each take a sip.

"Hmm, surprisingly accurate. Great choice!" I savor the smooth honey sweetening the drink. The scalded milk making it creamy. "Do we get what's in the bag now?"

Deran laughs, shaking his head. "Have at it."

Curious, I open the bag and find cinnamon rolls. "Yum!" I reach for one, then pause. "They're safe to eat, right?"

"Yes. Someone at the market makes them."

I frown. "But they're in a *Santini's* bag."

"They are."

Then I remember the bags shoppers bring to the market Deran is referencing, and I get it. "Ah! Of course." I bite into the pastry, then roll my eyes. "Hmm, wow! These are delicious!"

Deran merely chuckles, leaning against the kitchen counter, content to sip on his coffee. "We'll leave as soon as you've eaten."

Sudden anxiety tightens my gut as I remember what we're doing today.

Deran sighs. "I was hoping my positive spin on the start to the day would carry you through any nerves."

I offer a tentative smile, not sure my mouth manages the right shape. "Thanks, I appreciate your efforts."

"But nothing's going to make you less apprehensive?"

This time, I don't feign the confidence I don't have. "No." I bite my lip. "Your gadget will get us out, no problem?"

"The test I did two weeks ago, then again this morning, confirms it should."

"You already went there this morning? What time were you up?"

"Earlier than you."

I grimace. "I can't believe I slept so late. My only explanation is eating food without the serum. Does that sound right?"

"Yes, it was the same for me. Or, at least, initially."

"Nooo, don't tell me it wears off."

Deran shrugs. "I guess you'll find out." He pushes off the counter and collects a backpack I didn't notice because I was too focused on the pastry bag. "I have something to show you." Deran hands me a silver triangle, slightly larger than my palm, almost a quarter-inch thick and bent in the middle so it has a graceful curve.

"What's this?"

"Something to help you breathe in the zone."

My glance is dubious. "Really?"

"Go on. Look more closely."

Intrigued, I inspect the oddly shaped piece of metal. Then I see them. The tiny holes covering the surface, the small rectangular opening on the inside of the curve. Using my nail, I slide the rectangular cover, then grin when it pops off and I spy the filter inside. "Oh! Brilliant! But how do you keep it on your face? Do you have to hold it there?" I turn the silver triangle over, looking for hidden strings.

The smile on Deran's face is confirmation I'm keeping him amused this morning. He pulls out a... scarf? When he passes it over, my eager hands grab it. I soon find the pouch sewn into the seam, joining inner and outer edges. With deft movements, I slip the filter inside the mask, then place the filter over my nose, wrapping the long ends of either side of the scarf around my head. I grin at Deran, delighted.

He's openly laughing now. "You like this invention?"

"I do!" I inhale tentatively. "You're sure the filter works?"

Deran rolls his eyes. "Please! You don't think I'd make something defective!"

My eyes widen. "You made this?"

"You're not the only inventor."

"Well, color me impressed!"

Abruptly, Deran looks sheepish. "Thanks, but not that difficult to make when you have access to the right materials and training."

The implication sobers me. "Which I assume the people in the zone don't?"

"Correct. Also the reason I have the scarf. Face coverings are commonplace there. No one looking at us will think twice. We'll just be two more faces in the crowd. No reason for them to think we've got filters hidden in our scarves."

"Clever." I pause. "You don't think we'd be okay breathing the air there without these?"

This time, Deran's laugh holds no mirth. "Absolutely not! My parents and I barely survived the two hours we were there last time. Took a month to hack that gunk out of our lungs after we got back."

There's no need for a response. If Deran says the filters are necessary, I believe him. "Thanks for making these."

Deran nods. "Eat up! We should get going."

Although I'm not really hungry anymore, sudden nerves twisting my stomach again, I'll need the sustenance. I force down the pastry, offering the other one in the bag to Deran.

"No, it's yours. I ate mine on the way here this morning. I thought you'd like a spare to snack on when we got back."

I beam, then wrap my arms around his neck, tugging his head down to mine. "Thank you. You know me too well!" I kiss him, intending it to be brief, but when he tucks me closer, I don't object.

This time, his kiss is tender, as though he can expose his very soul to mine through our joined lips. My own soul opens in response, and I experience an intimacy that leaves me wondering how I ever thought a kiss was just a kiss.

When Deran pulls away, his eyes are deep winter seas. I've never seen the gray so dark, no trace of the silver brightening those eyes when he's amused. I'm still gazing into those dark depths when he grins, breaking the spell. "Let's get going before we spend all day canoodling in your kitchen."

I laugh. "Canoodling?"

"Get over it. You learned a new word."

Still chuckling, I allow him to lead me out of the apartment, my mask and scarf safely concealed in his backpack. As expected, we hop onto the trundle, riding almost to the end of the tracks. Or what I guess would be the end of the tracks. This must be housing for the lowest tiers, furthest from the center where CC HQ is located. Where the grounds around CC HQ are immaculate, this area is derelict, the streets filled with litter. No malls line the lower levels of the apartment buildings, and open space is nonexistent. Just one dreary, low-cost building dumped on top of another.

Why have I never thought to ride the trundle all the way to its conclusion? *Does* it end? If we're in an artificial biosphere, shaped like a dome, the tracks likely keep circling. If this is true, then the only way the trundles pull into the stations with minimal delay is if there's more than one.

Deran eyes me as we exit at the stop he's chosen. "What's going on in that head of yours?"

"Have you ever ridden the trundle all the way to the last stop?"

"It doesn't end. The trundle runs a continuous loop."

"I figured as much." I study the area we're in. "Why here?"

"Lowest tiers, meaning the people they care least about, so virtually no cameras."

"Ah, easier for us to accomplish our mission."

Deran nods, then leads the way through a veritable maze of alleys between the buildings. As we pass through gloomy passageway after even gloomier passageway, I scan for cameras, but Deran's words are proven true. No cameras on the tops of the buildings or watching the intersections.

"Fascinating, isn't it?"

I glance at Deran, unsure what he's referring to.

"The sense of freedom."

Now that he mentions it, a strange, oddly exhilarating sensation *has* accompanied me since we stepped off the trundle. I smile. "Wow, who knew?"

Deran nods, and his hand twitches, like he was about to reach for mine, before he remembers where we are and drops it again. Obviously, we're not totally clear. We traipse on for another ten minutes and four seconds. The alleys get narrower and darker, until Deran stops abruptly. "This is it."

Deran points at the wall preventing further passage, the dead-end blocking this alley. I raise an eyebrow. "Seriously?"

Grim-faced, Deran nods, then pulls a device from his pack. I scoot closer, keen to see what it does, but all I spot are a set of lighted bars, glowing red. Deran touches a button on the side, and the bars turn orange one by one, then fade to yellow and finally green.

"Follow in my footsteps exactly."

I'm almost too curious about Deran possibly stepping through a wall to watch where he's placing his feet. Noticing my distraction, Deran halts, waving a hand in front of my face, snapping his fingers. "Here, watch my hand."

As he moves it toward the wall, it suddenly vanishes. I gape, about to move closer again, when Deran pulls his hand back and places it on my shoulder, stopping me.

He's studying me again. "Okay, now you've seen what it looks like, how about watching my feet and doing what I asked? Follow in my footsteps *exactly!*"

His stern tone finally helps me grasp the gravity of the command. My eyes shift downward, and Deran sighs in relief.

"Excellent. Easy does it."

He creeps forward. As soon as his foot leaves the ground, I'm careful to place my foot precisely where his was. I'm so focused, I don't notice I'm struggling to breathe until I'm suddenly gasping for air.

An involuntary cough escapes, my lungs irritated. My nose hairs feel as though they're being scorched brittle by the toxic air. My eyes water. Panicked—I'm losing track of Deran's footsteps—I bump into him. He catches me (I really should stop making a habit of this!). I wheeze, still not finding the air I need.

Then, blessedly, the mask he made for me covers my face, concealed in its scarf, and I gulp air greedily. My eyes still stream, but Deran's thought of that too. He holds out a pair of goggles, and I snatch them, desperate to give my eyes the same relief as my nose. We stand there for a few minutes, regaining our equilibrium.

When I can breathe and see again, I examine my surroundings. Underfoot, dirt as rock hard as concrete, covered to varying depths by rotting detritus except for the parts where narrow tracks mark the paths used by workers. Ahead of me, boxy factories in every direction as far as the eye can see. None have windows, all are rendered the same monotonous shade by accumulated grime and toxins. Their walls rise, encasing the misery within, then disappear into the murky pollution overhead, squatting malevolently over the entire area. The noxious gases are an oppressive black cloud obscuring the sun and painting the landscape with a bleak gray light.

I remember this view. Isn't this what every house in my row looked out on? I turn, eager to see what's behind me, and I blink. The dome, gunmetal blue, stretches up behind us, but some sort of filter on the inside obscures the dome's interior. I'm about to take a step back toward the dome, when I remember the way we came in.

I glance at Deran, and he raises an eyebrow. "Do we have to be as careful where we put our feet on this side?"

"No."

Curious to see what the shell's made of, I stretch out a hand, only to have it disappear the same way Deran's did.

"Here." Deran adjusts its position.

This time, my fingers encounter a cool, smooth surface. Intrigued,

I move my hand between the two areas, unable to differentiate them visually, but quite capable of feeling the difference.

A question in my eyes, I face Deran. He nods, grim-faced. "I knew you'd find it fascinating."

"How?"

Deran points at his device. "My gadget. Let's confirm this is your greenhouse glass. Do you remember how you made it?" I roll my eyes, and his stern expression softens. "Yes, yes, I know, you don't forget. But humor me."

I sigh. "Fine. Microscopic wires run through each glass plate. There are, primarily, three different wires: titanium to lend strength, copper to facilitate heat modulation, and the third, well... it's actually a specialized type of fiber-optic cable to carry the commands for making angle adjustments to individual plates." I glance at the reflective shield on the dome. "Apparently, they added something else to facilitate reflection on this side and projection on the other side. I'm assuming that's how they can make the dome disappear. Satisfied?"

He merely nods and waits. I'm about to ask him what he's waiting for when I get it. "Oh!" My mouth and eyes make equally round Os. "Your device taps into the fiber-optic cables and... moves the glass plates out of the way?"

"I knew you'd get it. I'm not sure if the plates sliding over one another was part of your original design, but my gadget uses that feature to make a hole in the dome wherever I want. Then I use their own technology against them and corrupt the data feedback, so the breach appears as a glitch to any security monitoring the dome."

While I marvel at Deran's ability to even figure this out without access to the blueprints, the bitterness of yet another betrayal overrides it. "You know what Cygnus told me that feature was for?" Deran shakes his head. "To allow air into the greenhouse, to make windows if we needed them."

I snort. "I should've known better! Windows, indeed!" I raise a finger. "Although, in my defense, I asked Cygnus why windows were necessary when the greenhouses have excellent ventilation systems." I pause. "Do you think that's how he circulates air through the dome?"

Deran catches on right away. "Could be. I've never really thought about the problem, but it would have to work like a life-support system, right? I mean, without air circulating in a sealed dome, we'd all die."

"Sealed?"

"It has to be to keep toxins from the zone out."

I nod, though I'm beyond feeling shocked by these revelations. Whether it's the plethora of information I've had to absorb since the failed test for Cygnus, or simple overload from everything else that's happened, I don't care to analyze it. I'll process it later.

For now, I want to get what we came here for. "Which way to the people you know?"

26

Deran sets out ahead of me. I follow, the paths between the factories too narrow for two people to travel side by side. We remain silent, Deran's long legs eating up the distance and me trotting to keep up. Just as well I'm fit.

We wind through the factories. Not a soul passes us on the street. "Where is everyone?"

After a quick backward glance, Deran turns to watch where he's going again. "Had to be sure you weren't joking. They're at work, Chiara."

Of course they are! Why would the conglomerate allow anyone a shift off when they can work them all day every day with only minimal downtime for sleep?

More memories assail me. The hurried meals, cramped living quarters, Mom and Dad always at work. This is the reason Xanin and I grew so close. We had to take care of one another and then, later, our younger siblings. I thought we had so much free time because I only remember what it was like for me. As kids, we got to roam the area, play with our friends, spend our days how we pleased once we'd done our chores.

No school, never any school. Saddened by the thought of all those kids who'll be illiterate for the rest of their lives, I realize the reason. Keep the population uneducated, and they won't know to rebel to regain the liberty stolen from them.

Deran grabs me and yanks me from the corner we were coming up on, then stuffs me behind his broad back. With a squeak of surprise, I open my mouth to ask what he's doing, but he quickly lifts a finger to his lips.

I hide behind Deran, peeking over his shoulder. The beetles march past, faces straight ahead, batons held high and ready. I'm surprised they don't turn their heads to scour their surroundings, but won't regret they don't. Most likely, their failure to glance around is the only reason they don't see us. The corner we're hiding behind hardly provides enough cover.

They stomp down the main street, fading from sight, then sound.

Another memory returns to haunt me. How afraid I was as a kid. *All* the time. The constant terror. Because then, exactly as Deran is now, we had to be vigilant every second of every day. Constantly alert for the threat of monitors. If they caught us, we were in for a beating before they dragged us back home and told us to "stay where we belonged."

As a kid, their beetle suits fueled my nightmares. However, as an adult, I recognize their purpose. The hardened plastic exoskeletons protect their bodies should anyone try to attack them, and the piece running from head to chest, which reminded me of a beetle's thorax, is most likely an air filter. Further, that single giant convex eye formed by the black reflective shields over their faces not only hides the breathing apparatus, but serves the same function as the goggles Deran handed me.

While the monitors are still terrifying, I can now see exploitable vulnerabilities should I ever need to escape one. Get rid of their mask or breathing filter and they'll be distracted long enough for me to escape.

Deran takes my hand, and I give him a grim smile before we slink away. Deran soon picks up the pace again. I'm wondering how much further we'll have to go when Deran turns down a short lane, toward the row of houses behind the factory.

So many images flood back. I flounder against the tide. Then it overwhelms me, and the tears come. These houses are so like the ones I grew up in. The same slipshod construction, the same tiny spaces for windows and door, the same dirt running all around the house. Dirt that turned to mud any time we were fortunate enough to get rain, which might have happened once a year. If it could even be called rain. But when it did, oh! Mud we loved clomping around in, tossing at one another, molding into shapes. A whole new playground, lasting only a few brief hours.

In my mind, I see my mother outlined by the light of the lantern in our kitchen. Hear Xanin's taunts as he flicks the mud balls he has on the end of a stick at me. Remember the way Tavi would run between us, playing first for one team, then the other. Frankie was still a baby.

Deran's hand grips mine, squeezing. Although my tears are silent, he's fully aware of them behind my mask and goggles. Right then, the goggles fog up, the moisture too much for the confined area. Keeping my eyes scrunched closed, I yank the goggles off and quickly rub the lenses with the edge of the scarf, then shove them back on. A little streaky, but they'll do.

As Deran leads me to one home, there's no need for words. We let ourselves inside (another memory—no locks in the zone, at least, not for the workers) and sit down at the kitchen table. I check the time as I remember something else. Everyone has to leave the factory for thirty minutes at lunchtime. I don't remember why, but the siren would blast through the constant sound of running machines.

On cue, the siren blares, and I glance at Deran. His smile is tight, the skin around his eyes equally so. "He should be here soon."

I nod, keeping my hand in his. The touch reminds me I'm not alone. Then I hear the people. Shortly after, the door bangs open.

I leap up from my chair, ready to bolt, but recognition shines on the man's face as he enters his home and spots us in his kitchen.

"Deran! I never thought I'd ever see you again!" The man rushes forward, arms open, and embraces Deran heartily. "How are you? How are your parents?" Deran's demeanor shows he's touched a nerve, and the man frowns. "No, come, sit! Let's do this properly. Tea?"

Deran nods. "Thank you, David. Tea would be lovely. Meet Jane."

I almost don't keep the surprise off my face. Why didn't Deran warn me he wouldn't be using my real name?

David runs a cautious eye over me, questions flitting across his face before he smiles. "If Deran brought you, I'm pleased to meet you."

He doesn't say he trusts me because I'm with Deran, but it's obvious. I raise an eyebrow at Deran, and he shakes his head. *No, I don't need to leave. I'll be fine staying here while he speaks with David.*

Kettle on the stove, David sits down with us. "Now, tell me what happened."

His bluntness surprises me until I remember he only has thirty minutes before he has to be back at work—including the time it will take him to get there. Deran must be aware of this too, because he explains his parents' fate in five terse sentences.

David's face pales, and he licks his lips. "I'm sorry, my boy. I know how close you all were."

"Thank you, David. But we're here on another matter."

"Please! Whatever I can do to help."

"Have you heard anything about a place where they might imprison people from the dome? Like a detention facility?"

David frowns. "Why would they keep those folks here? For starters, they'd choke on our air and die before seeing out a month."

"Jane's brother is missing. We're trying to find him, but it's possible he may no longer be in the dome."

"No whispers?"

"None. I've tapped all my sources, but no one's heard a thing."

This is news to me. When did Deran have time? And who are his sources?

David taps his chin thoughtfully. "So you thought they brought her brother here?" Deran nods. "Well, it's possible, but I've heard nothing."

Deran sighs. "I was afraid you'd say that. Any word yet on where they take the people who disappear?"

"Nothing. Not for lack of trying on our part. They still take them away in those APCs, so it's impossible to follow them."

My mind boggles. So much I'm not understanding, just guessing at by reading between the lines. I keep my attention on the present so I can ask Deran questions later.

Deran frowns. "The same ones you told us about when I was here with my parents? They lift vertically, have no windows and are solid hunks of metal able to withstand explosive blasts?"

"Yep, them's the ones. 'Armored Personnel Carriers' is what the monitors called them. Tough little suckers. We don't have anything powerful enough to take them down."

Deran thinks. "If I made you a tracker, could someone attach it to one?"

David considers the question. "Well, the APCs are only on the ground long enough to drop the new rotation of monitors and their supplies. Then they load up with the monitors finishing their rotation and leave."

"Roughly how much time from when they land to when they take off again?"

"Twenty, maybe thirty minutes?"

"Is it a guarded area, or do they need an open space to land in?"

"Both. They have special areas set aside near the bunkhouses where the monitors stay. The APCs land and take off there."

Mind clearly on the problem, Deran leans back in his chair. "Meaning there would be surveillance on the ARC at all times?"

"Yes. But if you could make us another one of those gadgets you gave us for the meets, we could potentially get someone in and out undetected, have them place the tracker."

"You have a candidate in mind?"

David tries to hide it, but his eyes slide toward me before going back to Deran again. "I do."

So, no names while I'm around. That's okay; I don't need to know who's getting the job done, just that someone's willing and able. I offer

David a sincere smile. "Thank you. From my family to yours. Please pass that along to whoever you have in mind. I sincerely appreciate the risk they'll be taking."

David studies me as though trying to make sense of me and who I am to Deran, but he's too polite to say anything. If I were in his position, I wouldn't let that stop me. Asking questions means staying alive. Well, the right questions.

"I'll let them know." David glances at the clock. "Time for a quick cup. Then I must get back."

He rises. For the first time, I note how carefully he moves. Another memory returns with blinding clarity, one I've pushed so deep it takes my breath away with its vindictiveness. How many times did people we knew succumb to easily treatable ailments?

I suck in air, and Deran's gaze flies to mine. I'm quick to reassure him. "Nothing to worry about. Just something I remembered. There's no medicine here, is there?"

The statement immediately draws David's attention. "You're from here?"

"A long time ago. There are many things I've forgotten." No point explaining how my memory was corroded. Another realization strikes. This time, I shoot up out of my chair, too shocked to remain seated.

Deran's still watching me. "You thought of something else?"

I nod, unable to speak past the fury that rages, the blinding need to strike out, to smash things. With deliberate, stiff movements, I force myself to sit down, but my hands shake with repressed anger, and my cheeks burn. Deran must understand I'm beyond explaining because he turns to David, asking about someone else they both know.

Effectively distracted, David answers Deran. They may as well be speaking a foreign language for all I understand. The relentless rush of blood pounds through my head as I seethe, trying to control the rampant violence I'm barely leashing.

I've realized why I've forgotten so much.

Not only did the coercion serum fog my mind, make logical thinking difficult, it also robbed me of my memories. How often did thoughts of the past bring on those awful headaches? Headaches which only increased in intensity the more I tried to dredge up the past. But now Deran's freed me from their food, their insidious serum.

And I remember *everything*.

27

By the time we leave David's home, enough memories have returned so they no longer overwhelm me every step of the way. As a result, I can process my surroundings on an entirely different level.

Zone and dome are night and day, famine and feast, adversity and opportunity. Everywhere I look, I see CCs greed. They've plundered the earth, hijacked every resource in their mission to increase their wealth, their power, regardless of who or what they left behind in their trail of devastation. There's no one left with the resources to stop them. The conglomerate controls everything: water, food, domes, relationships, family size, weapons, people. The list goes on.

From the fraction of the world visible to me as I follow Deran—and my slowly returning memories—I know what I'd find if I ventured beyond the factories. A barren wasteland. Abandoned buildings crumbling to dust because they aren't essential to keeping the wheels of the conglomerate turning. Who cares about houses or hospitals or schools for the workers? They're a drain on resources.

No, leave them to live on the land where toxic rain falls, where the soil is so ruined nothing will grow for the next hundred generations. Allow them to breathe the filthy air. Let the useless scraps of fabric they wrap over noses and mouths as filters remind them how worthless they are.

My glimpse inside David's cupboards confirmed what I already suspected. Food remains scarce; even offering us tea must've been a sacrifice. If the canned and preserved slop CC calls sustenance here is in short supply, fresh food is non-existent. As for water... I recall all too well the way we recycled it at every opportunity.

I may have been only six years old, but I knew the value of water. Our planet's most precious resource, and was it looked after, treasured, as it should've been?

A derisive snort escapes, and Deran glances back at me. "What?"

"How naïve I was to think they had restored the world! What was I thinking? Just restoring even this tiny section of hell would take decades. Yet I believed Cygnus."

"In his eyes, he *has* healed the world—the domes, those tiny sections where he lives, are all that matter, right? If only they'd do that for the rest of the world, too."

"If only." A bitter truth hits home. "Nothing will ever change as long as CC's in power."

The thought is beyond depressing, and we slump into silence again. Then I frown. "I've seen them, you know?"

"Seen what?"

"The greenhouses. Cygnus took me there when I was working on that project. Deran, there were miles and miles of them. With so many, the people here should have plenty of food."

Deran spares me a withering glance, but says nothing, and I realize what he didn't say. Do I really think the food in those greenhouses was for the masses? My heart sinks even further. The only people CC is feeding with those greenhouses are the people in the dome.

Listlessly, I turn my head to the side, trying to find something to distract me. When my eyes land on the blue shell of the dome, I'm not sure what I feel. Until I spot what I never saw when we entered. A mass of pipes exits the dome, with no effort made to hide what they pump out. Even through my air filter, the odor of noxious fumes is unmistakable.

Sickened by the sight, fresh anger flares. Not only does CC flaunt the shiny shell of the dome—they add insult to injury and pump their toxins back into the zone. How short-sighted are they? Don't they realize eventually it will become their problem again, when all their workers die in this lethal environment they've created and they have to pick up the slack?

I stop so suddenly I almost fall over my own feet. Deran turns. Face reflecting his sudden alarm, he rushes back to me, patting me down, and searching for signs of injury. I wave a hand, too stunned and breathless from the revelation to tell him.

He waits until I finally squeeze the words out. "I'm on the verge of creating something extraordinary, a self-sustaining energy source, a machine with the power to change everything, to allow us to clean this polluted world. But what if Cygnus doesn't care? What if he wants the machine so he can build more robots so he doesn't have to bother with human workers?"

Deran says nothing, face grave, eyes inscrutable.

I blunder on. "Think about it. If they keep treating the world outside the dome like that," I stab a finger at the offensive pipes, "like a dumping ground for toxic waste, the workers here will die. But without workers, they lose everything those workers provide. The rich and entitled living in the dome won't take a loss of their luxuries sitting down. They'll rebel. If Cygnus wants to keep his power, his position, he'll need to keep the wheels of supply turning. And the only way to do that is to replace the workers who've died with robots."

Deran runs a hand through his hair, but the spikes don't stand more on end as they usually do. "It's an excellent theory, but I don't think it's the only reason. You know Cygnus better than almost anyone else. Have you ever known him to go after a single objective, without having other reasons?"

I start. Deran's right. "You reached that same conclusion about the people here before me, didn't you?"

"Yes. After coming here when Carys died, my parents couldn't stop talking about how many of their friends had died, how much the conditions had deteriorated."

"And when Cygnus suddenly wanted to build a machine to generate endless power using little to no resources, you added that knowledge and figured this was the real reason he wanted it. Why didn't you tell me?"

Deran shrugs, his eyes leaving mine to scan our surroundings. "Would you have believed me if I'd told you before you'd seen the state of this place for yourself?"

I don't answer the rhetorical question.

Eyes stopping their scan to find mine, Deran touches my hand. "Look, we need to get back. Can we talk then?"

"Get back? We're not seeing anyone else?"

"No need. David was top of my list for answers to our questions. If he doesn't know, the others I had in mind as backups in case we couldn't find David, certainly won't. Can we go now?"

I sense his uneasiness, and I remember who might come marching around the next corner at any moment. "Sure, sorry. Let's go."

Deran picks up the pace. The closer we get to where I suspect he brought us in (the place is a maze!), the more I sense his growing tension. "Deran, what's the matter?"

"I'm not sure. Something just feels wrong."

His words are not reassuring. I increase my speed, goading him on from behind. By the time we reach our exit point, we're both panting. Hurriedly, Deran pulls his device from the pack and points it at the dome. I turn my back to his, keeping my eyes peeled for any sign of trouble coming from the opposite direction.

At his soft curse, trepidation coils a tight fist around my heart. "What?"

Deran taps the side of his device, then shakes it, before redirecting it toward the dome. None of the bars change color. They remain an obstinate, angry red.

"Deran?" No answer. "Deran! What's happening? Why isn't it working?" I attempt to keep my voice down. Whether it was Deran's earlier sentiment or this unexpected hiccup, I'm suddenly skittish, aware of the fine knife edge we're balanced on.

"My best guess is because—"

"They're working on the network!" We say it simultaneously. Eyes wide, I stare at Deran. "Why would they do that?"

Grim-faced, he shrugs. "I've heard talk. Sometimes they run extra security on the dome."

Icy perspiration trickles down my spine. "How? And for what reason?"

"Closest I could figure, they add another layer to the existing program, which fixes all the plates in their sealed position."

"They freeze the network?" My voice has a grating, screechy quality.

"I think so. Difficult to ascertain when you have to cobble bits and pieces of information together."

"But why do something so asinine?"

"If I have the right of it, they only do this when they're having problems with the resistance."

I gasp. "Meaning what? Do you think CC knows we're missing?" Near hysteria in my voice now. "Do they think the resistance kidnapped us?"

Deran puts his hands on my shoulders. "Calm down. The only thing we know for sure is that my device isn't working. There's no need to drive ourselves into a frenzy conjuring crazy reasons why they've frozen us out."

Still grappling with the problem, I focus on some calming breaths. "Okay, okay. I hear you. But how will we get back?"

Deran runs a hand through his hair, still remarkably flat considering how many times he's done that today. "There is another way out, the one my parents and I used, but we'll probably be detected. I can't hide us going back in."

My mind slams to a blind stop. My fear is inhibiting thought. Consciously, I suck down the fear, focus on the problem again. "Our options, then, are to stay here and potentially be discovered by the monitors or go back and certainly be caught by the SerSents?"

Deran nods, face solemn, eyes never leaving my face.

"How long will the filters in our masks last?"

"Roughly forty-eight hours."

"At least one thing in our favor! Well done!"

This time, Deran manages a wry smile. "Something I could plan for. But will it be enough? Can we get back before it's time for work on Monday?"

I pull down my scarf, then do the same to Deran's before giving him a quick kiss, spurred to giggling by his shock. "Yes, I can take a moment to enjoy something in my life that's wonderful. Besides, you were smart enough to consider we might be stuck here for more than a day. Makes me really thankful now I didn't talk you into bringing us here after work this week."

A glorious smile at last. "Me too."

"So, what's the plan?"

"We find somewhere close to hunker down and wait it out."

"We're not going back to David's?"

"No. We still don't know why the dome network is out. For all we know, there could be an issue on this side, which would mean—"

"Patrols," I finish for him. "And finding us there would put David in danger."

"Yes, so we'd better find somewhere to lie low, preferably close to the exit, so the patrols aren't a problem if we have to make a run for it."

Deran leads us to a nearby building. I'm not sure why I thought we'd have trouble getting inside, considering the lack of locks, but I'm nevertheless surprised when Deran twists the knob and the door opens.

Cautiously, he steps inside. We find ourselves in a narrow hallway. Dozens of hooks along the wall are draped with clothes. I raise an eyebrow. Deran shakes his head, and we back out. As we scurry to the next building, Deran answers my question. "A place that requires its workers to wear special clothing is not a good hideout."

"Agreed."

We try door after door, making it further into some buildings than others before Deran finds some reason to dismiss them. Then he opens one, revealing utter darkness. We try to see past the impenetrable shadows. Foiled, we slip inside, closing the door behind us and feeling our way further in. The soft glow from Deran's comm link lights the space, and all is laid bare for us to see.

Debris clutters the floor from one end of the building to the other. Overturned barrels, smashed cabinets, the twisted metal frames of what were once chairs. The silent machinery would give it away if the jagged edges of a crater on one side didn't.

I inhale sharply. "That machine exploded!"

Jaw set, familiar tic moving the muscles, Deran surveys the scene. We both know the only reason this factory would be abandoned, and not restored, is because hidden danger lurks here. "Yes, but some time ago, if the accumulated dust and debris are any sign."

"Still, that doesn't mean whatever made this area unusable has dispersed. Do you think the air's safe? Will your filter remove toxic particles?"

Deran shrugs. "It's already removing most of what's in the air, but I can't promise anything out of the ordinary won't make it through the filter."

A sobering thought. Do we stay in the one place we can safely find shelter, but risk air that might kill us?

With a grunt, Deran takes the decision out of my hands. "Let's risk fifteen minutes, see how we feel. Then we can take it in increments, assuming we survive the first fifteen. We're unlikely to find a better spot. Here, we have places to hide and trash to cover our tracks with."

"Sounds like a plan."

Together, we move deeper into the building, rearranging the trash to cover our passage. A set of stairs leads up to a landing where all the windows were blown out. Air from outside circulates in, at least giving me the illusion of ventilation and alleviating some of my fears.

Deran must feel the same way. "What do you think? A reasonable place to hide out for a while?"

I nod, and we move toward the far end of the landing where a stack of crates still stands, remarkably untouched. Although I try to read the labels, it's a wasted effort. Smoke residue and time conceal whatever was once printed there. With a sigh, I sink onto the floor behind the crates, leaning back against the wall. When Deran slides down next to me, then tucks me into his shoulder, I snuggle in, finally feeling safer.

But for how long?

28

Deran nudges me, and I startle awake. When I move, my muscles are stiff. I groan. "How long was I asleep?"

"A couple of hours."

"What?" I look around blearily, then remember where we are and the dilemma facing us.

"Before you ask, yes, we're safe. No apparent side effects from the air here, so we stick with our plan. Hide out here, check back on the dome as often as we can, and hope we can get back home before Monday." He notes my rising agitation because he hurries to add, "This isn't a reason to worry either. I've been thinking while you were sleeping. If I increase the power output to my device, I might be able to increase the interference it generates."

My frenzied mind latches onto a problem I can solve. "Right—with more power, you could potentially break through a frozen part. What do you need?"

Deran doesn't hide his grin. Or was that his plan all along—to give me a problem to solve so my mind would be on other things?

"Some copper wire and a transistor, or two, if we can manage it."

I immediately think of the surrounding machinery. "Totally possible. If you point me in the right direction, I'll start looking."

"No arguments?" Deran's eyes twinkle.

"None. Machinery is your domain. You'll know the best places to look."

His somewhat bashful grin makes me smile. Deran extricates his arm from behind my head. (Did I sleep on him all this time? I must've if he's rubbing his arm to restore circulation.) Then he strolls across the landing to look down on the machinery below. Exactly like the supervisors who worked here must've once looked down on their workforce.

Deran crooks a finger, and I hurry over. "There. You see that long, blue pipe running along the far right side?"

I squint into the gloom. "Yes."

"Start looking in that rectangular box midway along it."

"Okay. Where will you be?"

"Over there." Deran points at a spot a little further down. "I'm sure I don't need to remind you to be quiet and hide your tracks."

"Will do. Let's get those supplies."

Skulking downstairs, we move to our assigned posts. Carefully, I ease the box's door open, expecting squeaks. Instead, my mouth drops open. *Empty!* Not a single wire. Not even a screw or scrap of metal. I scurry back to Deran, hoping he's had more success. But his expression tells me his control box was as empty as mine.

Sticking together, we make our way down the (assembly?) line. We check every compartment, but the place has been stripped bare. For some reason, this reminds me of the way I used to scavenge pieces for my inventions as a child. Are these gutted boxes the result of similar efforts by the people here, or was anything valuable deliberately stripped by CC after the explosion?

Irrelevant! I doubt we'll find what we're looking for, but the memory has reminded me of other options. I keep my voice low. "Deran, I think I know where else we can look."

Hope springs into his eyes, and I grin. He was feeling just as desperate as I was. "Where?"

"I'll show you. We need to get back outside, behind one of those long, flat factories."

A brief silver streak in his eyes is the only sign he finds my description amusing. "Fine, but I'll take the lead."

I won't argue. He's been sneaking around far longer than I have and is more likely to keep us from getting caught. We slip back to the same door we entered through, and Deran cracks it open, peeking outside before deciding the way's clear.

Then we hurry out, slinking along the side of the building, facing away from the main route any passing patrols would use. Too busy looking behind me for those patrols, I don't notice Deran's stopped just past the corner I'm rounding. I run smack into him.

"Ow!" The muttered complaint cuts off as I spot the issue. We stand rooted, facing the stranger (sans mask) openly gaping at us, much the same as we're probably gaping at her behind our scarves.

She's the first to recover, closing her mouth and crossing her arms. Snarky defiance settles on her sensuous features. "What are *you* doing here?"

Several things about the stranger strike me simultaneously: she's shorter than I am (which is saying something!), making her look like a kid at first glance, but her smooth leather outfit encases a woman's toned body, and her eyes are hard. Tough, calculating, challenging.

Deran steps in front of me, shielding me from the girl. He's reached the same conclusion: she's dangerous. Deran raises pacifying hands. "Look, we mean you no harm. We were just visiting a friend."

"Sure, and I suppose you can give me the name of your 'friend?'"

We can't give her David's name! What if she reports him? Before Deran can answer, I issue a challenge of my own. "Who are you to be making demands of us?"

The hefty weight of her intense gaze lands on me, and I regret saying anything. Eyes cool, she gives me the once-over. "Clearly, someone who belongs here, whereas you obviously don't."

"What makes you so sure?"

The stranger snorts derisively. "Please! You've got dome written all over you. Your clothes are a dead giveaway, as are those breathing masks you're trying to hide so ineffectually."

I glance at my clothes, still wondering how they told her where I was from. She's wearing leather, isn't she? Last time I checked, no one here wore that.

Then again, I am working from memories at least a decade old. The only person I've seen since we got here other than the monitors is David, and his clothes lined up with those childhood impressions.

I'm about to ask another question when Deran places a hand on my arm, interjecting smoothly, "We're not dome spies, if that's what you're thinking. We came to visit a friend, but now we seem to be stuck here."

Her smirk bothers me, as if she knows something we don't. She crosses her arms, a foot tapping the ground. "Uh-huh. I'm still waiting for a name."

Deran sighs. "We visited David Esterburg. My parents were from here, and my sister and I were born here."

Not even the slightest change in stance, but she suddenly grins. Her impish smile transforms her face, making her look like a pixie who wouldn't swat a troublesome fly. How wrong people making that assumption about her would be! The stranger offers a hand. "I'm Ava."

The radical turnabout in her attitude stuns me, and I lag behind Deran in offering our own names. Just as well. I wouldn't have remembered to call myself Jane. I try not to let it bother me, sure Deran has his reasons, but I make a mental note to ask him when we're alone again.

Introductions over, Ava gestures for us to follow her. "This way. You're not likely to get back through the dome again soon. I have a place you can hide."

Without a backward glance, she slips into the increasing gloom. Night is approaching. A quick check of the time on my comm link— too early for twilight. Then I remember the polluted skies overhead, dampening the sun's power, and answer my own question.

Grabbing my hand, Deran starts after Ava. I hang back, and he stops, turning back to me. "What?"

"How does she know David? Are you sure we can trust her?"

Another swipe of his hand through his hair, followed by a sigh. "If we're going to make it through the night, I don't think we have a choice."

"Fair enough," I grumble, before allowing Deran to pull me along after him again.

Expertly, Ava guides us down alley after alley, darting between factories and warehouses and abandoned buildings like she was made for this. Not once do we ever hear a patrol, let alone encounter one. Just as I wonder how deep into this world she's taking us, she slips inside a derelict shed dwarfed by two towering factories on either side.

She stops just inside the door before bending down. With an ease betraying her strength, she tosses a section of the floor up. I half expect it to go flying across the room until I spot the hinges, keeping it in place.

"A trapdoor!"

Ava rolls her eyes. I want to take offense, but Deran's pushing me down the stairs to the level below. After almost losing my footing, I growl at him. "Stop! I can't see. Let me go at my own pace!"

I catch the flash of silver and guess Deran's grinning behind his scarf. "Now, now, no biting. But you need to hurry."

Disgruntled, I mutter under my breath as I feel my way down the stairs. I'm nearly to the bottom when I remember I could've used my comm link to light my way. The realization only annoys me further. By the time Deran drops to the floor next to me, I'm fuming. Clearly, he knows what this woman's about. But does he tell me? No! Does he defend me? No! Does he stop to consider I might—*what was that?*

Straining to hear the sound again, I stop breathing. Then muted voices filter through. Panic rips into me, a live snake squeezing the life out of me, fangs bared. Remembering how paralyzing that fear was earlier today, I fight it. The voices are muffled, unmistakably overhead. Breath still coming in quick gasps, I peek up, then run my mental projector backward, doing a few quick calculations. *We're under the factory floor of one of the adjacent buildings!*

Eyes round, I glance back at Deran. He dips his head in acknowledgement, and we both maintain our silence. Ava slides past, then beckons for us to follow again. We travel some distance through a confusing network of maintenance tunnels and rooms, before we're dumped into a chamber, apparently a dead-end. This time, only the soft hum of machinery running overhead breaks the silence. As near as I can calculate, we should be under the center of the factory now. A scan of the room reveals a locked steel cabinet, four chairs and a table, and four camp cots.

"You may be D-Dunces, but you're smart ones, I'll give you that. You kept quiet," Ava grudgingly admits.

Slapping my hands on my hips, I glare at her. "D-Dunces?"

"Yeah, you know, the mindless idiots who follow the conglomerate's orders without question, taking your cushy lives for granted, never thinking about the cost to the rest of humanity for the luxuries you enjoy."

I'm about to tell her what I really think. Only that's exactly what I was until Deran helped rid me of the coercion serum. "Well, maybe if you weren't so ignorant, you'd know the reason we were D-Dunces!"

Impish smile lighting her face again, Ava raises an eyebrow. "So, she has a spine."

Deran steps between us. Either he's afraid we'll come to blows, or, more likely, he's worried I'll disclose who I really am. I pause. Why *is* Deran keeping my identity secret?

Then it hits me. All those parties I was forced to attend every time Cygnus advanced up the ranks. While he never mentioned I invented the machines making him so successful (of course not!), countless images of those parties exist. Anyone who looks can find me, figure out who I really am, calculate my worth to the conglomerate. Disguised behind our scarves and not dressed up, I might avoid recognition, but if he said my real name, I'd be an obvious target. He's been keeping my identity a secret to protect me!

My sharp intake of breath turns Deran's eyes my way. I want to hug him, thank him for caring about me. But his grim expression is a deterrent; he knows I've put some things together. I'm pretty sure he hasn't guessed what exactly, but enough to know I'll be careful about what I say from now on.

His gaze releases mine. Ava's watching us, her eyes far too shrewd. What did we reveal to make her look like she just struck a rich vein of rhodium? I bite back the retort teasing the tip of my tongue, about keeping her eyes to herself. Next to me, Deran relaxes, accepting I'm going to keep my unspoken promise to maintain my silence.

Ava must realize she's getting nothing more from me. She flounces over to a steel cabinet against the far wall, unlocking the tumbler with a practiced hand. With a flourish, she flings the doors open. "Help yourselves."

Curious, I glance inside. Outrage immediately boils to the surface again. With difficulty, I restrain myself from attacking her. So much for the people here not having enough food! The cabinet is stuffed to overflowing with nonperishables. I remain where I am, a silent protest that she has so much when David had virtually nothing.

"It's not all mine."

I find Ava watching me. No, analyzing me. I've seen that expression on my own face too many times to not know what it means. She's trying to solve a puzzle, and that puzzle is me.

What if she's a *permanent* puzzle solver, and she decides I'm too much of a risk?

When Ava bursts into rambunctious laughter, I growl. *Now what?*

"For a D-Dunce, you're remarkably easy to read." She swings off the wall she was leaning against and reaches into the cabinet for a can of peaches. "If you're not having something, I'm not waiting for you." Ava drops into a chair at the rickety table, pulling a multi-tool from her pocket and opening the can. Switching to a blade on the tool, she spears a peach and pops it into her mouth. "I meant what I said. This isn't all mine. It belongs to a group I know. We only use it in emergencies, and I'd say today qualifies."

Why do I think there's more to that last statement? But I get a whiff of the sweet syrup coating the peaches, and my stomach grumbles. I turn so Ava can't see my face and raise an eyebrow at Deran. He gives an almost imperceptible nod.

Deran allows me to choose a can first, then selects his own before we join Ava at the table.

"Here." Without asking, she grabs my can, opening it for me, then opening Deran's, before pushing them back our way. "Sorry, this is my only blade."

Now why don't I believe her? But I'm hungry enough not to care, either about that, her not sharing her weapon, or why she's suddenly so affable. Careful of the jagged edges around the rim, I pluck out a pear (I couldn't have the same as her!). I bite into the soft juicy flesh, relishing the sugary syrup filling my mouth.

Deran does the same with his can of… beets? Before I can question his choice, he swallows his mouthful and studies Ava. "So, what group do you belong to important enough to have a cabinet full of food in an underground hideout?"

29

Ava's smile is sly. "I didn't say I belonged to the group, just that I knew them."

Deran nods. "Sure, and I'm supposed to believe they'll let a mere acquaintance have access to a place like this."

With a shrug, Ava pops her last peach into her mouth. "Believe what you will. How did you leave the dome undetected?" Curiosity gleams in her eyes.

I think Deran's going to answer, but then he plays her game. "Did I we say we had?"

Laughter fills the room, and I realize Deran's laughing with her. I crush the stab of jealousy, glancing from one to the other, uncertain what's so funny. Then it clicks. *Duh!* They both know the truth about the other, so there's no need for answers.

Ava has access to this place because she belongs to the resistance. And Deran and I wouldn't be worried about getting back into the dome if we hadn't left unnoticed.

Irritated by their continued mirth, I concentrate on the pear I'm fishing out of my can. There's too much syrup, and the slice is too far down, so it slips away whenever I touch it. I succumb to the urge to drink the syrup, keeping the can far enough from my lips I won't cut them, but close enough for the syrup to dribble into my mouth.

Careful to keep the can at an angle that won't let the solids suddenly slide down and smash all over my face, I slurp the nectar. When the syrup's all but depleted, I shake the remaining pears toward the top of the can and snag the slightly deformed piece eluding me before.

As I slide it into my mouth, I catch Deran watching me, amusement filling his eyes with those silver glints. I grin. "What?"

"You weren't letting them go, were you?"

"No, they're too good to waste."

Movement to his left. Ava's watching us again. Time for her to do something other than study us like lab rats. "Can you show us a safe way to the dumping grounds behind those long, low factory buildings?"

Ava's eyes sharpen. "How do you know about those?"

I'm not giving her an iota of information more than she needs. If Deran wants to give her specifics, he should take the lead. "Can you get us there?"

"Why?"

"Why do you think?"

Deran gets the hint. "Since you are who you are, you may have a more effective way of getting what we need: three feet of copper wire and two transistors."

I sense Ava's excitement, although to look at her, you wouldn't know it. She'd do well in the dome, keeping her true feelings hidden. "I can hook you up. When do you need them?"

"The sooner the better."

"In that case," Ava slides her chair back, and rises, "I'll be back. Stay here. Rest if you can."

Then she's through the door, disappearing back down the corridor we came in on. I wait until she's out of sight. "Do you still think we can trust her?"

"Yes. If nothing else, she has more to lose than we do. If she gives us up to the resistance so they can ransom us back to CC, we could not only tell CC where this safe house is, but also what she looks like."

I grimace. "Unless she or the resistance plan on killing us the moment they have their ransom."

"There's always that possibility," Deran concedes. "But I doubt it. She wants something, and I'm guessing it's what she thinks we have: a way in and out of the dome undetected."

"What makes you say that?"

"It was the first question she asked after bringing us here, ergo, what she's most interested in."

"She could just as easily have meant to make conversation."

"I disagree. All she's done since we met is watch us."

My snort is definitely not ladylike. "You mean scrutinize us!"

This elicits one of those cheeky grins I love. "She getting under your skin much?"

I roll my eyes. "You seem to get her much better than I do. So explain your reasoning further."

"Besides being the first question she asked, did you notice how her eyes lit up the moment I told her what we needed?"

"Aah, yes! But then why tell her?"

"We need the components, and she's the quickest, most assured way of getting them. While we have our motives, she has hers. No doubt she's hoping I'll fix my device here, where she can see it, and potentially learn what it is and how it works." The silver suddenly fills his eyes, making them shine with delight. "But we won't allow that."

I grin, eager to put one over on Ava. "How?"

"You'll be keeping her far from me and my device while I work on it."

"I doubt Sirena's easily distracted. She's seems the 'honed-focus' kind."

"Sirena? You mean Ava?"

"I'm calling her Sirena; as in Siren-A. First-class temptress of men and all kinds of dangerous."

Deran's laughter is a balm to my soul. "She'll love that!"

"She won't find out." I chew my lip. "But how do I distract her?"

"I'm sure you'll come up with something."

"At least I have time to think about it." I push my empty can around on the table until Deran's hand meets mine, putting an end to the restless movement. My eyes find his.

"You'll do fine. As long as she doesn't see the circuitry, we're golden. I believe you can keep her occupied for the few minutes it'll take to add the components."

I raise an eyebrow. "A few minutes, that's all? You won't break what already works trying to boost the signal, will you?"

Deran chuckles. "I think I can be trusted to know what I'm doing."

My hand catches his. "I do trust you. It's her I don't. Do you really think she knows David?"

Wonder fills Deran's eyes. "I couldn't say, but if she does, then he's tired of living this life and wants a better one. Not only wants it, but he's willing to fight for it."

"Nothing ever comes easy, does it?"

Deran shrugs. "I've learned if you want something, you must go after it. No point hanging around in the shadows, hoping it'll be handed to you on a platter. Although, I'll admit, meeting Ava is the rare exception to the rule."

"How so?"

"I always doubted the resistance existed. I mean, if they were real, surely, I'd have found something by now."

The mention of whispers reminds me of his conversation with David. "When you asked him about people disappearing, what did you mean?"

"When we visited last time, David told us people had been vanishing. Just there one day and gone the next. There was no apparent pattern. Not the same area, time, or method of abduction."

My throat goes dry. "The same *method* of abduction?"

"Some simply disappeared off the street. Others were called to their supervisor's office while at work and then never seen again. A few were taken from their homes and families in the middle of the night."

The intensity of Deran's gaze deepens, and I struggle to get the words out. "You mean, like what happened to Xanin?"

"Exactly. This is the reason I thought David could help."

I expel the breath I was holding. "Except, unlike my brother, someone here followed them and saw their family member being put into the APC. Is this why you offered to build a tracker?"

"Yes. If we can work out where those transports are going, we have a hope of finding Xanin."

Deran's too far away. Rising, I move to his chair, sit on his lap, and wrap my arms around his neck, then kiss him. "Thank you."

"Always." We sit still, enjoying the contact. "Speaking of revelations, what else came to you while we were at David's that you didn't want to discuss?"

I quickly explain how my memories and headaches seem to be related. "Tough to believe, but I think they've engineered the serum to work with long-term memory, so it not only represses the ability, but gives you a headache to discourage further attempts."

Deran's arms tighten around me. "Not enough they have to coerce people into doing what they want—they have to steal their memories too?"

Resigned to the reality, I've overcome my earlier anger. I rest my head on Deran's shoulder, finding peace and joy in what I can. Time's too short not to take advantage of the precious moments when I have them. I'll think about my revenge on Cygnus another time.

Approaching footsteps make us leap to our feet. I look to Deran for guidance, and he gestures for me to take a spot on the opposite side of the entrance. He means to attack the person coming in, hopefully overpowering them, so we have time to make a run for it.

Ava enters, and the tension leaves my body in a whoosh of air. She stops in the doorway, glancing between Deran and me, a wry smile on her face. "What? You were going to beat me with your bare hands?" Not waiting for an answer, she waltzes into the room, moving to the cabinet. She pulls out a steel bar I hadn't seen lying on the back of a shelf. "Next time, at least get yourselves a weapon." Ava places the steel bar on the table, then empties her pockets.

When he spots the wire and transistors, Deran's eyes gleam. "You got them."

A smirk from Ava. "I told you I would. Now, are you going to fix whatever got you in here undetected?"

That's my cue. I amble up to the table like I have no ulterior motive, waiting for Deran to remove his device and set it on the table.

Deran shoots Ava a glance. "Can I borrow your multi-tool?"

Wordlessly, Ava hands it over, positioning herself behind Deran. The perfect place to watch exactly what he does over his shoulder. I stroll around and nudge her out of the way, placing my hands on Deran's broad shoulders. "I believe you've taken my place."

Without comment, Ava moves, her eyes never leaving Deran's hands, almost salivating as Deran readies to remove the cover. I slide between Ava and Deran, blocking her view. My body screams at the awkward angle. With a curse, Ava jerks first to one side, then the other, trying to see past me, but I keep myself firmly rooted.

Her hand lifts—she's planning to move me physically. I raise my arm. As she shoves me, I latch on, pulling her with me. We both topple sideways, landing on the floor in a heap.

Fortunately, she landed at the bottom. I grin. Turning the air blue with her curses, Ava wriggles trying to free herself. I pretend to struggle to get off her, all the while making sure I stay on top, keep her down.

Another almighty heave from Ava and she tosses me aside like a rag doll. I scramble up. She's her on her feet already, turning back toward the table. I flop sideways, snagging her foot with my hand, and tug. Ava lands right back on the floor.

At the fury in her eyes, my glee turns to fear. *Uh-oh!* I backpedal, but Deran steps between us. *He's finished! Yes! Thwarted the conniving minx!*

Realizing she's lost, Ava is rightfully mad at us. "You two planned this, didn't you?"

Before I can get my snide comment in, Deran speaks. "I'm sorry, Ava. Until we know we can trust you, I'm sure you understand a little caution?"

"I haven't earned your trust by bringing you here, keeping you safe, not disclosing your location to the monitors?"

"Not yet. Admit it. You only helped us because you wanted to know how we got in undetected. None of what you've done so far proves we can have faith in you. In fact, it tells us the opposite."

Ava crosses her arms over her chest and studies Deran. "Not all brawn and no brains then." Her gaze passes from Deran to me, then back again. "Fair. What *can* I do to gain your trust?"

30

My snort is derisive. "That's not how trust works! It doesn't happen like that!" I snap my fingers. "It takes time."

"I understand. So how do I start earning?"

Ava's maddeningly calm tone riles me further until I realize there *is* something. "If you're serious, I'm here to find my family. Any idea where they might stash people from the dome?"

Ava's expression instantly neutralizes. *She knows!*

"What? Tell me!" Although I don't want to ask anything of this girl, let alone beg, I'll do whatever's necessary.

Ava regards me, eyes wary. "I may know something, but don't count on it. What makes you think your family are here?"

"I'm not certain they are. I only know they're being kept where I can't find them."

"This may be blunt, but how do you know they're still alive?"

"Blunt is an understatement." But then I remember who I'm talking to and why. "I saw them eleven days ago."

"You see them often?"

"No, about once every few months."

Ava grunts in disgust. "Naturally. Just often enough to make you remember who you work for and what you have to do to keep them safe, right?"

Stunned, I gasp. "How do you know?"

"You're not the first person I've met with the same story." She pauses, considering. "Can you ask for another visit?"

"Yes, but there's no guarantee the request will be granted."

"Make the request. And make sure they can't deny you."

"How does this help?"

"If you get a visit with your family, it'll be easier to track them back to where they're being kept, meaning the information I provide will be accurate, not an educated guess." Her dedication to this mission surprises me before I realize where this is headed. On cue, Ava follows my exact line of thinking. "You know this is a big ask, right? You also understand trust is a two-way street. If I supply this information, what do I get in return?"

"Name your price." The words are out before I have time to consider them. I have no right to offer Deran's invention as payment, but she'll likely ask for money. Isn't that what all these renegade organizations need?

"I don't want your cash."

Yet again, she's surprised me. "Then what?"

"How about some of that Nanogo you hoard so rabidly in your dome?"

My eyes widen, but didn't I point out the lack of medicine here earlier? "How much?"

"A dozen canisters will get you the information you're after."

Deran answers. "Done."

I stare, wondering how he's going to get his hands on that many canisters, but he wouldn't have said he could deliver if he didn't mean it. I glance back at Ava. "Well?"

She extends a hand to Deran. "Deal."

They shake on it. For the first time since coming here, I feel a glimmer of hope.

Ava turns her attention my way again. "Do I need to warn you about eyes and ears?"

"If you mean the ever-present cameras, no."

"You also know not to send any comms from any workstations or use any device where the keystrokes can be tracked for messages about that family meeting?"

Panic sucker-punches me, and I stagger back. Deran steadies me, his face looming over mine, concern clear. "What's wrong?"

Horrified, I gaze up at him, whispering the words. "We forgot they can track us through our comm links. They're not listening in, but they know where we are."

Deran's sudden smile cuts through his angst like the sun after rain. His words are equally low. "You don't think I didn't take care of that?"

He doesn't explain because Ava's crept closer in an attempt to hear us. Determined to leave her in the dark, I keep my mouth shut.

"Anything wrong?" Ava fishes when Deran releases me to stand on my own two feet again.

"Just a mild panic attack." Not a lie, except it may not be about what she thinks.

The momentary flash of annoyance in Ava's eyes is satisfying, but I keep my grin to myself. Perhaps I was a little harsh calling her Sirena. Or maybe I'm only more gracious now because I know she's more interested in Deran's gadget than him.

"Is your device fixed? Are you ready to leave?" Now that she's finagled as much information as she thinks she can get, it seems she's in a hurry to get rid of us.

Deran nods. "We are."

"Then follow me."

"Wait!" They both turn to look at me. "How will we do the exchange? And when?"

"I'll find you when I have the information. You just make sure you get that meeting." Given Ava's matter-of-fact attitude, this won't be the first time she's slipped into or out of the dome. But how does she avoid detection? And what if my family are transported by APC? Can her group still follow them?

As I ponder the problems, Ava leads us back through the overwhelming tunnel network. We finally exit using stairs leading up into another abandoned building. Not the same one she brought us in through. These tunnels are more extensive than I thought.

In this factory, the machinery is rusted almost beyond recognition. Most likely, a relic from the days before the world became toxic, although why the conglomerate would leave it here instead of razing and rebuilding like they did with everything else they considered useless, I can't fathom.

Besides, I'm more interested in where Ava's brought us. This building is almost directly opposite the building Deran and I hid out in earlier. Was our meeting really accidental? Or did she follow us from David's (which could explain how she knew who he was), then watch us from a distance?

Either way, we've been in her sights for longer than we knew. I hurry after Deran; I don't have time to consider the implications. When we reach the dome, Deran aims his device. Breathing suspended, I watch the bars. This time, they change color, and air whooshes out of me. In seconds, Deran's beckoning for me to follow, his eyes the only warning to watch where I step.

As I pass Ava, her disappointment is obvious. I want to gloat until I glimpse the determination under it. She's only letting us go so easily because she has backup plans to get her hands on his device.

When we make it through, Deran signals the need for caution is over. I rip my scarf and mask off, eager to be rid of them. Helpful as they were, wearing them was irksome. Deran turns to take us back to the trundle, but I put a hand on his arm. I can't think of a safer place to ask. "Why did we have to be so careful going in and out of the dome?"

Deran considers me for a second. "If I tell you, promise you won't freak out?" I steel myself, then nod. "CC has booby-trapped any roads or alleys that end on the dome."

I know he's not telling me everything. I raise an eyebrow.

"Fine!" Deran runs a hand through his hair. This time, the spikes respond, standing taller. "They use landmines. I'm guessing they don't want any possibility of 'leeches' entering the dome."

Swallowing hard, (I promised not to freak out!), I think before I speak. "How did we avoid them?"

"This little beauty not only allows us to sneak in and out—it also has laser and infrared scanners to map the mines."

Instantly, I know what else it does. "And it also creates some sort of dampening field, like your music player, so they can't use our comm links to track us?"

"Bingo!"

"Pardon?"

"Sorry, something I learned from my parents. It means you got it."

"Oh." I want to say more, but the reminder he could learn things from his parents growing up only reminds me I couldn't. I turn my mind elsewhere. "Just so you know, when you get home, you'd better either hide that device where it's impossible to find or destroy it, because I'm betting Ava's planning on swiping it."

Deran grins, that wonderfully wicked smile turning my insides to mush. "You don't think I saw that?"

"Just checking." Because I can, I lean in and kiss him. Deran takes advantage of what I intended as a brief sign of affection and pulls me close, kissing me mindless. I'm not complaining.

When he draws back, I smile. My grin is goofy, but I don't care. "Shall we linger a little longer?"

Deran laughs, the hearty tone warming me. "Enticing as that sounds, we should get home." His eyes are wary again. "Whatever made CC run extra security on the dome is still active. If we hadn't made those modifications, we would never have made it through."

His talk of modifications reminds me of one last thing I must ask before we move. "Remember how we discussed CC monitoring our keystrokes?"

"Yes, why?"

"When I was changing the data yesterday—and the day before—I understood why the Director punished me for keeping my projects and processes in my head, why he forced me to start keeping actual records, to commit those thoughts to a tablet."

"So he could duplicate your inventions without you?"

"Yes, but also so he could turn them into something else." I glare at the dome. "Turns out I knew even as a kid not to trust him, but somehow, he short-circuited that preservation instinct." Inhaling deeply, I stand taller. "Well, no more!" My grin is feral. "He'll never get the plans for the cold-fusion device from me. I've taken steps to circumvent his keystroke monitoring, but I wanted to know if you have."

"As much as I can. The team and I work off the data you give us, so if you've changed the plans, we'll build it to match because what's on your cube comes through to ours. Should the team have questions, I'll say the alteration is needed to correct the problem."

Deran doesn't need to reiterate his request not to know how I build the machine the "right way." Believing I can make the necessary changes to repair the machine without either him or his team knowing how shows his confidence in me.

I squeeze his arm, quick affirmation of this silent acknowledgment, but this wasn't what I was asking. "Yes, but have you made any notes for yourself about the machine?"

"Why do you think I keep pens and paper?"

I'm reminded of his first, covert handwritten note to me. "You've written everything on paper?"

"Yes, but the materials are expensive. So, I've been working on a way to counteract the keystroke tracking. I wanted us to have an untraceable way to communicate. As soon as I perfect it, you'll have your tablet."

A surprised half-giggle burbles out. "When do you sleep?"

"Only when I have to. There's too much to do."

Deran's continued wariness, his reluctance to engage in anything frivolous, abruptly breaks through. "Right. Let's go."

Offering a brief, grim smile, Deran turns, and we leave. We've gone about thirty feet before we reach a break in the buildings. We halt, unable to believe our eyes.

Fire stains the night sky with a ghoulish orange glow. Only a few blocks away, flames lick up the side of an apartment building.

Deran's the first to manage speech. "What in the world happened while we were gone?"

31

Deran and I are too stunned to move, but the surrounding mayhem, increasing in pitch and intensity, makes us realize we can't stay here.

Deran grabs my hand, gripping it firmly. "Stay close and keep your head down."

He says nothing further as he tries to navigate a safe path away from the chaos. Despite his attempts, there are too many obstacles. Although it's almost midnight, people rush about, agitated ants before an oncoming storm. I can't blame them. I've never seen a building on fire either. A fact that's even more disturbing now that I know we're stuck in a confined environment.

Snatches of conversation from the people we pass increase my turmoil. I can't believe what I'm hearing. *An explosion. Two people died; others were injured. CCs reporting a power generator blew up.*

The last one is perplexing. I know how the generators work because Sarissa provided this information in the research pack when I started the cold-fusion project. It was essential to figuring out how I would integrate my invention with the existing infrastructure, assuming I could get it to work. Based on that knowledge, a generator explosion is extremely unlikely. Further, the power plant in this sector is at least two blocks from the burning building. How could the explosion have affected this building without touching the others in between? It doesn't add up.

The number of people on the street has doubled. Abruptly claustrophobic, I cling to Deran's hand, fearful we'll be separated. I wish the people would all go home until I realize the milling crowds work to our advantage. More people mean we can hide ourselves more effectively and potentially disguise where we've been and for how long as we slink back to our homes. Or disappear back into the zone if the fire burns out of control.

To our consternation, for the first time ever, the trundle isn't running. Another reason the people are so rattled? Fortunately, we overhear the frightened whispers before we reach the nearest platform, warning us of the breakdown—and of patrolling SerSents.

We scurry away, back into the shadows of the alleys, where cameras are scarce, and don't stop until Deran finds a place safe enough for us to rest. As we crouch behind the piles of broken furniture, Deran sighs. "At this rate, we should've spent the night in Ava's room. At least we would've had cots to sleep on."

I shudder. "No, I'd rather be here. If we'd stayed, I probably would've had nightmares about the beetles coming to carry us away."

"The beetles?" Deran chuckles, the first sign of his usually effervescent disposition resurfacing.

Delighted I could restore his mood, I explain. Deran reaches into his pack and pulls out two wrapped sandwiches, bringing me to a stop mid-story. "Ooh, yum! Why didn't you bring those out sooner?"

A flash of white as Deran smiles in the muted light filtering from a lamp at the end of the alley. "I didn't want to share with Ava. I know you wouldn't have."

"You're right. Your food is too good to split with anyone."

A soft chuckle. "And here I thought it was because you didn't like the woman."

"She was just so… so… condescending!" I take an aggressive bite of my sandwich, almost nipping my fingers. Sufficient warning to make me realize I've also almost finished the mouthful without tasting it. "Let's forget her. I want to enjoy my meal."

I sense rather than see Deran shaking his head, but he obliges, and we eat in silence. Every bite seems more delicious than the last, and I sigh when I polish off the final crumb. "You never make enough."

More soft laughter, and I can't resist. I want Deran's arms and body blanketing me as much as his laughter. I scoot closer and snuggle into his muscled shoulder, relaxing into him when his arms wrap around me. I'm exhausted, but also too wound up to sleep. My mind spins, streaming through everything.

I lift my chin so Deran can hear me. "You said you and your parents got into the dome a different way. How?"

"The waterfall."

"The one marking the city's western boundary?"

"Do you know another?"

I slap his arm playfully, satisfied his humor seems fully restored. "How did you know it was there?"

I feel him shrug. "I'm not sure. Seems I've known it was an access point to the zone for ages, but I can't recall when or where I gained that information."

"So, what? You just… walk through?"

"Pretty much."

"But don't you reach the other side sopping wet?"

The rumble of his laughter deep in his chest is pleasant under my fingers. "The waterfall's not real. It's part of the illusion."

I bolt upright, the action moving me away from Deran's chest. "I knew it! There was always something off about that waterfall."

More chuckles. "And what do you mean by that?"

I turn in his arms, facing him. "Do you know how many times I calculated the volume of water flowing over that cliff and came up with a ridiculously large answer? How often I told myself if that amount were in fact tumbling over the cliff, water would flood the valley?"

"You knew the dimensions for the calculation?"

I wave a hand. "No, of course not. The trundle doesn't go way out there. I used guesstimates. I always meant to check them, but never remembered by the time I got to work." Something else occurs to me. "Do you think I kept forgetting because of the coercion serum?"

"Possibly, but knowing you, it's more likely your mind was on work."

"Logical, I suppose. Am I seeing ghosts in every problem again?"

Deran nods. "I think so. I warned you this would happen once your mind was free of the serum. Now that it is, consider applying a logic filter."

I nod, then settle back onto his chest. "Why do you think you can get through the dome at the waterfall, but nowhere else?"

"Maybe they're using so much power from your little glass tiles to generate the illusion, there's not enough left to keep the shield in place effectively. You can answer better than me."

I ponder the problem, then accept Deran's explanation. No point wasting time on an irrelevant problem. I'm more interested in something else. "How do you think Ava gets in and out?"

"Hmm, I wondered the same thing. She doesn't have a device like mine, or she wouldn't have been so interested in it. She also doesn't use the waterfall, or she would've been caught, like my parents and I."

"No answers then?"

"None that I've been able to come up with."

I turn to another problem. "Do you really think an explosion caused the fire?"

"Yes, there were distinctive scorch marks, and the way the glass was blown out for a hundred yards from that building is confirmation."

"What do you think caused it?"

Deran's head turns my way, his eyes glinting in the dark. "What are you thinking?"

"CCs generators have failsafes to prevent accidents. Also, no way a generator blowing up caused a secondary explosion and a fire in a building two blocks away."

"How do you know the generator's two blocks away?"

As I explain where I learned it, I reach the only logical explanation. I don't finish my sentence, breathing the answer. "The resistance!"

"That would explain the extra security CC's running on the dome. But why would the resistance blow something up? They've never been violent before, never taken overt action. That would make them active targets."

There's only one explanation "Something must have changed in the status quo."

"Agreed, but what?"

I shrug. "I don't know. If Ava comes through with the information, I'll ask. Which reminds me—how do you have access to so much Nanogo?"

Deran's voice holds all the anguish of the memory. "After visiting David, my parents and I began stockpiling it. His wife had just died from pneumonia, totally treatable and something she should never have succumbed to. We couldn't stand by and let him, or their other friends, suffer because of a lack of essential healthcare. But we never got it to him because my parents died before I found a way to make it through the dome undetected."

Pieces fall into place. Deran didn't just recently create his device to get me into the zone. He's been working on it for some time, possibly years. No wonder he didn't want to share it with Ava. Then there's his bond with David. Such deep friendships don't happen when you've met a person only once; or at least once as an adult. For them to form so quickly, there has to be a shared event of such magnitude, it binds the parties irrevocably. The deaths of those close to them both would've qualified. I realize what Deran's giving up, the gift he's offered me.

"Thank you for being willing to part with the Nanogo, so I might learn where they're holding Xanin."

When Deran simply nods, I understand it's not only for Xanin; it's also for the many others taken from the zone, separated from their families. My heart expands, almost unable to comprehend Deran's ability for such compassion. His life has been so much harder than he's made it sound.

I tuck myself closer, wanting him to know how much I care, needing him to understand he's not alone in his fight anymore.

Deran's arms tighten in response, and we take comfort in our embrace.

Before I'm ready, Deran's moving. *Just when I was getting warm and comfortable! If he'd given me a few more minutes, I might've fallen asleep.* But better I didn't; I'm already stiff. I rise and stretch, trying to coax my aching muscles into relaxing. Then we're off again, Deran leading us back toward the part of the city we're more familiar with, where we'll have to do our best to elude the increasing number of cameras.

When we reach a spot roughly midway between our homes, Deran pulls me deeper into the shadows of a grove of trees. I have to hand it to him. He's led us back through a series of parks and open spaces, all without cameras. Doesn't mean the odd surveillance drone didn't spot us, but it makes where we came from more of a mystery. Hopefully, one they won't ever have the time or inclination to figure out.

Seeming uncomfortable, Deran rubs the back of his neck. I grin. There's a first time for everything. "What? Spit it out."

"Can I make a suggestion?"

"Sure."

"Please know before I do, you should take this at face value. I have no hidden agendas, no expectations for anything you're not ready to give."

Mystified, I nod, clueless.

Still looking unsure, Deran takes the plunge. "Considering they were still running security on the dome, the explosion, the pervasive sense of unrest, I think… I'd like to suggest… I'd feel better if you spent the night at my place." Before I can respond, he hurries on, eager to reassure me. "At least there, I can keep an eye on you, keep you safe. I have cameras in my apartment to warn if someone's been there, and I also have a few safety measures to alert us if we weren't careful enough, and they come for us."

I could've done without that last part, but I know where he's going with this, and I melt. I draw him into my arms this time. "Thank you. I appreciate you taking care of me."

Deran relaxes, a relieved smile touching his lips. "Glad we got that settled. My home it is, then."

32

Twenty-three minutes and sixteen seconds later, we're back in Deran's apartment. I flop onto his couch as soon as we enter, totally worn out.

"I'm going to check on things." Deran's careful to avoid specific mention of his security feeds until he knows we're safe. "Make yourself at home. Grab some food if you're hungry. I'll be back soon. Then you can have my bed, and I'll sleep on the couch."

Too weary to do more than grunt acknowledgement, I sink further into the comfy cushions. I don't remember Deran returning or carrying me to his bed later, but he must've because I wake the next morning wondering where I am.

Alarmed, I sit up in the strange bed, then realize I'm still fully clothed except for my shoes. About to freak out for real, my eyes land on a guitar adorning the chair opposite the bed. Last night's events return in a deluge. I yawn and stretch; I should check the time. Then I smell the coffee.

Following my nose, I find Deran in the kitchen. He grins, a slow, lazy smile. "If I didn't know any better, I'd think you slept your weekends away."

My eyes fly to the clock, mortified to find it's almost noon! "I guess yesterday took more out of me than I realized."

"Stressful situations will do that. How do you like your eggs?"

"Scrambled." I slide onto a stool at the kitchen counter, my mouth watering as the first salty tangs of bacon tease my nose. My stomach growls. I need something to keep the hunger at bay. "May I have some coffee?"

Deran grins, like he knows why I'm asking, but says nothing. I could kiss him. In fact, I *will* kiss him. When he passes the mug over the counter, I place a hand over his, using the stool to gain enough height advantage to lean across and kiss him. He blinks in surprise, and I plop back onto the stool, giggling. "You don't have to look so surprised every time I kiss you!"

Shaking his head, he chuckles. "That's not the reason. I'm almost impressed you managed that without falling off the chair."

A startled half-laugh escapes. "Yes, I suppose with the track history we have, you probably expected me to fall over the counter and crash into you."

Still chuckling, he turns to check on the food. "I didn't say it."

He divides his attention between the eggs, bacon, toast, and chopped vegetables as I take a sip of coffee. I almost spit it back out. "Uh, more cream and honey, please?"

Deran grins, reaching for the cup. "Not demanding or anything when you first wake up, are you?"

His continued teasing makes me smile. After he's added the requested ingredients, I take another sip. "Ah, much better. It'll be perfect when there's food to go with it."

"Miss Impatient," is all Deran says before we're both laughing again.

We enjoy quiet companionship as Deran puts the finishing touches on our meal. After sliding a plate of food my way, he sits on a stool opposite me.

I need no invitation. The food is as wonderful as the savory aromas promised. As I relish each mouthful, I don't speak, just eat. When my plate is empty, I sigh. "Thank you. That was exquisite."

"You're welcome. I enjoy cooking for you—you're always so appreciative!"

I get the hint, rising from my stool this time to walk around the counter. He turns toward me, and for once, we're the same height. *Nice! I won't have to crane my neck to reach him.* I give him a kiss worthy of the thanks the meal deserved.

With my arms still draped around his shoulders, I smile. "So, what's next on today's agenda?"

Deran smirks. The villainous smile makes my stomach feel as though butterflies just took flight inside. "Oh, I can think of a few things…" Then he sighs. "But most of those will have to wait for another day. We have too much to do and not enough time. Today should be spent discussing how you'll assemble the machine correctly while keeping Cygnus ignorant of the details."

I feel like he dumped a bucket of ice water over my head, feeling the need to sputter and gasp, unprepared for the brutal return to reality. Although I want to protest, go back to the easy conversation and flirting, Deran's right. No wonder he sighed.

"Ugh, if we must."

"We must."

Grumpy, I drop my arms from his shoulders and amble over to the couch. *Snap out of it! Xanin needs you. Deran needs justice for Carys. Stop thinking about yourself!* My little pep talk does nothing to bolster my mood. Deran plops beside me, a tablet in hand with wires coming out of it, and the tide turns sluggishly.

Deran's eyes crinkle with amusement. "Yes, I thought this might interest you—our first discussion point today."

I'm too intrigued to care that he's teasing again. "What is it?"

"The tablet I told you about, the one I'm trying to break the encryption on so we can communicate, record what we need to, without CC monitoring us. I'm hoping you can help crack the last firewall. Or maybe the last few firewalls."

"I think Ferret can help."

Deran quirks an eyebrow. "Your device that could help me piggyback into CC's camera system?"

"That's the one. Shall we fetch him, then continue working here, or do you want to work at my place?"

Rising, Deran offers me a hand. "Let's work here because this is where my supplies are. But a train ride to your home and back sounds like a pleasant diversion. Shall we?"

No shocker when we find the trundle up and running again, but the round trip takes longer than expected because we stop in at the market on the way back. After eating lunch there and shopping for Deran's weekly food supply, we don't enter his apartment again until mid-afternoon. Once more, and before we do anything, Deran checks his security feeds, while I unpack the groceries, both of us eager to get on with our task.

I stroll back to Deran's room in time to catch him pulling his supplies and the modified tablet back out of their hiding place—a loose floorboard under his bed. "Isn't that the first place someone will look if they come hunting?"

"I'm open to suggestions. I don't have a handy panel behind my kitchen closet like you do."

"I'm sure we can find a better solution." As Deran sets up his supplies, I wander around. Then my eyes fall on his windowsill. Unlike mine, made of stone, his is wood—rotting wood. I pick at it.

"Stop! I don't want to replace that," Deran grumbles.

"No, I think you should, except when you do, use something that looks weathered, but isn't."

Deran looks at me like I've lost it. "Chiara, I'm used to your occasional nonsensical sentences, but what are you rambling about? We have work to do."

I grin. "I thought you wanted a better hiding spot."

Deran considers my statement for all of a second, before striding over and examining the area more carefully. "You're right. If I rebuild it so the wood slides in and out, the gap between the outer and inner walls will allow me to slip things in there. Narrow, but if I don't make it too deep, I shouldn't lose things." He continues inspecting the space, visibly making mental notes of the supplies he'll need.

When he turns and grins, I know he's done, and I smile. "Ready for today's next mission, then?"

Deran nods, and we move back to his setup on the kitchen counter. I study the circuits and wires exposed on his experimental tablet before selecting one to hook Ferret up to. "That should do it."

I flip Ferret's switch, keying the hack request; then we wait. Oddly, Ferret doesn't break through in seconds, as he's done every other time. When we're still waiting ten minutes later, I can't help myself. "Wow! There's better security on the tracking software than at the bank!"

A quirk of Deran's lips. "And how would you know that? Been hacking banks lately?"

Too late now to realize I should've thought before speaking.

Hurt flits across Deran's eyes before it's gone. "I thought we trusted one another."

I pull him into a hug, get him close, so he can see I'm not lying. "No, it's not that. If I give you this information, I'm putting you in an impossible position. You may be forced to expose it if you're ever..." How do I say this without sounding like I'm expecting us to fail?

"Caught and interrogated?" Deran finishes. I nod. "I'd think that was my decision to make. And I want to know. Unless you think it might jeopardize whatever you're planning to do with the cold-fusion device. Then keep it to yourself."

I grin. "I've been making chards."

Deran's eyes go so wide and round I burst out laughing.

"You haven't!" Deran says, voice betraying his doubt.

"I have. Don't look so shocked. It's not that difficult. Especially when you have access to a personal lab where privacy is guaranteed and you can print cards."

Deran leans back, eyes filled with wonder. Then he chuckles. "I thought I was being a bad influence on you. I may have to rethink that." He tugs my hair affectionately. "Why were you creating chards?"

As we wait for Ferret to grind through the firewalls, I explain the need for cash that can't be traced if I want to get my family out.

"And chards are the perfect solution," Deran concludes. "Smart. If I give you my bank information, will you make some for me?"

"Sure. You thinking of using them at the market?"

Deran nods. "And a few other places. They'll come in handy when I want to buy more supplies for my less-than-acceptable side endeavors."

I laugh. "Such a diplomatic way of describing illegal activities."

"Speaking of which," Deran picks up a compact motherboard from the counter, "we may as well make you your own device for getting in and out of the dome. Then if you have to leave in a hurry, you can."

This talk makes what's coming up all too real. I can't bear the thought of leaving without him. "If I have to go unexpectedly, where will we meet in the zone?"

Deran's eyes have lost their silver streaks, his face grave. "Best if we don't set up a meeting place. I'll find you if it comes to that."

Selecting another component from the counter, Deran adds it to the board. Neither of us wants to continue an abruptly dark conversation. "Tell me what you need and I'll pass it to you."

We work this way for a while, me fascinated by Deran's design and asking questions, him explaining the process. Abruptly, Ferret beeps, and we both jump.

"Ferret's done!"

Turns out there was no need for my superfluous statement. Deran's already reaching for the tablet, disconnecting Ferret, pressing keys, running tests. Too nervous to sit still, I pace the small living room, waiting anxiously for the result.

I see the smile before I hear the answer, and I know Ferret's excelled. "It worked?"

"It did. Here, come see!"

I thought Deran would simply remove the tracking, but he's added a sub-routine to generate snatches of coherent text pulled from a variety of sources, mimicking notes. His tablet hack allows no recording of our real search history or work, filling the space with fake information instead. "This way, it won't look like you're working on a tablet they can never find tracking information on."

"Wow! And you think I'm the genius!"

Deran only laughs before pulling me into his arms and kissing me. I'm just as elated. This "silent" tablet opens up a whole new host of possibilities. But Deran's kissing me giddy and I can't think about those now.

When Deran releases me, I'm still on cloud nine until my stomach growls. "Well, that was rude."

Deran moves back to the kitchen. "I'm on it."

"Let me help."

"Sure, but it's only sandwiches after our massive lunch."

"I still want to help. I must know how you make them taste so good."

"More likely it's the untainted food and nothing special on my part."

"Don't be so modest. Your mom taught you well. Have I told you I look forward to the meals you leave me?"

Turning, Deran winds his arms around my waist. "Why, no, you haven't."

I grin, understanding. "Well, I do. Your meals are the highlight of my day. Thank you." I kiss him. Then offer another when he asks if that's all they were worth.

Once we finally get to making dinner, and I can think clearly again, I'm keenly aware of time slipping by, too precious to waste. If I want results, I should focus on fixing the problems, not flirting! What was I thinking? *Okay, I wasn't. But I can change that.*

Deran's team finished dismantling the machine on Friday, which means we rebuild tomorrow. We need to address this. I pick up the tomato Deran's asked me to slice. "How are we going to rebuild the machine without giving Cygnus the ability to duplicate it?"

33

Over the kitchen counter, across from me, Deran grins. "I'm glad you asked. Remember when I told you this morning hacking the tablet was our first discussion point?" I nod. "Well, we have several more, and I'll start with what I haven't yet told you. Last week, whilst my team was dismantling your cold-fusion device, I had several chances to slip away when the work required no oversight."

My grin matches his. "And what did you do with that time?"

"Put it to excellent use, of course!"

"Deran!" I'm tempted to throw a carrot at him. "Stop teasing and tell me what you did!"

Chuckling, Deran butters the bread. "I added a few countermeasures to several key areas."

"You mean, you went crawling around in your ducts, and put them there?"

"Some, not all. Several cameras in the workshop were too distant to be affected by my gadgets in the ducts. For those, I placed my countermeasures in convenient, alternative hiding places. Unfortunately, I still haven't found a solution for one camera in the far section of your lab floor."

"You're going to make me ask, aren't you?"

Another cheeky grin. "I wouldn't feel smart if you didn't."

Rolling my eyes, I indulge him. "Fine. How are your gadgets countermeasures?"

Deran wipes his hands on the kitchen towel. "Give me a second." He disappears into the bedroom, returning a few seconds later.

When he places a gorgeous silver ring with an intricately worked metal band and a deep-sea-blue topaz at its center on the counter, I glance up at him, uncertain.

He laughs, shaking his head. "Oh, no, it's nothing like that! Perhaps I should've explained first. Pick it up."

Unsure where he's going, I obey. I can't resist running a finger over the beautiful metal band. When my finger reaches the topaz and snags on something, I understand. Inspecting the spot, I find the tiny protruding piece of metal. To a casual observer, it would appear as a piece the smith forgot to smooth out, when it's actually the tiniest button I've ever seen.

Curious, I press the button, waiting for something, but nothing happens. Deran's laughter fills the room. I throw the carrot at him. "Not funny! Stop sniggering and tell me what it does!"

Deran's eyes stream. Though I shake my head, I succumb to laughter too. When he eventually contains his mirth, he explains. "Your face was priceless. But," he raises a finger, "the switch worked exactly as it was meant to: showing no visible effect, but discreetly working where it can't be seen."

More confused than ever, irritation rises again, but before I can demand he be more specific, he interjects. "Come, let me show you." He offers his hand, a peace offering.

I accept, and he latches on, eagerly leading me back to the bedroom. For the first time, I see where he's stashed his surveillance equipment. "Oh, brilliant! This is a much better hiding spot!"

"I'd hide more there if I could, but as you can see, space is limited."

I inspect the light fixture. As with all lower-tier apartments, it's a simple spherical disc, the size of a dinner plate and about five inches thick. A rotating piece at its center lowers the lighting option selected by the user.

Deran's altered this so the piece holding the selected bulb moves down even further, exposing a five-inch gap between the bulb and main disc above. In this gap, he's inserted a tiny tray which extends outward. It holds his "surveillance equipment": a cube for collecting and storing the information from the cameras and a mini-holographic projector for displaying it. I touch the tray, impressed when I find it cool to the touch.

"You added a thermal barrier so the heat from the bulb won't affect the electronics?"

"Naturally." Deran taps the tiny tray, and it retracts into its space above the bulb, then slips up out of sight into the light's can with no effect on the "soft daylight" offered by this selection. Another tap on the outside of the can and the tray drops down again, Deran's satisfaction obvious.

His animation contagious, I grin. "You really are quite the inventor, aren't you? This is incredible!"

"If you like that, wait until you see what your ring did."

Now I laugh. He's like a kid, eager to show off his toys. But what toys these are! I'm jealous. Using the holographic interface on the cube, Deran bring up the feeds from the cameras, the other third of a typical system, and evidently scattered throughout Deran's apartment.

Deran swipes through the feeds until he reaches one showing only static, then scrolls through the menu, rewinding the feed.

And there we are in the kitchen, making sandwiches. Deran leaves the kitchen, returning with the ring and dropping it onto the counter.

I giggle, and Deran grins. "Yes, my reaction was funny. But what do you expect a girl to do when she's suddenly presented with a ring?"

No answer as the feed gets to the part Deran was interested in. "Watch!"

The moment I press the button on the ring, the feed turns to static. "Ooh! A way to create interference on CC's cameras!"

Now I understand Deran's excitement. I can't help myself. I grab his hands and bounce around on the floor, a mad impromptu dance. Deran chuckles but goes with it. When I abruptly feel silly, then self-conscious, I stall mid-leap.

"Don't stop! I was having fun watching you." Deran's teasing tone and the glimmer of silver in his eyes makes me wonder what he's thinking. Before I let the thought run its course, I turn away, sure I'm about to blush, although why now, I don't know. I pretend to inspect his surveillance tray again.

Then his arms slide around my waist as he comes up behind me, pressing his chest to my back. "I'm sorry. Too much teasing?"

His tone is gentle, and I melt into him, leaning my back against his chest and relaxing. How did I get so lucky having someone who understands me better than I understand myself?

"Yes." I turn in his arms, draping mine over his shoulders. "Remember, I grew up without a family constantly pestering me, so I'm not good at teasing or dealing with it when I'm teased."

Deran moves a stray curl off my face. "I'll remember that." His kiss is tender, his touch equally so. I groan, dissolving. This time, however, Deran keeps the kiss short. When his lips break from mine, I'm left with the sweetness of the kiss, so I don't object.

"Let's get back to dinner and making plans, hmm?"

Deran's question reminds me of my earlier sentiments about romance, but I'm oddly reluctant to rush off. A sigh escapes, my only indication I reluctantly agree with him.

Back in the kitchen, Deran explains how the button disrupts the signal the cameras send to the control center for a varied length of time, no less than five seconds, no more than two minutes.

"Why the two-minute maximum?"

"The SerSents watching the feeds take just over two minutes to isolate the camera's position, then get someone there to inspect it, meaning by the time they arrive, there will be no hint of what might've caused the problem."

I eye him suspiciously. "How do you know?"

Mischief written all over his face, Deran grins. "How do you think?"

"You tested it?" The question isn't quite a shriek, but close enough, a strident attestation to my distress he went through with something so dangerous.

"Don't worry." Deran puts a placating hand on my arm. "I was in the ducts. They couldn't see me."

My snort telegraphs my lack of faith in the level of safety this provides.

Deran ignores my concern, apparently believing it, and my skepticism, unwarranted. "There are a few caveats. Don't use the ring repeatedly in the same location and try to use it sparingly. Too many static-filled screens without a viable explanation will probably mean they do a more thorough search for the cause, and we don't want that."

"So what do I do when I need more than two minutes to make an 'adjustment' on the machine?"

"Ah, glad you asked. I have a few other tricks up my sleeve."

I giggle, earlier concerns forgotten as I cave to his charms again. "Of course you do!"

And we're back to the face of a kid eager to explain his toy. Or, in this case, toys. Deran has not only the gorgeous ring which blocks the camera signals within a ten-foot radius, but he's created a mini remote allowing him to crash the lighting for our floor, several floors simultaneously, or other floors entirely.

"You mean to make it look like our floor isn't the only one with issues?"

"You catch on fast. The goal is to make it as difficult as possible for them to realize the actual area they aren't meant to be watching is the workshop. I want them to think those cameras going on the fritz and the lighting issues are part of a larger problem. Here, try this."

Deran hands me an electric adjustable wrench, a tool I'm familiar with, and I press the power button. The claws clamp down on themselves. "What's so special about it?"

"It works the same way as the ring, except the effects last as long as the wrench is powered."

Immediately, I understand. "A scapegoat to blame the glitches—or some of them—on, if we need a reason?"

"Exactly. Anyone determined enough to find a reason will soon see the correlation between the wrench's use and the camera static if they're sharp enough."

Delighted, I rub my hands together. "What other goodies do we have at our disposal?"

This prompts a chuckle, and I smile, though I'm more interested in the box. Clearly, other things are in there and I want to know what.

Deran doesn't disappoint. In short order, he brings out a cube, a gigantic piece of paper, and a tiny mirror with a hinged base allowing for varied preset angles. "The cube is identical to the one in the lab, except it doesn't work. It has our blueprint on it, minus a few details, but several subroutines will cause varied errors."

"Such as?"

"Not allowing the user to pull the diagram apart and inspect the component parts, not turning on, and getting stuck on one part of the blueprint, amongst others."

"And this helps how?"

"I'm hoping we can create a diversion. Not as foolproof as turning the cameras off, but something else which might distract watching eyes if you need to switch something out and don't need more than a second or two."

"Clever!"

"I thought so."

Deran looks so pleased with himself I chuckle. "Okay, what's the ginormous piece of paper for?"

Unfurling it from the tight roll, Deran holds it up, revealing a printed blueprint of the cold-fusion device.

"Wow, that must've cost a mint!"

"It did, but CC paid for it. They're *still* going to be paying for it when we pin it up over a camera they added or altered the position of at the last minute."

I shake my head, giggling. "Can you imagine how apoplectic Cygnus will be if we block his view at a crucial moment?"

Deran nods, a gleam in his eye. "Like when we're testing the machine again."

My giggle turns to laughter. "I see you've thought about this. Fine, we'll save it for when I'm certain I've ironed out the kinks and we want to run a valid test."

"A valid test?"

"Oh yes, did I forget to tell you? I've got a few surprises of my own planned. One of which will be running several tests I know will fail. Between my plans and your gadgets causing intermittent glitches in their recordings at key moments, I'm now confident we can successfully hide the working version of the machine."

Deran's laughter is infectious. We dissolve into uncontrolled hysterics. When he can, Deran wheezes what he was thinking. "Cygnus better buckle up. You've so got it in for him."

"I do, and every reason is his own doing. Payback will be immensely satisfying."

"Justice indeed."

"What's the mirror for?"

"See this? Magnetic base, so I can attach it to the drum on the machine and—"

"Redirect the laser to shine directly into a camera instead of the drum, blinding that camera?"

"Aw, Chiara! Do you have to guess everything?" His tone suggests equal measures of annoyance and admiration.

"Sorry!" I give him a quick, consolatory kiss, my hands lingering on his muscular arms. "I'm just having so much fun! It's seldom I meet someone who thinks like I do. I didn't mean to crash your party, but you don't understand how intriguing it is to guess the purpose of your toys. And what incredible inventions! So many ways to make it look like we have nothing at all to do with them, let alone their recordings failing at critical moments. Moments they won't know are critical until it's too late. Have I told you I think you're a genius?"

A quiet huff before Deran smiles. "If I can make your eyes shine like that with guessing games, I can live with it."

"Glad to hear it." Then I remember the mindhunters. "You know all these failsafes and misdirections only counteract part of the problem. What will we do if they send mindhunters?"

Deran's brow furrows. "I thought you worked out the frequencies for Tandize's song? Won't that solve the problem?"

"Only if we use it the same way as the ring—sparingly and only when absolutely necessary. Besides, you know I still need to test it. Until I do, we can't rely on it. Even if it works, what if Cygnus stations a squad of his goons on the workshop floor 24/7?"

My anxiety spirals again, until Deran grips my upper arms, turning me to face him, then nudging my chin up so our eyes meet. "One problem at a time. For now, we have a few tools at our disposal. If we need more, I'm sure we can come up with them. We'll deal with additional problems as they present themselves, so don't get worked up about things that may not happen."

He pauses before adding the rest. "Although I believe your concern about Cygnus sending mindhunters into the workshop to watch our every move and monitor our every thought is justified. Especially with all the problems they're going to have getting an accurate picture of how we build the machine. It's only a matter of how much time we'll have."

I draw strength from his touch, his quiet assurance, and his conviction we can pull this off. "In that case, we'd better make sure we get the cold-fusion device up and running in record time."

34

Deran and I finish dinner, then move to the couch with our tea. The conversation bounces from further ideas for subverting the conglomerate's spying, to the most efficient way to rebuild the machine, to the explosion and its cause (CC media are still blaming a faulty generator), to our families and, finally, the resistance and whether they'll truly find Xanin.

I don't realize how late it is until the yawn slips out. "Oh, sorry!" My hand moves belatedly to my mouth. Now that I've registered my weariness, I see the same exhaustion dragging on Deran's features. "I should get home."

Deran cocks his head. "You sure?"

"Yes, I think it's safe. No one's looked at us even remotely sideways today, and the aftermath of the explosion is keeping the SerSents too busy to worry about us."

When Deran's surprised by his own yawn, he nods. "Agreed. Let's get you home. But first..." He rises, holding out a hand to me.

I accept, and he leads me to the kitchen. Suddenly solemn, he tugs me into the cocoon of his arms, face earnest. "You know I'll always do my best to protect you?"

I nod, mystified by this sudden change in demeanor.

"Then will you wear this as a reminder?"

He takes my right hand in his and holds the ring he made in front of a finger. My ring finger. Thoughts scrambled, I allow two facts to surface above the melee. Not my left hand and this ring is more than a beautiful accessory. It's a promise.

"Yes!" My answer is as breathless as I feel.

With infinite care, Deran slides the ring onto my finger. The fit is perfect.

I take a moment to admire how it looks on my hand, turning it this way and that, using the time to compose myself. Despite this, tears shine in my eyes when I look up at him. "Thank you."

Wordlessly, Deran's embrace tightens, and he kisses me. I soak in every sensation, not wanting the kiss to end. Because, somehow, he's made even this kiss convey his need to care for me. Shattered doesn't even begin to describe how this makes me feel after so much time taking care of myself.

My arms tighten around his neck, wanting him closer, as safe as he's made me feel.

By the time he ends the kiss, I'm no longer thinking. But he doesn't draw back, holding me as he studies my face. "Time to get you home so you can sleep."

We part reluctantly, and although I protest the need for Deran's protection, he ignores me. Ten minutes and twelve seconds later, we're entering my building. I'm determined to get him back on the trundle as quickly as possible so he can catch up on his own sleep because I think he needs it more than I do.

As we trudge down the empty mall corridor to the resident's entrance, a rough voice calls out behind us. "Excuse me, ma'am?"

Immediately alert, I tense. Deran steps in front of me as we turn, ready to face the threat. Although it's shadowed here, I recognize the face. Putting a hand on Deran's shoulder, I move past him. "Evening, Sam. How are you?"

"Good, thank you, ma'am. Humblest apologies for disturbing you, but you dropped this on your way in."

I'm about to disagree when Sam moves ever so slightly. The light shifts, allowing me to glimpse the plea in his eyes. My gaze drops to what he offers, and I automatically reach for it. My mind screams this is all kinds of wrong, but I must act as normally as I can to keep Sam free of trouble. "Thank you."

"Yes, ma'am. Take care and, again, apologies for the interruption."

Sam melts back into the shadows, disappearing. Still stunned he dared approach, I finger the object in my hand. A barrette, like any of the countless others I use for tying my hair back. But that's not all. My fingers curl protectively around the precious, concealed cargo, and I turn back to Deran.

As expected, his face gives nothing away, but I sense his questions. I debate my options.

Which will keep Sam safest? While I'd love to run back to Deran's home, that's probably the worst choice. So I offer Deran an overly bright smile. "Shall we?"

Deran follows wordlessly. This time, instead of waiting for the elevator after my biometrics are confirmed in the resident's lobby, I lead Deran toward the stairs. He doesn't question the move, simply follows. However, when I lead him down to the basement, I sense his surprise. Despite this, he keeps his peace.

Rather than aiming for the incinerator right away, I duck behind one of the steel girders marching across the space in straight lines, crisscrossing the area. As soon as I'm sure we're out of sight of the cameras watching the incinerator (the only ones I've been able to detect), I pull Deran's head close to mine, keeping my voice to a whisper.

"Sam gave me a message."

Deran's eyes widen, but I see understanding. Excellent! He remembers Sam. Carefully, I remove the tiny scrap of paper meticulously folded and concealed between the barrette's plastic outer piece and the metal clip on the inside. How Sam got pen or paper, let alone the barrette, I don't know, but I'll have to find a way to repay him.

My fingers tremble as I open the paper, clumsy as I fumble my way through nerves. Then Sam's note is revealed.

They came. Beware your apartment.

Terror strikes. My knees go weak; my breathing hitches. So many thoughts all at once. Who are "they?" I can only assume SerSents or, worse, mindhunters, if the second sentence is any indication. And what does that even mean? *Oh, Sam! You could've gotten into so much trouble if they caught you with this note!*

Deran is the first to move, the first to understand. "We can't go to your apartment. I bet they've bugged it. We should go back to my place."

"No!" The single word is vehement, raising Deran's eyebrows. "Sorry, but no. Sam took an insane risk giving me this warning. I won't make it obvious he did. I'd never forgive myself if he got into trouble."

Deran runs a hand through his hair; the spikes are back, more on end than ever. "Fine. We'll go to your apartment. But only so you can ostensibly pack a bag to bring back to my place."

I lift my chin. "No. I'm spending the night in my home. You can come in and see for yourself no one's there. We'll limit our conversation to inconsequential topics, and then you'll leave, telling me you'll see me at work and thanking me for helping you this weekend so you could get the order of things right in your head."

The muscle in Deran's jaw tics again; his fists ball, ready for a fight.

"Please! I don't want Sam paying for this. After leaving first the clothes, then the food, it's possible I've already landed him in hot water. Instead of adding to his burdens, revealing he helped us, I want it to look like all he did was hand me something I 'dropped,' and all we did this weekend was work on how we would reassemble the machine."

Deran's fists unclench, arms dropping to his sides, his face assuming the gray cast of weariness once more. "Fine, we'll go with your plan. But," he raises a finger, "if there's even a hint you're in danger, you come home with me. Understood?"

"Understood." Now that we agree, I pull tomorrow's lunch he prepared so carefully from my pack, removing it from the brown bag and stuffing it into the plastic one with my breakfast. It bulges so much it won't close. No matter. It'll keep, and I have what I needed. I place Sam's note inside the brown bag, crumple it into a ball, and then dart to the incinerator and toss the bag inside.

Instantly, it bursts into a tiny ball of flame, consumed in under a second. Satisfied, I turn and lead Deran back up the stairs to my apartment. When I open the door, I half-expect to see the same chaos I found after someone came looking for the slide from Tandize's microscope. But everything is exactly as I left it. Almost.

Using my mental projector, I compare my apartment when I left this morning to now. The pillows are angled differently, the picture on the wall is a millimeter off center, and one screw on the extractor fan in the kitchen isn't quite tightened all the way.

Deran was right. "They" bugged the place while I was gone. I just hope they left after they finished. Pretending a carefree attitude, forcing a relaxed posture belying the tension I feel, I stride into my apartment. Deran follows me into the entryway where I turn to face him.

"Thanks for seeing me home. You didn't have to, but I appreciate it."

Deran's voice is as mild as my own. "It's the least I could do after you spent your weekend working through how we'd reassemble the machine. Mind if I use your bathroom before I leave?"

"No, go ahead."

As Deran moves toward the bedroom, I drop my pack onto my couch, ensuring a cushion falls and partially obscures it, then massage the back of my neck, pretending to work a sore muscle. I must make it look like I was too tired to care about unpacking, just left things where I dropped them. Loathe as I am to leave Ferret out in the open, it would be worse to remove him with eyes watching my every move.

I stroll into the kitchen, pouring myself a glass of water and sipping as I lean back against the counter. Deran appears, his face revealing nothing. Carefully, I release the breath I didn't realize I was holding. No one waiting for me in the furthest rooms of my apartment then, or Deran would've given some sign I should leave.

"Would you like something to drink?"

Deran shakes his head. "Thanks, but no. I've taken up enough of your time. Sorry I made you work so late. Hopefully, you can sleep in tomorrow, and by the time you get to HQ, I'll have finished level one on our plan."

Managing not to choke on the water I just sipped, I swallow the mouthful. *Wow, he's really getting into this deception!* "No, I'll be there on time. Although we've worked out the most expedient way to rebuild the machine, I want to be there in case we overlooked something."

"Fair enough. I'll be on my way then. See you tomorrow."

He heads for the front door, and I follow, letting him out. Only our eyes admit our disappointment at our lost farewell kiss. Then he's gone, and I'm closing the door. I don't fake the yawn, yet I'm still alert enough to remember one last thing I must do before heading for bed.

I pick up the morning newspapers, left on my entry table when Deran and I came in. Pretending to scan the headlines, I head for the couch. Then I rub my eyes, roll my shoulders as I walk past the couch, and drop the newspaper over the cushion covering my bag. Hopefully, I didn't make that look too obvious. If someone breaks in and tries to steal my bag, the rustle of paper will alert me.

I fall asleep the moment I crawl into bed, fully clothed. Without knowing where the cameras are, I'm certainly not getting undressed for anyone, not even partly. I face the same dilemma the next morning, wondering if they put cameras in my bathroom. Giving myself a sniff, I decide I don't smell too bad. I can probably make it through the first few hours of work and then nab a shower after a light workout—even though it's the last thing I want after the weekend we had.

But the gym visit will serve another, greater purpose. I make a show of adding two sets of workout clothes to my bag before grabbing some "subterfuge" food from my monstrous refrigerator and leaving.

After furtively dumping the conglomerate's swill, I eat the somewhat stale sandwich from Deran on the ride in, then find nothing amiss when I arrive at work. No SerSents with stun sticks waiting at the entrance, no mindhunters ready to chase me down, no sign of anyone more interested in me than usual.

Relieved, I ride the elevator up to the gym floor. Ferret burns a hole in my bag all the way. But the gym is as quiet as the rest of the building (so far, anyway!). I wander around the locker room, pretending I'm switching out clothes when I'm actually squirreling Ferret back into his hiding spot.

With one less thing to worry about, I head up to the R&D floor, where I dump the rest of my things in my office before checking on my team. Since no one has questions and there are no delays on my department's other projects, I turn toward the workshop.

Mentally, I run through the plans Deran and I made yesterday, touching the ring still on my finger. A small beacon I draw comfort from. When I run my finger along the intricately fashioned metal, enjoying the tactile contact, I abruptly realize this will draw attention to it. I move my hand to the elastic band at my wrist instead, reminding myself to use that instead.

Today will be stressful, rebuilding the machine while making sure Cygnus can't copy it. My hand strays to my lab coat pocket before I adjust its trajectory to swing next to my body as I walk. When I left my office, I placed my dictation device in my lab coat pocket, along with a few other items I'm planning to use. Items Deran is unaware of, as per his request. I'm as armed as I can be, except for one last thing.

I spot it the moment I walk into the workshop, inconspicuous on the tray with all the other tools: Deran's modified adjustable wrench. We agreed leaving it with the rest of the tools would mean anyone could use it, so Deran and I will occasionally be oblivious to its effect on the cameras.

Further, use of the wrench won't be tied to a specific person. We're hoping this, together with the fact that it could've been added at any time, even in engineering, where all tools are drawn, will keep our team safe. By adding a second department in HQ, widening the pool, we won't put a target on our team's back. We can only hope we've done enough.

Deran spots me and waves. Gesturing for his team to follow him, he makes for the workbench on the one side of the workshop where we hold our informal meetings.

I smile as they assemble. "Good morning! I hope you had a restful weekend because we have an intense week ahead of us. Deran, have you filled them in on how we'll proceed?"

"I have. We've already started with the basic frame again, same as last time."

As I turn to look at the machine, I spot them. Two minus men, just entering the workshop. Panic takes hold for an instant before I crush it, putting Goldbach's conjecture front and center, mentally calculating the three primes whose sum might equal my randomly chosen 43,289.

Mid-calculation, I realize this is the perfect time to test the recordings on my dictation device. Deran's team are all gawking at the minus men, so my stare is nothing out of the ordinary. Covertly, I slip my hand into my pocket, pressing the play button. I keep my hand there while my eyes remain glued to the intruders, watching for the slightest sign of discomfort. Nothing, no hint of the recording having any effect. I toggle the button, allowing the second recording to play, the one I made based on frequencies. Still no effect.

Since I can't turn up the volume, the only alternative is moving closer. I square my shoulders, then march over to the stony-faced men, standing in the doorway as if deciding what to do. Perhaps waiting for their next orders?

I get within a few feet before realizing I can't get closer without them hearing my recording. Not breaking my stride, I hit the "off" button. "This is a restricted area. Leave."

The two men blink at me, processing my words, before marching back out the way they came. Flabbergasted, I stare after them, then turn to find Deran and his team equally dumbfounded. Numb, I make it back to them, noting the question in Deran's eyes. But I can't answer him outright. "Nice of them to leave without complaint. Best we take advantage of their absence and get on with our work. There's no time for sleeping."

A spark in Deran's eyes is my only hint he caught the clue. He asks his question in a teasing tone, but his eyes remain serious. "No time for singing as we work, either?"

I smirk. His phrasing gives me an idea for a name for my little invention: Lullaby. "If you must. I guess we'll grin and bear it."

The rest of the team bursts into laughter. The momentary tension broken, we pick up where we left off. But the unexpected appearance of the mindhunters in the workshop, combined with Lullaby's failure, make me uneasy.

I need to sabotage the machine, and I'd rather not have to do anything covert with mindhunters present. While I'm fine for these next few minutes at least, I must find a solution. An idea pops into my head, and I think I know how to get answers—if only I can get Deran to take me there.

Because next time, the mindhunters may not be as amenable.

35

Deran's team and I work all the way through to noon, fitting the machine back together like the intricate puzzle it is. I lean back from the piece I've been working on. After running a hand across my sweaty forehead, I clap my hands to get the team's attention.

Work ceases, and I speak so everyone can hear. "Time for lunch. I need you fresh and focused for our next session. Take an hour and eat, or grab a power nap if you can."

Tired sighs and grateful glances tell me I've made the right call. Tools are literally dropped where the team were working with them as they hurry out.

Deran raises an eyebrow. "Shall we?"

I nod. "Lunch outdoors so we can clear our heads?"

"Yes. Fresh air and sunshine will do more for me than a power nap. Besides, I want to run this next section by you again, one last time, before I assign tasks to the team."

"Sounds like a plan."

We don't speak as we leave the workshop. I'm careful to set the force field in place as I normally would when leaving the workshop unattended. Satisfied I've done what I can to keep our decoy wrench and Deran's other diversions safe, I smile. "Workshop is secure. Let's go."

The slightest twitch of his lips is the only sign he understands I'm not taking ordinary precautions. We stop at my office for the lunch he provided, then exit the lab floor, elevator, and finally the building itself, in silence.

Once we're outside, I let Deran lead. He'll know a safe place where we can discuss the morning's events. I'm not disappointed by the grassy knoll, shaded by trees on one side, flanked by gently sloping hills on the others. People won't be able to hear us past Deran's modified music player—and they won't have a clear line of sight either.

We sink onto the grass, making ourselves comfortable and retrieving our sandwiches. I don't wait, plunging to the core of the problem. "You were right. Lullaby didn't work."

Deran's confusion clears in an instant. "Oh! Your name for the songs?"

"Appropriate, don't you think? If I can ever get it to work, it should be the soothing sounds of a lullaby to those people, lulling them into closing their eyes, ears, and minds."

Chuckles as Deran shakes his head. "Again, I'm glad you're on my side." He chews through a mouthful. "Why do you think it didn't work?"

"I don't know. I tried both the recording you gave me and my frequency-matched version, but neither worked. Obviously, I'm missing something." I hesitate, but now is the time to ask. "Deran?"

Eyes instantly wary, Deran studies me. "Yes, Chiara?"

I squirm, grasping for words. "I'm going to ask you something, but say no if it makes you uncomfortable."

"Okay." He draws the word out, not sure he'll like what I'm about to ask.

"You told me you'd once seen the surgery." There's no need to elaborate because Deran's eyes tense, and I know he understands why I'm reluctant to say more. "Can you take me so I can see for myself? I'm hoping to find clues to fix Lullaby."

I hold my breath, but after considering the request, Deran nods. "We'd have to go during work hours. I suggest lunchtime tomorrow."

"Thank you, but why then?"

"They're used to us going out over lunchtime, meaning they won't be unduly concerned if we suddenly disappear. Also, the sooner you get your answers, the sooner we'll be free of those menaces when you need them gone."

"Tomorrow lunchtime it is, then. In the meantime, if those men come back, can you find a reason for us to avoid assembling the drum today? I'd prefer not to sabotage the machine without something in place to counteract them."

"I can. Although next time," Deran grimaces, "don't tell me which part you're messing with. Just that you need time."

I grin, pleased with myself. "Who said I was doing anything to the drum?"

Deran laughs, the sound music to my ears. "Oh, you're good. I didn't even suspect your cutoff point was random."

"I'm getting better at this subterfuge thing." A strained smile from Deran. "What?"

Putting his sandwich down, Deran touches my hand with his finger, the briefest contact before his eyes find mine. A storm rages there. "Chiara, I'm sorry I never put a surveillance system in your apartment before CC got there."

I frown, unsure why this is such a problem. Then I get it. "Oh!"

Deran nods. "Yeah." He picks at a blade of grass. "If we hadn't been warned..."

There's no need for him to finish that sentence, and I shudder, the consequences too horrific to contemplate. I shake the thoughts away. "Let's not dwell on what might've happened. Yes, we got lucky. Next time, we just need to be more proactive." A gleam enters Deran's eyes —he's already ahead of me. "What did you do?"

"I came in early this morning and cleared your personal lab for cameras, then added surveillance of my own, so you'll know if they decide to bug it too."

"Ha! Let them just try now!" I cackle, tickled by Deran's actions.

"You're not mad?"

"Why would I be?"

"It is your private lab. I wasn't sure if I'd be overstepping."

Although I want to hug him, reassure him physically, I limit my touch to the briefest whisper of my hand across his, making the contact look accidental. "I think we're long past that mark."

Deran recognizes and accepts the contact, his eyes shimmering with silver again. "I'm glad we agree."

This settled, we fill our remaining time with idle talk. Then it's time to head back. The moment we enter CC HQ, I feel the weight of watching eyes again.

I sigh, but when Deran quirks an eyebrow, I shake my head. We go our separate ways once we reach the R&D floor, him back to the workshop and me to check on my team. After answering questions, I'm satisfied I can return to my project.

By the time I reach the workshop, the basic frame for the cold-fusion device is taking shape. I'm about to ask where Deran is when an almighty screech breaks across the room. Metal rending is not a pretty sound, and I bolt for the source.

Koni crawls out from under the machine, a grimace on his face and a broken long bolt in his hand. "Sorry, boss. I over-tightened this one. Do we have a spare?"

At first, I think he's talking to me until I hear Deran behind me.

Deran runs a hand through his hair. Is the action genuine? Was this a delay he engineered or a complete fluke? Because, without that long bolt holding the drum in place, none of the work that follows can happen. I scan the workshop. No sign of mindhunters. Did Deran delay work on the drum as a precaution?

Deran's tone is grim. "I doubt we have a spare. Run down to engineering and see if you can find one, then look where you wouldn't expect one to be if you can't find a spare. That should teach you to be more careful next time."

Koni looks sufficiently chastened for me to believe this might have been pure error on his part. Doesn't mean Deran didn't do something to the long bolt before Koni worked with it. Deran's posture bolsters my suspicions. Does he look a little guilty? He would hate reprimanding someone on his team if he knew it really wasn't their fault.

"Also, make sure you get a dozen more of those long bolts on order," Deran calls after a retreating Koni.

When Koni disappears, Deran turns to me. "I'm sorry. I know you were planning to work on the drum this afternoon. You'll have to wait until I get another piece to replace this one." Deran scowls, lifting the piece Koni just tossed into the trash. Then his eyes widen. "Wait a minute!"

"What?" I breathe, knowing he sees something I can't.

"Give the man a medal! I think Koni just found our problem. See here?" Deran points to a part of the bolt below the sheared-off section. "That's metal fatigue. I'm willing to bet this destabilized the entire drum."

"Meaning this faulty component is possibly the reason our second test failed! Now I feel justified calling for a rebuild."

While I know this wasn't truly the problem, I'm back to wondering whether this really was an accident. Either Deran's an excellent actor, or we had a genuine stroke of luck.

One thing's certain: Koni won't be getting into any trouble for "breaking" the piece. If anything, they'll commend him for being part of the solution. No accident after all. Deran orchestrated not only the problem, but ensured Koni wouldn't suffer for the error.

I want to reach out, touch him, this wonderful, thoughtful man, but I'm all too aware of the cameras. Instead, I offer Deran a disappointed smile. "I suppose I can find something else to work on. Several projects in the lab would benefit from my more active involvement. Will you come find me when you've replaced the bolt?"

"I will, but don't expect it to be today. In fact, if Koni has to order the part, we're looking at Wednesday."

Feigning discouragement I don't feel, I nod, then leave. The afternoon drags despite the mental demands of the projects I assist with. When I attempt a half-hearted workout (have to keep up impressions!), I give up after twenty minutes, barely having worked up a sweat and not in the mood to shower here. I leave for the day, earlier than usual, and the evening stretches ahead of me, an unbearably endless horizon. Restless, I do something I never ordinarily would—I go shopping. Sarissa would be proud.

Aimlessly wandering the mall wastes a couple of hours before I find my way back to my apartment. Restless, I realize I never got a real workout today, and avoided the subsequent shower. Though there've been plenty of times at the lab I went more than a week without a proper shower when on a deadline to finish a project, I still feel the need to get clean. *Oh, for when I was oblivious to everything and could lose myself in my work.*

Disgruntled, I stand in my bathroom and stare at my shower before I get an idea. Grinning like a loon, I command my shower on, waiting for the room to fill with steam before I disrobe and step inside. *Try to see me naked through all that!*

As expected, my shower refreshes like nothing else, its spa-like sprays, heated air, and fragrant lotion each doing their part to lift my spirits. I leave the bathroom feeling more like myself, but I'm barely five steps into my bedroom when exhaustion sets in.

People say stress is the silent killer, and I can't deny it. The only other time I've been under such extreme pressure was when Cygnus first brought me here, separated me from my family, and kept me in that facility where they ran all those tests. Compared to then, I now have the freedom to sleep when I want, so I can release some tension in the best way possible. I crawl into bed, determined to make the most of the time I have available, and I'm asleep in seconds.

The next morning is torture as the clock makes its eternally slow way around to noon and my meeting with Deran. Finally, it's time and I amble over to the workshop, ostensibly to check on progress. I'm relieved to find no mindhunters in sight.

The moment Deran spots me, he calls for a break and strides over to join me. "How about lunch out today?"

I feign surprise. "Won't that mean we may go over our allotted hour?"

"It may, but we're as stuck as you are now. Until that bolt arrives, there's nothing we can do. Tracking says it should arrive in two hours, so I've given the team time off until then. We'll work late tonight to make up for the lost progress."

"In that case, I won't pass up the opportunity. What are you in the mood for?"

"I've found an amazing diner I want to try again. How about it?"

"Perfect. Lead the way."

After stopping at my office to shed my lab coat, Deran ushers us to the elevator on the R&D floor, waiting until we're inside before informing me he needs to make a stop on the way down. He's been as generic as possible, both about the restaurant we're supposedly having lunch at and where we'll be stopping along the way.

When we stop on a floor I've never visited, he leads me through a chaotic office area stuffed with tiny cubicles. "What level is this?"

"Admin." Deran grins as though this explains the pandemonium.

I'm not sure it does, but I stick to his side, wary of slipping into the waiting eyes of any cameras he may not have disabled. At the far end of the room, we leave the bullpen and slip through a door and into a poorly lit corridor.

From there, it's down a staircase at the end of the corridor, then through a space under construction. Deran retrieves a pair of hidden coveralls, which he hands me with instructions to don.

This accomplished, he places a ball cap retrieved from one of his pockets on my head, before leading me down more stairs (not the same stairs I run up and down to get to the gym!) until we finally reach a mechanical room. Deran motions for me to keep quiet, then grabs my hand and pulls me along behind him until we reach a massive metal pipe in the far corner.

Deran releases me, then quietly opens the access panel on the pipe and gestures for me to enter. One glance at the grimy interior and I understand the coveralls. I slide inside, scooting a little way down one of several pipes leading off horizontally from the main entrance. Deran follows me, securing the access panel from the inside, then pointing at another pipe leading in the opposite direction. "This way. No loud noises, please."

His clipped instructions evidence his tension, even though I can't see his face and any carried in his body is masked as he moves through the ventilation duct ahead of me.

I'm intrigued by the small windows onto the other parts of CC HQ the vents in the ducts provide. I glimpse snatches of familiar areas, but far more I've never seen before. We crawl on, climbing down by bracing our bodies against the strong ducting, then crawl some more.

I'm thankful now for my hours at the gym. I never would've been able to do this without either the strength or cardio training I've gained there. When I'm nearing the point of exhaustion, thinking I'll need to ramp up my workouts, Deran slows. When he cautiously moves so he's on one side of the vent, motioning I should take the other, I know we've arrived.

36

Leaning close so I can get the widest angle into the room, I take in the view.

We're directly above some sort of operating room. Two masked men, gloved and garbed in blue scrubs, set up surgical instruments and check equipment. Task completed, they leave, and the room's quiet—for all of a few seconds—before two more men enter, differentiated by their green scrubs.

I wonder at the significance, but sudden, terrified screams pierce the air, seeping into the room through the closing door. For a second, I think I'm imagining things, but then the persistent, gut-wrenching shouts penetrate the closed door, getting louder. By the time the door swings open a second time, my heart is in my mouth, expecting something barbaric.

A boy about my age strains against the two mountainous men holding him, fighting with all his strength, but his resistance is futile. Suddenly, his words are intelligible. "You can't do this! I don't consent! Take me back to my family. Let me go!"

I go cold. Whoever this boy is, he does *not* want to be here. Why would they perform the procedure on someone unwilling? My eyes find Deran's, and he shakes his head, indicating he has no answers either.

When I return my attention to the room, the boy's guards shove him onto the operating table, still screaming and struggling. They confine him with straps specifically placed there for that purpose. My stomach turns. Can I really sit here and watch, let them do this?

Every instinct I have yells at me to run. *Run! Get away!* For once, I resist. I must stay. I don't have a choice. If I want to know how to overcome the mindhunters, I have to know how they're created. Swallowing my apprehension and disgust, I steel myself. There's nothing I can do for the boy, no matter how much I want to free him. I have no army backing me who could break us free of CC HQ, even if we could get him out of the operating room, let alone off this floor.

If this boy must be a sacrifice for the knowledge I need, I must make it count. I stuff all thoughts and emotions into that too-small box in my brain and focus on the "procedure." I dare not look at Deran, knowing my tenuous self-control will break. I close my mind to the boy's continued struggles. To my relief, his wretched cries finally cut off as the anesthesia administered via a mask takes effect.

If only I could see more clearly! I wish the operating table was under us, but a vent overhead would've compromised sterility.

"Ungrateful Zeech! Doesn't he know how lucky he is to have the gene? Without it, his life would remain as miserable as it always was."

I almost fall through the vent. Deran steadies me, his face one big question mark. I shake my head, trying to breathe, trying to remember *how* to breathe. I suck air in, but it goes nowhere. Black spots dance in front of me. I need air!

Deran's fierce pinch on my arm stutters my breathing back into rhythm. I'll take it. Thankful for the air suffusing my lungs again, I feast, keeping as quiet as I can even though I'm desperate to allow the air to make noise as it crosses my vocal cords, to release the groan deep inside.

As my breathing returns to normal, I rub my arm, offering Deran a grateful smile to let him know I understand. Some of the tension drains from his face, but my concerns for him are obliterated by all the connections happening in my head.

The gene! They can only be talking about one. Is this why it's important? Because they can turn people who have it into mindhunters? I'm light-headed again as the implications sink in.

I thought Cygnus took Xanin to punish me, to motivate me to finish his despicable machine. Instead, there could be a more sinister reason, one infinitely more practical for Cygnus and one that makes a lot more sense now that I know who Cygnus really is.

Trembling terror seizes my muscles. Relentlessly, my mind replays the moment I read about that gene in my file, stolen all those weeks ago. How I wondered if it was even relevant, considering my mother didn't have it, despite the opposite being true for all her children. But if the gene meant they kept us kids around to turn us into monsters, why let Mom live?

My mind spirals to even darker places. Is it possible my dad had the gene? Could this be why Cygnus took him from us all those years ago? The lie Cygnus gave about him being on a space mission now seems far more appealing.

Deran's arms curl around me, supporting me, his long legs wrapped around my body like a cocoon. I sink into the powerful embrace, drawing strength. The dizziness recedes. If not for Deran's support, I'm not sure I'd be able to witness the rest of this procedure.

The world beyond the vent snaps back into focus as I remember where I am and why. I can't let my emotions ruin what we came here for. I must make this young man's sacrifice count! Patting Deran's arm to reassure him, I lean forward, peering through the vent.

The taller of the two men speaks. "Cranial cradle."

So, he's the surgeon, and the other man is his assistant. Absolute focus subdues revulsion and regret; I absorb every detail of the procedure.

The assistant moves a dome-like apparatus over the teen's head. Made of shiny steel, hundreds of tiny maneuverable metal tubes line the underside, interrupted only by a thicker central panel holding a compartment, but my glimpse is too brief to be certain. Then the dome is over the boy's head, and the assistant moves aside.

The moment he does, the surgeon places his hands on two sensor pads on the dome's exterior. As the surgeon moves his hands over the sensor pads, dim green lights appear and disappear under the dome. While the angle we're at doesn't allow me to see exactly what's happening, I can guess. The tubes hold lasers. Perhaps for slicing through the scalp, accessing the brain? When the green lights vanish, I tense, waiting for the next step.

An audible click. Something was released from the mechanism over the boy's brain. *No, inserted—the implant!* Must be from that compartment. I crane my neck, trying to get a better angle, hoping to see the mystery piece, but no luck. Then blue lights play peek-a-boo from under the cradle. The same tubes, but this time used as a tissue welder to close the cut?

In under ten minutes, the procedure is complete. The surgeon lifts his hands and nods at his assistant. He removes the cradle, then the anesthesia mask from the teen's face, revealing no evidence of the procedure. I'm astounded. I'd at least expected hair removed at the incision site.

At that moment, the teen stirs. I press my nose against the vent, hoping for a better view. The young man blinks, face a blank slate. His eyes roam the room, taking in his surroundings. None of his earlier rebellion remains, no smidgeon of resistance at all. Just perfect, implacable calm. Terrifying in its implications.

"J270-Z, how are you feeling?" The question comes from the surgeon, now waving an unfamiliar device around the young man's head. From the way he studies the device, moving it at different angles, he's getting readings.

"I am well." The young man's voice is robotic, holding no inflection.

Appalled, my eyes find Deran's, and I meet equal shock. Clearly, he hasn't seen this before either. We turn back to the room, but I'm not sure I want to learn more.

The doctor continues his scans, ignoring the young man. Not that he seems to mind. He's oblivious to the world around him, content to lie there unmoving, arms and legs still strapped to the table.

With a satisfied smile, the doctor snaps the device closed. "Record him as registering eight on the scale and send him for training."

Training? I shudder to think what that means.

The associate makes the note, then walks toward the doors, opening one and speaking to someone outside. Next moment, the same guards who brought the boy in return, pushing a wheelchair.

A wheelchair! My eyes fly to Deran's a second time. This was the floor he got the wheelchair from, that day when I needed help with an inebriated Sarissa.

But there's no time for further contemplation. The guards—or are they orderlies?—release the ties binding the young man, then ease him off the table and into the wheelchair. As they wheel him out, I realize I heard no one mention his name. To them, he was just a number. Merely a tool.

Then again, why would I ever think they'd deign to call a zeech by name? The reference now makes sense: not "z" for the last letter in the alphabet, as Sarissa told me, but "z" for zone. Leeches from the zone equal zeeches. And zeeches have no rights. If they have the gene, they're turned into mindhunters, regardless of their wishes.

Sickened, I want to rush back up the duct, away from the horror of this operating room, but the surgeon speaks again. There's more I can possibly learn. I swallow the bile.

"Sterilize the cradle and prep for our next patient. I'm getting coffee."

No offer to get his assistant any. Just barges out of the OR, banging the doors on his way out, grating victory smirk still on his face. Obviously accustomed to this, his assistant removes the wrap from the table, throwing the tray of unused instruments into a metal canister and then wheeling it out of the OR. He's back a second later. He must have left the canister in the corridor, presumably for someone else to collect, and now he enters a small, glass-enclosed room attached to one wall of the OR.

Before I can see what he does next, sudden movement explodes behind me. Something is thrown over my face.

Panicked, I struggle against the smothering fabric, frantic to free myself. They've caught us!

Deran's soft snarl reaches my ears, and rough hands push mine out of the way. "Stop fighting. I'm trying to help."

All at once, I understand what he's doing, and I relax, allowing him to finish, then watching as he dons his own air filter and scarf. I didn't realize he'd brought them with, but he must've seen this part of the process before. When it comes, I'm thankful for his foresight. Pale blue gas floods the OR, blasting through the room at speed, lifting my hair even here in the ducts. The slightly acrid tinge to the filtered air I breathe is the only indication of its decontamination effect.

Minutes later, the gas swirls into a vortex, sucked up and away through the exhaust vent in the corner opposite to the assistant in his glass room. He waits five minutes before deeming the air clean enough to breathe again, then approaches a control panel next to the operating table.

Metallic clanking draws my attention to the robotic arms supporting the cradle from the ceiling as the assistant commands them. Another clank; then the arms cart the cradle to the far end of the room, where a large steel box slides open as the cradle approaches.

The box swallows the cradle, supporting robotic arms and all. A second later, a high-pitched whistle sounds as steam billows up and out of the top, reminding me of an ancient pressure cooker. The piercing whistle dies a slow, wailing death. Then the doors of the box slide open, and the robotic arms carry the cradle back to the main area of the OR, now swathed in a protective plastic coating.

I search for the assistant. Just as I wonder if he also went to get coffee, he returns, dressed in fresh scrubs. No rest for the wicked then. Excellent!

The assistant pushes yet another button on the control panel, and a fresh sheet of paper spews out, covering the operating table. Then the man carefully removes the plastic covering the cradle with gloved hands.

He looks to the door, impatience plain as the bulbous nose hiding behind his mask. On cue, the door opens, and someone in green scrubs wheels another set of instruments in. Without thanking the person, the assistant reaches for a sealed plastic envelope. When he uses a pair of inordinately long tweezers to collect the contents, I suspect what I'll see. It makes sense now why the boy's head showed no sign of surgery.

I'm not disappointed. He removes a tiny chip. *The implant!*

If not for Deran hanging onto my arm, I might have pushed through the vent as I lean closer for a better view. But the chip is too small. The tweezers all but obscure it, and then the assistant blocks my line of sight.

Frustrated, I wriggle, wanting a better angle, but the assistant moves out of the way. He flips the lid off the chamber in the center of the cradle and inserts the chip. Satisfied my suspicions are confirmed, I lean back. About to gesture to Deran we should leave, I stop when the door to the OR swings open and the surgeon returns.

They're about to do this again. I don't think I can handle more, but if we move now with the OR suddenly quiet, they may hear. Resigned, I study the surgeon. He, too, wears clean scrubs. A fresh mask covering his face, he ambles up to the operating table and inspects the area.

Before he can comment, the door bangs open, and a girl, barely a teen, stalks into the room. Her attire makes it clear she's the patient. She marches up to the operating table, then lies down, making herself comfortable.

The surgeon raises an eyebrow at his assistant before addressing the girl. "Are you ready, Candice?"

She gets a name! She's humanized. Given a choice. Unlike the boy who came before. I can only conclude she's so special because she's from the dome. Bitterness turns to fury at the injustice.

The girl nods, her disdain for the men operating on her obvious. Not the smartest response, considering they will be working on her brain. She's at least five years younger than the boy. Superior attitude aside, how can they allow someone so young to make a choice this life-changing?

Or did her parents have no say in the matter? Perhaps she has none, because it's the only plausible answer. No, I correct myself, not the only answer. But the other—that her parents are encouraging her to do this for the benefits they think they'll reap—is too abominable to contemplate.

"I need verbal confirmation, my dear," the surgeon says.

"I'm ready. Get on with it, so I can stick it to those supercilious tier sevens who've been lording it over me at the academy." She closes her eyes, eagerly accepting the mask offering anesthesia.

Sickened, I turn to Deran. His grave eyes confirm this isn't the first time he's seen someone so young undergoing the procedure.

The moment the anesthesia knocks the girl out, the assistant mutters. "Bossy, isn't she?"

"Not for long." While it could be my imagination, the surgeon sounds smug. "Cranial cradle."

This procedure is identical to the preceding one. How boring it must be to repeat the same thing over and over again. As before, in under ten minutes, the surgeon steps back from the cradle, then nods to the assistant, who removes the anesthesia mask.

I expect the girl to come around as quickly as the boy, but she takes far longer. When she does, her eyes are unfocused, her movements uncoordinated. "Bluh bebe amshh ist. Ashu su fir ugh. Mun ah de teshkat." Her lips continue moving, gushing more gibberish.

Chills pimple my skin. I know what I'm looking at, but I'm desperate to deny it.

The surgeon sighs. "Candice, can you hear me?"

No response. The girl just lies there, eyes vacant. Drool slides out of the corner of her mouth, pooling on the paper sheet under her head.

"Candice, if you can hear me, blink." No sign she heard the man. "Move your finger."

Nothing. Just those empty eyes. I'm correct. I want to scream, yell at the doctors, tell them they have no right messing with people's heads like this. Look what they did to someone so young!

The assistant slaps her face, but even that draws no response. "Probably not fully through puberty yet. Serves her right for thinking she knew better."

The surgeon doesn't comment, just snaps his gloves off. "She's gone. Terminate her."

I'm too shocked to react, the statement so cold I can't comprehend this could be a fellow human talking. Then my mind makes another connection. *This is why they haven't turned my younger siblings into mindhunters yet. Why they took Xanin now instead of sooner. He was the only one fully through puberty.*

As I stare numbly, the assistant grabs a long, thick needle off the nearby surgical tray. Holding her head still with his free hand, he plunges the needle through the girl's eye into her brain. Trauma reverberates through me, and I heave, my body desperate to purge my stomach's contents.

Deran shoves me back up the duct. I want to object, but then understanding slams into me. I remember where we are, why I can't throw up—why I can't even make a sound. Of my own accord, I scurry away from the gruesome scene. I'll never forget it.

Just the thought makes my gorge rise again, and I hurry along the duct, eager to get further away before my body betrays me. I reach another opening, this vent revealing a large, open area with no-one in sight.

When I halt, gulping down the fresh air, Deran's insistent nudging starts again, but I turn, placing a hand on his arm. Too afraid to speak in case someone hears, I hope both my eyes and the gentle pressure I exert on his arm tell him I'm okay—or at least won't give us away.

In the subdued light trickling in through the duct, Deran's face is ashen. Mine is equally colorless. Words superfluous, we gaze at one another, struggling to come to terms with what we just witnessed.

Gritting my teeth, I swallow the bile teasing the back of my throat, crush the fear attempting to consume me. I must get past this. For myself, for Deran, for my family. For Xanin. We have to get out of here. We have to stop the conglomerate.

Resolved, I roll back onto my hands and knees, then butt Deran with my shoulder, nudging him into an awareness of my need to leave. Still dazed, he takes the lead again, and I follow, all the while trying not to dwell on the harrowing implications of what I learned today.

Despite my efforts, the thoughts threaten to drown me. If I'm right and they took Xanin now because he's past puberty—because they could successfully turn him into a *mindhunter*—did he survive the procedure? If so, has he also been sent for "training?" The next time we meet, will he be a fully fledged, unthinking, uncaring, inhuman mindhunter who doesn't recognize me?

If this is true, I can only help my brother now by getting my hands on an implant, studying it, figuring out how it works. Determine whether an implant can be safely removed or, if not, how its effects can be nullified.

But how do I steal an implant without getting caught?

38

The trip out of the ducts passes in a blur. I only register we're free when Deran tugs my coveralls off. We're back in the construction zone. Fingers numb with shock, I fumble to help.

Then I'm free, and I take a deep, calming breath.

Deran's worried eyes study me. "Will you be okay? Should I invent some excuse for you to not be in the workshop this afternoon?"

"No!" My reply is sharp. "Sorry, I didn't mean to bark at you. But no, I need to work. Something to take my mind off… everything."

Deran's expression tells me I'm not alone in wanting to forget what we saw—and not the only one who reached conclusions—but we both know we can't discuss them here.

Needing touch, but unsure about cameras in the construction zone, I settle for a hand on his arm. "I appreciate your concern, but the best way to help me is to let me sink my teeth into a problem I can solve."

"Understandable. Do you want lunch before we go back?"

My hand touches a stomach still unsettled. "No, thanks. Food's the last thing on my mind. If I get hungry later, I'll eat then."

With a curt nod, Deran leads us via a circuitous, multi-floor path back to a bank of elevators. Not the same ones we used earlier, and not on the same floor. I didn't know these elevators existed. I'm even more surprised when they deliver us to the R&D floor, near a seldom-used back entrance.

I key us in. After telling him I'll meet him there, Deran and I go our separate ways at the corridor branching off to the workshop. I didn't explain I needed to collect my little diversionary items before joining him. As I exit the corridor and enter the main lab floor, heading for my office, I spot them.

Mindhunters in the lab! Again! One part of my mind screams the warning as another attacks the mathematical problems I use as a shield. Or what I hope is a shield. I remember Deran's warning there's no way to be sure until it's too late. The minus men make a beeline for me, and I freeze. Opting for offense, I choose to confront them head-on.

As I march toward them, I'm aware my team has gone quiet, watching wide-eyed again. If I could see their limbs, I'm sure I'd find them quaking. I must be strong for them. Determined, I swallow the fear and address the intruders. "Please explain your presence here."

"The Director is asking for you. Follow us."

What? Why? Does he... Navier-Stokes's partial differential equations, used in physics for describing the motion of viscous fluid substances, saturate my mind. Keeping them uppermost, I nod. "Of course."

How I get my legs to move I don't know because, frankly, I'm terrified. I'm tempted to run and hide. The thought prompts a realization, still hidden (or so I hope) under the endless equations absorbing most of my mind. *Another unscheduled meeting.* My steps falter; I shiver. Am I about to be "gifted" with another family reunion, sans a second sibling?

The minus men usher me into the elevator, then lead me past Hag Lady when we exit, not bothering to acknowledge her. Her irritation is obvious, but I have no time to savor the sight because I'm bundled past and thrust into Cygnus's office without so much as even a knock.

I stumble into the director's office, trying to get my feet back under me, standing where I am when I do. Pointedly, I lift my arms for the customary greeting (so glad I reminded myself not to forget this little detail on the elevator ride up!). I only slap my right hand palm down over left hand palm up, elbows elevated and straight out to the side, before Cygnus bellows, "Enough!"

Halting mid-action, I wonder whether he meant I should stop or if he was speaking to the minus men.

Cygnus barges past and slams the door. A second sign: something is dreadfully wrong. "Yes. I meant you!" Cygnus yells as he faces me. I've never seen Cygnus so… frazzled. Even his hair, normally meticulously groomed, is mussed. The gnarled collar of his uniform looks like it got caught between the door and drum of a sonic dryer, all twisted up.

My arms drop, as does my head (all the better to hide my face), my brain scrambling for an explanation.

A rough hand yanks my chin up, forcing me to meet his gaze. "What's going on in that head of yours?" Hazel eyes, glittering gold, scrutinize me. If not for the math equations, still running at the highest level of my thoughts, I fear my expression might give something other than confusion away.

Thankfully, the bewilderment is all Cygnus sees, and he drops his hand, grunting in disgust. "I told them you weren't responsible."

For what? "Pardon, Director Cygnus, but have I done something wrong?"

Cygnus snorts. "They said it was you, but I told them you were incapable of… never mind."

I wish he'd finished that sentence. *And who are 'they?'* I used to blame CC's Board for all the horrid things Cygnus did to me, so is this who he's referring to? Or someone else? Much as I want to ask questions, the "old" Chiara, the one drugged into oblivion, never would have. So neither can I.

Maintaining my silence is difficult, though. I concentrate on keeping my face devoid of any expression except distress. Isn't that how the old Chiara would've behaved? Beside herself, because she'd upset her beloved "Director Cygnus?"

Just thinking of the nickname he "allowed" me to use antagonizes me—speaking it since I've been in this room has been intolerable. But I'll do what I must to sell the ruse: I'm still his obedient, adoring slave. I pretend to fret, fidgeting my fingers together in front of me, keeping quiet as the mouse I was, but desperate to scream at him to tell me what's going on.

Cygnus paces along one of the side walls of his office, where massive windows span the floor-to-ceiling height. Finally, the pacing stops, and he whirls to face me, mask back on, his face serene. "Chiara, I must apologize for how you were brought here. I allowed others to corrupt my judgement. I didn't mean to scare you."

Third sign something's definitely off. Cygnus *never* expresses regret. *How would a mouse respond?* "No apology necessary, Director Cygnus. If there's anything I can do to help, you know I will. You've been nothing but generous to me and my family."

Whether it's because I'm no longer drugged or the state of Cygnus's mind, I discern the irritation that flares when I mention my family. Okay, a topic to either avoid or exploit if I want answers… but which?

Cygnus strides back to his desk, sinking gracefully into his lavish chair. He runs his hands over the leather armrests, then studies me. "Sit."

Again, I obey without question, reminding myself to sit on the very edge as I normally would've, ignoring the sudden, insane desire to lean back and make myself as comfortable as he has.

"How close are you to completing the cold-fusion device?"

Uh-oh! I thought we'd have at least another three days before he started whining. While the question is not entirely unexpected, I'm still failing to make the connection between it and his earlier behavior. Unless the conglomerate's Board are putting him under pressure? No, I worked that out—they're just there for show. Cygnus is the one running things. So why the desperation in his voice?

"I'm sorry, Director Cygnus. I regret I can't give you a precise estimate. When we'll finish depends on what we find."

"Explain."

"Now we're reassembling the machine, we've already found one faulty component. However, that component is rare, and we've had to wait for a new one to be shipped. There could be other delays similar to this one, delays beyond my control."

"But you believe these faulty components are the source of the problem?"

"Yes, as we rebuild, I believe we can return the machine to a functional state if we replace all components which may have been compromised in the initial test."

I refuse to think of the real reason I believe the machine failed, just in case those minus men out there can hear my thoughts over the tumult caused by Cygnus's disturbing behavior and the ongoing equations. A grin suddenly threatens escape when I consider how irritating the constant equations must be for the minus men, but I force it into submission.

Cygnus is back to pacing, not even bothering to watch me like the hawk he usually is. Who is putting pressure on him? In a flash, the answer comes to me. He needs this invention to retain his power! To keep his hold on his position, stop others from usurping him.

Although who the usurper might be I couldn't guess. I file the thought away, resolving to ask Deran if he's heard anything about dissension in the ranks.

"You're sure this will fix the problem?"

Inspiration hits. "Director Cygnus, may I be candid with you?" I twist my hands on my lap, feigning nervousness.

Cygnus's eyes sharpen. "What's the matter?"

"If I'm being honest, I confess to having trouble thinking clearly lately." My deliberate use of the vague time reference fits with what I'm planning, even though it's been months since he increased my dose of coercion serum. "I can't understand why. I've been eating my meals and doing my best to get the rest I need, but I'm still having trouble finding solutions. Do you think my blood sugar may be off again, like it was before?"

Resisting the urge to clench my fist, I hold back the anger thinking of how he's always blamed my "hypoglycemia." Time to turn the tables on him; let him see how it feels!

A glint of surprise shines in those golden eyes before being swept away by a mask of concern. "Why didn't you mention this before? You know you're supposed to tell me if you suspect you're having problems."

I shrink in my chair, hoping he'll see it as fear. "I'm sorry, Director Cygnus. This crept up on me, and I was too focused on resolving the issues with the machine to pay attention. But in the last week, it's become more prevalent, despite me eating more than I usually do."

The understanding in Cygnus's eyes confirms I've gotten my message across. *The dose is too high; she can't do her work.* Triumph glows in his eyes: he believes lowering my dose will fix the issue.

Time for the next stab. "Maybe it's my brother again." I sigh, dropping my head, but this time I don't have to fabricate my despair. "If I could just see him, perhaps that would help."

Instantly, Cygnus's lips thin, his eyes filling with that dangerous gleam I've learned means nothing good for me. "Chiara, we've discussed this. I can't expose you to any distractions—not until you finish the machine."

"Please, Director Cygnus, just let me talk to him! I know if I speak with him, even for only a few minutes, I can put my qualms aside so I can fully concentrate on my work."

"I won't repeat myself." Cygnus's voice is soft, barely audible.

I recognize that tone. Time to press those buttons I identified earlier and see where this goes. I knew he'd say no to Xanin, so let's see if I can get what I really want. "Please, Director, please! If I can't see him, at least allow me a meeting with my mother and little brother and sister." I infuse my tone with as much wheedling as I can, hoping this will drive the nail home. I need that meeting so Ava can find out where he's holding my family. The only way to keep them safe is to have them with me.

When Cygnus's face suddenly turns purple, I wonder if I overdid it. "Chiara! You are asking for the impossible! You have no idea what's going on, how difficult it is for me to pull those strings that get you those visits." He's back to pacing again, pent-up energy scarcely contained. His hands tug the collar of his shirt. "Do you even care what I have to do, or are you just that selfish?" The rant continues.

I never thought I'd see this—Cygnus skating on the thin edge of reason. And it didn't take much, highlighting the stress he's under. But from whom? The question remains. I must know to gain leverage. Also, it may answer why he wants the cold-fusion device so badly, give an inkling about what he really intends using it for.

Abruptly, Cygnus is in my face. "Are you even listening to me?"

I realize my concentration has wandered. Thankfully, I have a handy excuse, a believable reason I've already set up. "I'm sorry, Director Cygnus. This is what it's been like the last week. I can't seem to keep my mind focused for long."

Cygnus rears back like I've slapped him. Because he's so close, I see hate burning like fiery coals in his eyes. I inhale sharply before realizing the hate isn't directed toward me. To the people who are pressuring him then, attempting to take his position, his power?

Before I can consider it further, Cygnus is back in my face, so close I can smell the sharp bite of alcohol on his breath. No! Cygnus *drinking* on the job? I blink back the shock, then shrink further back into the chair, but he continues his pursuit, leaning so close his lips are mere inches from my own. "Marry me, Chiara! It's the only way I can keep you safe. Keep your family safe!"

I stop breathing. I'm not sure what to focus on: that I was right about his feelings for me, or that this is how he thinks he can keep my family safe.

"Well? Say something! It's not every day a man as powerful as I am proposes."

Of course he'd see it this way! Not whether I'm interested in him or even like him. Just that I'd want the power he offers. I realize what this marriage proposal is: an alliance. A way to secure his throne because without me, he's nothing.

He's using me again, same as in the past, selling it by saying this will help my family. Except I know him now. He won't lift a finger to protect them, not while dangling them over my head works to his advantage. Much as I want to reject his offer outright, tell him precisely what I think of him (and has he even considered I'm almost young enough to be his daughter!), I have to stay in character, play the long game.

"Um... er... uh, Director Cygnus, your proposal is... wow! I'm speechless. My apologies—this is something I've never considered, never thought I was worthy of." *Ugh! That last part is exactly what I would've said as a mouse.* I twist my hands again, hoping I'm selling the helpless girl routine. "Could you please allow me to discuss it with my mother?"

The last spike gets through. Cygnus pushes off the armrests of my chair, standing, staring down at me. Again, his mask is nowhere in sight. I can read his mental argument plain as day. Was he always so obvious, and the drugs simply kept me blind? Or can I see his inner turmoil because the alcohol has weakened his usually impenetrable exterior?

"I suppose a girl needs her mother at a time like this."

My surge of exultation—I'll get to see her—dies when I realize he'll coerce her into making me marry him. Doesn't Cygnus always get what he wants?

Confirming my reasoning, Cygnus smiles, that horrid, oily grin I now know means he thinks he's won. Time to act like he has.

"Oh, thank you, Director Cygnus!" If I'd been prone to giving him hugs in the past, I would've done so now, but he's not the sort. I jump up instead, bouncing on my toes like he's given me the best present ever.

Apparently, I'm convincing because that smile spreads, golden eyes glowing with the victory he thinks he has. "I'll set up the meeting. Mrs. Jacobs will let you know when it's been arranged. You may go."

Smug, Cygnus watches as I go through the motions I never finished earlier: slapping my hands as I should, then sliding them apart until my fingers catch at the ends, curling them up into a squashed delta symbol and drawing my hands together again. "All for one and work for all!"

"Indeed! All for one and work for all!"

When I leave his office, Cygnus is still gloating. I won't spoil it for him, not yet, but the day is coming. And what a day it will be!

ALSO BY BRONWYN LEROUX

Want more futuristic fantasy? Join Jaden and Kayla as they come face to face with a nightmare only they share… Pick up *Dawn of Dreams,* the first book in the *Destiny* series.

Feel like a little urban fantasy instead? Discover whether Forecaster wins her battle to regain the simplicity of the life she once cherished as Nylah. Get *Forecast of Shadows* now!

Other books by Bronwyn Leroux:

Breach (A *Destiny* companion novella)

Dawn of Dreams (*Destiny,* Book 1)

Dogs of Doom (*Destiny,* Book 2)

Doors of Destiny (*Destiny,* Book 3)

Duel of Death (*Destiny,* Book 4)

Forecast of Shadows

First Law of Attrition (*Laws of Attrition,* Book 1)

IF YOU ENJOYED THIS BOOK...

I would love it if you would please share it!

Reviews not only help other readers like you find great books to read, but they encourage authors like me. They provide both motivation to keep going, and insight into what else you might like me to write with you in mind!

You can leave a review at https://bronwynleroux.com/Attrition2Review

GET A FREE BOOK!

I love interacting with my readers and getting to know them as people. I also understand my readers hate spam as much as I do. For this reason, I only send the occasional newsletter with details on new releases, special offers and other bits of news you may find noteworthy. If you are interested in writing your own book, you can opt in for the additional bonus of weekly writing tips.

Enjoy these wonderful benefits, including your above-mentioned welcome gift, by signing up at https://bronwynleroux.com/ FreeBreach

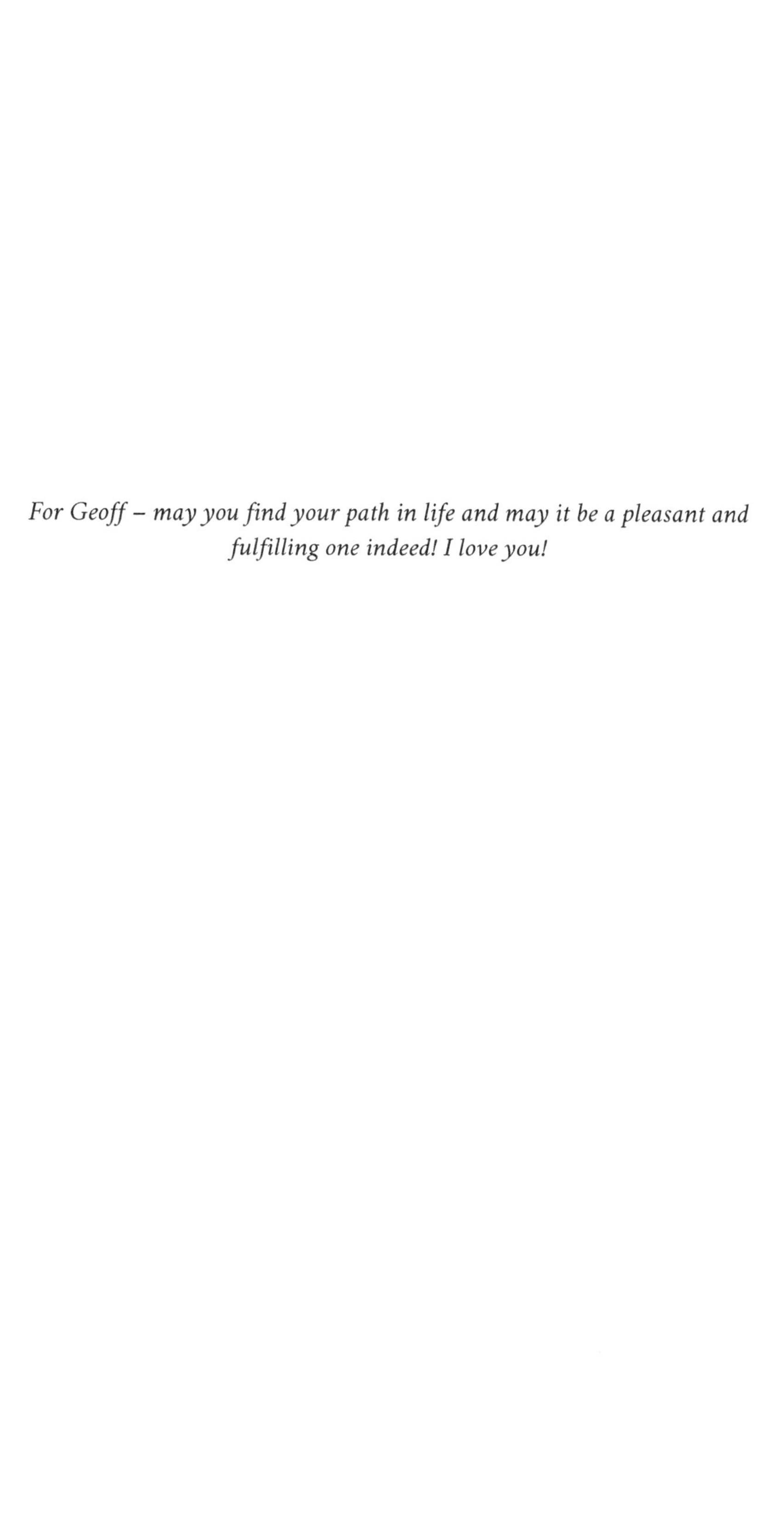

For Geoff – may you find your path in life and may it be a pleasant and fulfilling one indeed! I love you!

ABOUT THE AUTHOR

Born near the famed gold mines of South Africa (where dwarves are sure to prowl), it was the perfect place for Bronwyn to begin her adventures. They took her to another province, her Prince Charming and finally, half a world away to the dark palace of San Francisco. While the majestic Golden Gate Bridge and its Bay views were spectacular, the magical pull of the Colorado Rockies was irresistible. Bronwyn's family set off to explore yet again. Finding a sanctuary at last, this is Bronwyn's perfect place to create alternative universes. Here, her mind can roam and explore and she can conjure up fantastical books for young adults.